WILDFIRE

A NOVEL BY CALLIOPE JOHNSON

Chapter 1

Knock, knock. Hi Jenny, what's up? Sorry to bother you Grace but Lisa Kent is on line two and she's said it's important. Thank you, Lisa, I'll take it, could you please close my door on the way out. Yes ma'am, and don't roll your eyes at me missy! Well then don't call me ma'am, you know it's weird to me. I do and that's why I do it, Jenny says.

Ugh! I exclaim and roll my eyes to myself.

Hi Lisa, what's so urgent it couldn't wait for 45 more minutes until I get home? Oh nothing, just Mark sitting on your back porch with flowers, again. Oh no, why can't he just take a hint! I mean really, I have told him over and over that I am done. It's so frustrating Lisa, what can I do? Want me to turn the hose on him? Yeah, would ya? Don't tempt me Gracie, you know I will. No, no you better not... just ignore him and I'll be there when I get there, serves him right to sit and wait, ha! Ok sweetie, see you soon and I'll get the hose ready just in case. Thanks Lisa, you're a true friend, bye. Bye, bye, Grace.

Jenny? Yes ma'am? ugh! Jenny! Sorry ma'am... I mean sorry, Grace. Exasperated I tell Jenny, I have to go home...the EX. Oh no, is he bothering you again? Again? He never stopped; he takes small breaks. That's it. Grace, you don't have to put up with this crap, you should just get mean and blunt with him. Tell his sorry ass you just want him to leave you alone, friendship isn't in the cards for you two and he needs to take a hike. Jenny! That's very mean of you. I don't care Grace, you deserve better. Go on now and I want to hear all about it tomorrow. Will do Jenny, see you tomorrow.

What am I going to do about Mark? He's such an ass! I can't believe I ever dated him, he's so not my type anyway. What was I thinking? I mean really Grace, you like fun, adventure, and people...Mark is so serious and ready to settle down. He is very cute though, I guess that did sway me in his direction. Jeez Grace, you're talking to yourself in the car. ugh! I'm a loser, truly.

Walking around the side of the house to the porch I see him sitting there...waiting. Mark? What are you doing here? I have told you many times that this is over, you can't keep showing up whenever you want. Grace please, I just want to talk to you. Don't you think you owe me that much? You did just toss me aside without a reason. Without a reason, I exclaim! Have you lost your mind; I gave you a reason a-lot of reasons if you want to be specific. Let me recap for you: We do not suit, you are too serious, it wasn't going anywhere, we're way too different & I just wasn't feeling it. How about all those reasons? huh? Did you forget? Grace, just stop it. You know those aren't real reasons and they certainly aren't good enough for me to just walk away. You can't just say in general terms "we just don't suit" and expect me to understand. I thought we had a good thing going, that we both wanted the same things... to build our careers, save money and eventually start a family. You asked me out, remember? I suited you then, didn't I? Flushed, Grace sighed and sat down on the patio chair next to him and took a deep breath. Listen Mark, I know I asked you out...of course I did, just look at you. You're gorgeous and sweet, I thought maybe we could see where it went. I am sorry if I ever gave you the impression that I was more serious than I was or that I was thinking about future plans. You have to admit, I never told you that, did I? I talked about travel and adventure, that I wanted to see what there was for me out there in this huge world. I never said a word about kids or marriage, and I certainly don't plan to be in the corporate world or chasing big promotions forever. That's why I studied environmental engineering. Mark looked down at his shoes while she went on about what she wanted. Not looking up to meet her beautiful hazel eyes he said, I just thought if I could show you what love was and how a real adult relationship could be you would change your mind and let me make you happy. Oh Mark, don't you see? You can't make me happy; I have to be happy with myself. I would be miserable in that world you described; it would suffocate me. You deserve someone who wants the same things you do, someone who looks at you and only sees that amazing future you both want. I know she's out there waiting for you; she just isn't me. He looked up to meet her eyes then and as brown eyes stared in hazel, he knew she was right. Grace, I feel like a fool. You did tell me; I just didn't want to see it. I still don't. It was a long moment until Grace said, Mark I'm sorry. But if I had dragged it out any longer it would have been harder than it already is. I just want you to be ok and to be happy. Can you promise me this won't happen again? Showing up like this only makes things worse. I know Grace, he said as he stood up. I promise I won't bother you again, but if I see you out or we bump into each other, promise me one thing. Promise you'll wave or say hi, don't just ignore me. Oh Mark, I would never ignore you. You're not a bad guy and you didn't do anything wrong. Let's just part as friends and when we see each other we'll only have good feelings with waves and hellos... Ok? Sounds good Grace. Here take these flowers anyway. No, I couldn't. Oh, just take them, put them on your table or give them to Lisa. I know she's been watching me this whole time, he said as he looked up at her window the curtains swishing when he did. Grace laughed, yup that's Lisa alright. Ok, hand them over. And Mark... Yes Grace? Take care of yourself. You too Grace, he said and then turned to walk away. Grace watched as he left, then headed over to Lisa's.

Flopping down on Lisa's sofa I exclaim, it's finally done. Really? How did you manage that, Grace? I just told him the truth, the whole truth. That he wasn't ever my type and that if I led him on, I was truly sorry. He deserves someone who wants the same things he does. I mean he is such a nice guy and so good looking. Lisa if I was looking to settle down and have a vanilla sort of life, Mark would be my number one choice, but you know that's not me. I know sweetheart, you just have so much energy and curiosity in you. You need to be on the move and trying new things, having adventures, and meeting new people... It's who you are and that's wonderful, you should never try to change that or be someone else. I know all that, I really do. It's just sometimes I feel like you're the only one who gets that about me, you know? I mean not even my family can except that, and seriously my parents... who are they to judge anyone's choices? They were the biggest hippies ever! Woodstock and all that entailed... sex, drugs, and rock n' roll. The whole nine! They think I'm nuts to move all the way out here; they think I should have just settled down and made a life back home. How am I supposed to convince them that that just isn't in the cards for me? I don't know sweetie but listen; just be who you are, and they'll come around. They must remember how it was to be young and adventurous, I mean Woodstock? I saw that documentary, days of rain, drugs, and dancing in the mud. Yikes! Even you wouldn't do that Grace. I tell you Lisa, sometimes I don't think they can remember... Did I ever tell you how I got my name, how my sister got her name? No, I don't think so... I just figured Grace was a family name or something. Nope! My parents, being the hippies that they had been, named me and my sister after singers from Woodstock. You're kidding? I am not. I am named after Grace Slick and my sister after Janis Joplin, both played at Woodstock. WOW Grace! I never would have guessed that. Well at least your name has some meaning, my parents just picked my name from a book or something, thought it sounded sweet and wouldn't be too hard for me to learn how to write. OMG Lisa! That is too funny, but it is sweet and so are you. Yeah, yeah, yeah, so I'm told. Let's get some wine! I think a drink is in order, for the both of us. Absolutely, after that talk with Mark I might need the whole bottle.

Chapter 2

Good morning, Jenny! I am so glad it's finally Friday! I need a weekend like you can't believe. Don't you good morning, Jenny me like you're going to walk on past without telling me all about what happened with Mark. Rolling my eyes, I pause at the reception desk and level my eyes at Jenny, you know what Jenny? No, what? That's exactly what I'm going to do...at least until lunch where we can talk without any ears listening. Oh my, the story is that good huh? Well, I don't know about good but it's private and P.S. no one got the hose turned on them, I say winking at her and stroll off to my office.

Oomph, I exclaim as I drop into my big leather chair, I really love this chair it's so soft and enveloping. I could stay here all day and just hide out until time to go home.

A quick knock on the door, I look up and it's my boss, Terry. Morning Terry, I say. Good morning, Grace, how are you today? Oh, I'm fine, at least it's Friday, right? Well about that, that's why I'm here. Oh no Terry...what is it now? Well Grace, I'm sorry to tell you this but I'm going to need you to work this weekend. I know that's a bummer, and it is very last-minute notice. I'm going to need you to head up to Yosemite and help out with some water and soil sample collection and-testing. Geez Terry! Do you think you could've given me a little bit more notice? As it is I'm going to have to head home now and pack a bag and hit the road. I know Grace, and I'm sorry but you're the only one that can do it and they need the best. Rolling my eyes, Terry you don't have to lay it on that thick, I mean seriously... I'm going to go for you. Let me just catch up a few things here for an hour or so and then I'll head out grab a bag and hit the road. But you owe me one, and don't think I'm not going to collect. Laughing with hands up, Terry says oh I know you will. And I really appreciate it Grace, you truly are a rock here.

Terry closes the door, and I put my head back down on the desk and blow out a deep breath. Well, looks like I am headed out of town for the weekend, there goes my plans. Oh well I guess...

Driving home I hit Lisa up on the cell, hey girl. Hey Grace, that was quick I just saw you for breakfast. I know but as usual Terry's thrown a curve ball at me, and I have to go up to Yosemite for the weekend. Oh no! Why? We had plans to do some serious partying this weekend and get some good times in. I know I know Lisa, it's frustrating to me too. Let me see how quickly I can get up there help them out and get back, apparently there are some pretty important samples that need to be taken from the soil and water in an area. If I can get done quickly maybe I can be back by tomorrow night, and we can still have some fun. OK Grace that sounds like a plan, but if you're not back I'm going out without you. Well, you better somebody's got to have fun for the two of us, I say laughing.

A quick trip by my condo, and I'm throwing a bag together. It's fairly warm this time of year, but I'm still going to grab my khaki cargo pants and my boots. I definitely do not want to get cut up or eaten alive by bugs. Oh no I'm out of bug spray, I better stop by the sporting goods store and grab some so I don't come back looking like a polka dot Oompa Loompa. Wouldn't that just take the cake. Hmph!! Wonder if I need makeup...HA! Yeah, right who's going to see me, a squirrel, or a fox?? I shake my head at myself, quit being silly Grace, you're such a dork. A cursory look around and I take in my unmade bed, clothes on the floor, books everywhere...what a slob, yikes! No time for that now, I've got to go if I'm going to make it by dinner time. Keys?? Where did I put those? Oh right, in the bowl. Dragging my bag down the stairs, I grab the keys on the way out the door and punch in the security code, I rarely bother with it day to day, but this could take a day or two better to play it safe. Popping my trunk, I notice my Jeep is filthy, sheesh! Guess I'll drop it at the car wash to get detailed when I get back.

Zooming up the 41, I am jamming out! Rolling the windows down, the weather is so warm and sunny today. I just love the breeze and fresh air. Hair shoved into a ball cap, Pink Floyd on the radio, this is just about perfect. As I roll along it's getting greener and greener, bigger trees and less people. Just beautiful out here, oh I am going to sleep so good tonight in fresh forest air. As I think on it, I am actually sort of glad I got this assignment. A nice little break sounds perfect, nobody I know and no chance of bumping into exes. Laughing, I toss my head back and scream HELL YEAH!

I must be getting close; I glance at my GPS. 13 minutes to arrival. Oh, good because man do I have to pee so bad. Pulling up to the ranger station I notice a couple of pickup trucks, a picnic table and outdoor bathhouse. Hmmm, well looks like it's the outhouse for me. I stroll over so I can get this out of the way, opening the door I look in to see just how bad it might be... huh I am surprised, it's pretty nice. It kind of looks like a regular bathroom, tub and shower, toilet, and sink. Very clean I notice, sweet! I'll just get down to business then. All done, hands washed I head out the door and stroll on over to the ranger station. Knock, knock... glancing around as I wait, I notice how well maintained this station is compared to others I have seen. Hello there, you must be Grace Mason. Yup, that's me. Glad you're here, I'm Ranger Jenkins, but please call me Hough. Pleased to meet you Hough. Now, how I can help? As I understand it there are some soil and water samples that need to be collected pretty quickly. Yes ma'am, we are worried about some contamination, and we need to gather and mark samples from multiple locations within a 25-mile radius. That big?? Must be some serious or lengthy type of contamination. We suspect dumping of hazardous waste. Oh no! You're kidding, why would anyone do that? Ma'am people will do just about anything to save the cost of safely disposing the waste. Please call me Grace, Hough. Will do Grace. That makes me so mad, I will just never understand people's lack on conscience when it comes to destroying the environment. Well let me get off my soap box and get to work.

Ok Grace, here's a map and I've marked the locations where we need the samples gathered. Looking at the map I see 9 separate locations, thinking aloud I guess this will likely take me the rest of today and most of tomorrow. No worries, I'll get it done for you. You have all the supplies ready? Yes, ma'am, all bagged up and ready. I also put a pack together with protein bars, water and a fully charged walkie plus two reserve batteries. Well, aren't you just a gem Hough, you're making it so easy for me. Only one thing left, you wouldn't happen to have a spare can of insect repellent by chance. Of course, I do. He strolls over to the cabinet pulls the door open and reveals about fifty cans on the shelf. Well Hough, I would say you definitely have me covered for a couple years. Ha-ha, yes ma'am. Well, toss me a can and the pack and I'll see what I can get done before dark. I'm going to just grab a room at the Motel I saw out on the highway before I turned off so I can get started early. You could do that, not the greatest place though. I saw that but the next closest option is like 45 minutes away. Hey, why don't you stay here? We have a twin bed in the back, full bathroom right outside and a mini kitchen with microwave and fridge back there too. Really? No one uses it, I ask. Nah... We're far enough out we don't staff this station at night. After 8pm all calls route through the main station. Well then Hough, I accept. Do I need a key? Nah, I'll write down the code to the lock box. We keep the key in there now, after my partner lost the keys last time. That kid is a pretty good ranger but loses anything not tied down. Ok perfect, I say relieved I don't have to stay at the seedy motel. Hough went over to the desk and jotted down the code, turned around and grabbed the pack. I'll walk you out and load this up, I'm pretty sure you'll be fine in the Jeep...gets a little rough but nothing she can't handle from the looks of her. Absolutely, she's never failed me before Hough. Now if you need me, use channel 6 on the radio. I'll be here until 8 if you're back by then, but if not, I'll take a radio with me. Sounds great Hough, thanks for everything.

Chapter 3

Pulling out I glance at the map, where to start?? I think I'll hit that stop on the furthest side, that way I can work my way back tonight and start close tomorrow. Plan in place I head out. Driving along the grated road is easy enough, but then I realize I have to turn off on a sketchy utility road. Not worried at all, my Jeep's always got my back when the road gets wild. It's so bumpy back here, stray limbs whipping my roof and windshield. About 10 miles off the road, I notice the markers I'm looking for, well here we go. I grab my kit and some sample containers; it smells weird here. Odd, maybe there is some contamination I think. I use my tools and pull some core samples out of the soil. I think I'll hike around and do a few extras just to be safe. No water to take here so I'll head to the next stop, and think I can get two more today.

This one is about 4 miles from here, whipping my Jeep around I head out. No radio, ugh! I should have thought to throw a CD in the Jeep. I'm so spoiled by satellite radio, well that's definitely not going to work out here.

Oh crap, I exclaim! There's the marker, I slam on the breaks and throw it in reverse. I turn into the turn off, jeez it really is rough out here... I think as I'm bouncing around like microwave popcorn. It's a little darker back here but still enough sunlight to get the job done. I pull up to a clearing and notice a truck, another Jeep, and some sort of motor bike. Like a dirt bike. About 5 guys standing around talking. Hmmm...not sure this is a good thing. They all swing their eyes over to me. Uh oh, well, so much for getting away unnoticed. Maybe they're just hanging out, not doing anything bad like dumping a body or making a drug deal...Please let it be camping, I think to myself. I pull my Jeep up at an angle and put my window down. Hey guys! Nice day, I'm here to grab some soil and water samples but I can come back tomorrow. I hate to disturb your uh...er...camping, I stutter. Smooth Grace, real smooth. Like that wasn't obvious at all. I know I am as red as a beet right now. Glancing around, I see they are looking at each other and then me. One of the guys I couldn't see very well steps around and slowly strolls over closer a big toothy grin on his face, and what a face! Jeez, no I know I'm getting flushed. Get a hold of yourself Grace, it's just a pretty face and oh my... looking down I notice the body. Holy crap! H.O.T. As I glance slowly back up to the face, I am mortified. Totally BUSTED! He saw me ogling him like a sailor in a strip club five minutes off the boat. Oh lord, kill me now. Hey, he says. Hi, I reply shyly. Samples huh, you some sort of scientist? Environmental Engineer to be specific, but yes sort of. They think there may be some issues, so they called me in to collect the samples. Sounds like a fun job but you don't much look like any scientist I ever saw, he says looking me over this time. Environmental Engineer remember, and you see a lot of us, do you? Well, no, actually can't say as I ever have. I figured, but no worries and you're right you know. Huh? About what, he asks? I don't look like other environmental engineers, laughing I say at least not any I've ever met anyway. He chuckles at this. That's good Grace, I think, a joke that'll take the pressure off. Well?? He pauses for a name. Grace, I'm Grace, I say. Well Grace, I'm Jon. Why don't you just park and go about collecting your samples, we're just about to head out anyway. You are sure, I could come back or wait, it's not a problem. Nah, we're leaving some of these old guys got to get home for supper. I chuckle, well thanks I'll just get my gear and get it done. Before he turns, he sends me a little wink. What does that mean? And why is it making my heart pound? Gracie, Gracie I think, pull yourself together girl. He is a bad idea, just get your samples and get out of here. The truck pulls out and away, I notice Jon walk over to the driver's side of the Jeep to say something to the driver then the Jeep pulls away also and Jon gets on the motorcycle. Of course, he rides a motorcycle, sexy and a motorcycle. Just my luck or bad luck since he's obviously a bad idea. I march off to grab the first sample and try not to think about him anymore. Yeah right, I'll be dreaming about that tonight. What the?? I swing my head at the sound of a step behind me. What are you doing? Hands up, Jon says easy, easy I just wanted to apologize if we scared you when you pulled up. You seemed kind of nervous and I didn't want you to be worried. We're harmless I promise. Really? Harmless? You don't look harmless I say as I give him a quick up and down glance. He flushes and his eyes widen in surprise. I slap my hand over my mouth and turn 40 shades of red, I'm so flushed my ears are burning. I. AM. SO. SORRY. I say to him. I cannot believe that just came out of my mouth! He starts to tell me it's no problem, but I think I'm going to faint from embarrassment. I sway just a little and he reaches out to steady me by the arm. It snaps me back to reality and I look at his hand on my arm. He looks at me looking and I clear my throat. Well, I guess it's me who needs to apologize now I say, and we both look at each other and chuckle. Nah hun, no apology needed, you're probably right. He has the decency to flush at that statement and I smile. Well, thank you anyway, I admit I was a little nervous, you never know what you'll find way out here in the woods and me being alone and all. So, what is it you're doing there, Grace? I smile that he remembers my name and I explain that I am using a tool that removes soil samples. I need to get cores from a little deeper than the surface and at different levels so we can determine if there is any contamination and how much. You mean people come out here and dump trash? Trash, chemical waste, or something else just as hazardous to the environment. Damn! That's some serious bullshit! Exactly what I think too, I mean seriously why? Just to save some money they're willing to endanger wildlife preserves, the forests...like the planet for Christ's sake. Wow, I had no idea, I guess I never thought of it like that or at all really, but I can see why you get so upset. Yes Jon, I do get upset about it, it's why I went into environmental work in the first place. Really? So, you're one of those wacky green people? Oh, come on Jon, you don't have to be a whacko to care about the planet, you know it is our home. Alright he said hands up, you're right. I shouldn't joke it is very serious and I think it's good that there are people like you looking out for the planet. Well...maybe not the whole planet but I do what I can anywhere I am and today that means collecting about 15 different soil and water samples for about a half mile radius around here. You need that many? Yes, like I said we need different areas and levels to get the data we need. Seems like a lot of work and it's pretty hot out today, you sure you can do it? I mean I could stay and help you if you needed, he said looking so hopeful I almost laughed. Help, with what? Do you know how to use the tools or mark the samples? Nah, I am used to this and worse, it can be a real dirty job at times. No offense Grace, but you do not look like you're used to getting dirty, I mean the manicure the hair falling out of that cap... You look more like you belong in some office wearing power suits or some shit like that. Now wait just one minute mister! How do you get off assuming you know me like that by the way I look? Sheesh, I said no offense Grace, sorry I wasn't trying to offend you I was merely making an observation. An observation based on looks, didn't anyone ever teach you not to judge a book by its cover? You have no idea who I am, and you'd likely never believe me if I told you so I guess it doesn't matter. I realize I am standing with my hands on my hips, glaring at him as he is slowing taking a step back. I put my arms down and take a deep breath, sorry I snapped. Hands up in front of him he's looking at me oddly. What? Oh nothing, nothing at all. OH, just tell me, I'm not going to bite your head off. Okay, I was just thinking you look like you have a good little temper on you. I roll my eyes, book...cover I say and laugh. Well actually that is a correct observation, and yes, I do. We're both smiling at this point, and I just shake my head in mirth... back to work for me. So, want some help? Sure, you can hold my sample bag I say with a huge grin. Yes ma'am he says, smiling. Oh lord, not you too. Not me too, what? Oh nothing, it's just that my receptionist is always calling me ma'am and we're almost the same age. Makes me feel a little, weird, and old. Well ma'am, he stressed, it's a sign of respect and manners. But sorry, I'll try not to do it, no promises though. Whatever, let's go. Oh, and Grace?

Yes? I guess my other observation was right to. What do you mean I say looking puzzled? You know the one where you look like you belong in a business suit or something... Why would you say that? Because you have a receptionist. OHHH, well to be honest she's the receptionist for all of us, but yes, I do wear business suits regularly and you know what? What? he says leaning a little closer... I HATE them, I say! And we both chuckle. Let's go Mr. Observation.

We walk around and finish taking the samples. Looking up I notice it's getting a little too dark to continue today. What little sunlight there is left is quickly fading and casting long abstract looking shadows everywhere. Well Jon, I think we better head back it's getting darker, and I'd like to be back to the grated road before it's fully dark. Walking along I look over and notice the small lines around his eyes and mouth, like he smiles or laughs a lot. I like that, it's important to be happy and have humor in life. So, Grace, what will you do next? Next, I ask? Well tomorrow I have 7 more sites to collect from, I only got to two today and then I'll go home. No, I mean this evening, what are you doing this evening? Oh, well I suppose I hadn't thought that far ahead yet. Well, if you want you could come with me to this little diner/ bar I like to go to when I'm out this way. It's about 30 minutes from here, but it has great food, drinks and usually some pretty decent music on the jukebox. Umm, I don't know... I mean I don't really know you. Grace, we've been alone in the woods together for two hours, don't you think if I was going to do something bad I would have already done it? I mean why take you to a public place if my intentions are bad? Pausing I look at him, well you do have a point I guess, and I am actually pretty hungry. That settles it, let's load all this up and you can follow me. Alright, I guess it's better than coffee and protein bars at the ranger station. EWE, that is not an acceptable dinner Grace, good thing I'm here to rescue you. Rescue me, ha! Whatever! I say rolling my eyes.

Following him I start thinking, am I really following a stranger I met in the woods to some bar? I really have lost my mind. But he does seem genuine and for some reason I feel like I can trust him... which makes zero sense and is just more evidence that I truly am going crazy. Hmm? But he does look good riding that bike, but definitely not my type, I mean besides the bike because that looks like a lot of fun. Oh well too late to turn back now, looks like we're here.

Chapter 4

Betty's Bar & Grill huh? Looks like a dive, let's see if I survive. I park right up front next to Jon, close enough to the door to make a getaway if needed, I think laughing to myself. What are you smiling about Jon says as he walks over to me? Oh nothing, just thinking this place looks nice. He rolls his eyes at me a says didn't anyone ever tell you not to judge a book by its cover. I bust out laughing, touché Jon, touché indeed.

Chuckling we stroll in side by side, glancing around I notice it's a small place only 10 tables or so and 6 stools at the bar. Looks fairly clean too. There's a burly guy, mid height with a serious buzz cut behind the bar. He waves and says hey Jon, good to see you man. Who you got with you tonight? That don't look like one of your regular girls. Going bright red, Jon shoots him a look and says, thanks man. You just had to point that out huh? Well, you know I do what I can. He looks over to me and says, what can I get for you ma'am? I hear Jon chuckle, but I ignore him and say, how about a water and 2 shots of tequila. He whistles, you got it. Your regular, Jon? Yup, and I'll take 2 shots too. Okay he says, looking skeptical but turns to get the drinks.

So... I'm not like your usual girl, huh? Tell me what they are like so I can get the full picture? He's a dick, don't even worry about all that. Yeah right, now I'm really interested, you won't get off that easy so spill it Mr. Observation. It's really nothing so major, I'm usually just here with regular girls, you know. No, I don't know, so why don't you be a little more descriptive than "regular girls" I say using my best sarcastic voice and air quotes. Letting out an exasperated breath he says, you know girls with big boobs and low IQ's. Dropouts, strippers...etc. Get the picture now? Well, well, well Mr. Observation, I do believe you are blushing. Why are you embarrassed about your usual dates? No, I'm not. I guess I just never thought about how it might look until now. Not that I care, remember the whole book, cover thing? Yeah right, you are so embarrassed! You're beet red.

Shut up. Now I am laughing so hard I can't speak, he's staring. I clear my throat and compose myself, here come the drinks. Setting them down the bartender asks, anything else? Maybe some menus please? Yes ma'am, be right back.

Jon is just smiling at me, so what should we toast, ma'am? Asshole I mutter. What's that? We're toasting assholes, he asks. Yes, I say dryly, here's to assholes. I down my shot and turn the glass upside down. He does too and I reach for the other. Whoa Grace, what's your hurry? No hurry at all I say, then look him right in the and say, here's to "regular girls" cheers and I down that shot too. Wow that's pretty good. Jon quickly took his second shot and turned the glass over just in time to take a menu.

Taking the menu, I say thank you, I'll be ready in just a few minutes. Perfect, grab you another drink? Nah I'm good for now, I'll grab something else with dinner. Yes ma'am, he says as he walks away.

Hmm? Looks like I can have a burger or chicken, not too much on the menu. Yeah, it's a small menu but everything is good, and I know Ms. Betty keeps the kitchen real clean. Well, that's good at least, so what should I get?

I like the burgers, but they would probably make you a salad or something if you wanted. A salad? I'm hungry man, I need some meet. No, salad is out I say. I think I'll have a burger too, all the way. That a girl! I'll go up and order, you want fires? Of course, and mustard. Got it, be right back.

Hmm, nice guy, I think. Wonder what his deal is? Bet I can worm it out of him when he comes back.

He's strolling back over, here I go. Welcome back stranger. That's funny. Oh yeah, what's funny? Well, I said stranger, which we actually are. Strangers that is. True, I suppose we are. Well Mr. Observation, tell me a little about yourself then. Where are you from? How old are you? Whatcha do for a living? You know the usual. WOW, ok that's a lot of questions all at once. How about we play a game, you ask me a question and then I'll ask you one and so on. That's only fair, stranger.

Alright, let's play then. So, my first question…hmm? Ok, where are you from? Reno and you? Florida. Let's see... how old are you, Jon? 30, almost 31. You? Oh jeez, a baby. I'm 35. Grace, 30 is not a baby. Well maybe not but 35…jeez I'm knocking on 40. Older women are hot, don't stress about it. Easy for you to say.

Anyway, where were we?? Oh right, my turn again so Jon what do you do for a living? I'm in construction. I already know what you do, Environmental engineer. So, I'll ask you something else... Why did you become an Environmental Engineer? Oh, that's a loaded question but the short of it is this. I wanted to save the world and all that jazz, thought I would travel the world saving it one place at a time. But it only took me as far as California, first to Berkeley and then Fresno. Rolling my eyes and shrugging I add, I mean Fresno isn't bad and I have some great friends, but I am itching to get to the next step. Maybe South America or Africa. Uh, Grace... aren't both of those pretty dangerous? Oh, I don't know, probably in some areas but not everywhere. And if I work with the right agency I'd be protected. I don't know, sounds a little out there to me. Well, I've done lots of research and I could go places like Costa Rica or Argentina and be perfectly safe. Ok, if you say so. Well, I do, and it's my turn anyway. So, Jon, why construction? That's easy, one word…money. You can make a good living if you know what you're doing. And you know what you're doing I assume? At construction, yes. At life, eh… maybe a little. We both chuckle at that and here come the burgers. As they are put down on the table my stomach rumbles and Jon and the bartender look at me in unison. What, never heard a hungry woman's stomach rumble before? The only thing in there is tequila, which by the way could I get two more shots when you have a minute? Yes ma'am, you got it. Make it four Jon says. Be right back man. I look at Jon seriously, you know you don't have to drink me one for one. I'm quite the expert with tequila and I am not carrying you home if you can't handle it. Raising one eyebrow he levels me with a stare... carry me home?? No ma'am, I'm more worried about you. Ha! No need to worry, I am shots champion three years in a row in my sorority. Sorority huh?? Yes, what of it? They had the best parties, so I joined. Got a problem with that. No ma'am, I certainly do not.

I take a bite and my eyes roll back, mmmm! This is either a divine hamburger or I am so starving I can't tell the difference. Oh no, it's that good. That's why I come here whenever I'm in the area. So, what does bring you to this area Jon? Hey, no cheating it's my turn. Ok shoot? Grace, that's an unusual name for someone so young he says with a wink.

Family name or something? I almost choke on a laugh, coughing I grab my water. Clearing my throat, I take another sip before I begin. It's definitely not a family name, my parents were sort of... well they were kind of...Hippies. Hippies, he says curiously. What's that have to do with a name? I'm getting to that, hold your horses, here comes the tequila. I'll be at the bar if you need me. Thank you, I ask pausing for him to fill in a name... Oh sorry, names Mike. Well Mike, thank you. I'm Grace. Nice to meet you ma'am. Rolling my eyes, I turn back to Jon. Oh right, yes, my name. So, as I was saying my parents were hippies, and they met at Woodstock. Really? Yup. Well that still doesn't explain your name, Grace... Ok, ok so at Woodstock there was a singer named Grace Slick, ever heard of her? Are you telling me you are named after the lead singer of Jefferson Airplane? I guess you do know who she is, yup that's exactly what I'm saying. See, I told you. Hippies. Oh, and my big sisters name is Janis after the one and only Janis Joplin. Seriously? Your parents sound amazing. Oh, they are, not the biggest hippies anymore but they have their moments. So, Jon, any family? He looked down for a minute but quickly answered, no not anymore. My Gram raised me, but she passed a few years back. I have a group of great friends I consider my family though and we are very tight. Oh Jon, I'm sorry, I didn't know... we can stop playing if you want to. His head snapped up at that, no way Jose! It's my turn. Grinning he asked, do you have a boyfriend, Grace? I ask because I don't see a wedding ring. Nope no boyfriend I'm afraid, had one about 6 months ago but that's over...well finally over anyway and no, never married either. What do you mean finally over? We it's complicated. Mark, that's his name, he just couldn't let it go for a while. But he's all good now, I finally convinced him I was terrible for him, and we'd make each other miserable.

You make a guy miserable; I don't see how. Nope, nah uh. Well, it's true, Mark was sweet and kind. He just wanted this vanilla life with a vanilla wife by his side. It's just not who I am, family, kids, careers...same old same, day in, day out. No thank you, I need new, exciting, and adventure. I am not vanilla. No ma'am, you are not. I smile at this, well thank you very much for noticing. Alright Jon, tell me do you have a wife, girlfriend or do you just stick to the "regular girls"? Good lord that's going to get old fast. No, I've never had a wife, a few girlfriends but none right now. There are a few girls I "see" from time to time but no one serious and I like it that way, at least for now. I pick up my shot and raise it to a toast, here's to being single. We clink shot glasses and down the smooth clear liquid. So smooth, goes down like a warm kiss I remark, then flush a little. Why ma'am, I do believe you're blushing. Oh, shut the fuck up, but I say it with a grin and he grins back. Now let's shut up and eat, we can play later, I mean our game that is, but I blush again and I think I see a secret smirk cross his face.

I am stuffed to the gills; I need to stretch. I'm going to go over to the jukebox, wanna hear anything specific? Dealers' choice I say, pick something you like, and we'll see if I'm surprised. Deal, he says.

I stroll over to the jukebox, at least it's a newer model with a decent assortment. Let's see, Metallica, Bob Seeger, Hank Williams Jr, Reba, Debbie Gibson?? Who in the world stocked this thing I wonder? Oh, here we go, Free bird...but...maybe that's too cliche. I keep looking, hmm this is good. I pop in my dollar and select a song, that leaves me 1 credit, so I choose Free bird for my second song. As I am walking back to the table Black Bird by the Beatles starts to play and Jon just looks at me. The Beatles huh? I like it, I didn't see that coming but then Grace, I do believe you are an original. I don't know about that; just wait for my next song I say and wink.

Alright, well maybe I'll go pick a couple tunes myself. I watch him walk over to the jukebox and dig out a dollar, he pushes some buttons and is on his way back in under a minute. Hmm?? That was fast, I assume you know the selection well. Just then Free bird comes on. I do believe you're trying to tell me something about yourself Grace. I turn my head to the side and say as if I'm thinking of the right thing to say, like what? That I like birds or my freedom, maybe both I say with a small chuckle.

My song ends and what do you know, Somebody to Love by Jefferson Airplane comes on. He is wearing this stupidly silly grin. May I have this dance, Miss Grace? Oh, why not. It is a great song. He extends his hand and I follow him out to the floor. Twirling me then taking me by the waist we begin to dance around the small open space near the jukebox, faster and faster. I love it, the rhythm of the music the heat of his hands, I begin to let go and sing. Something I rarely do around people. By now I am belting out the lyrics and Jon is just looking at me, oh shit, he's staring. I stop singing and clear my throat, meanwhile we never stop dancing. He leans in a little and asks, why did you stop singing? You're incredible. Um...er...well, I stutter. I really don't sing in front of people. I guess I just got lost in the song.

Why wouldn't you sing for people, you sound amazing. Grace you are really good, like you could be on the radio good. Whatever Jon, I'm only average. You are not average Grace. The song comes to an end, and we stop dancing, he lets me go but we stand there just looking at each other. Then all of a sudden, the jukebox comes to life, and I crack the biggest grin. Crazy Bitch huh?? What? You don't like Buckcherry? I roll my eyes, of course I do, it's a great song but tell me Jon are you trying to tell me something about me or you? At that we both crack up and drag our butts back to the table. He lifts his shot glass and says, here's to crazy bitches, whoever they may be and winks before tossing back his shot. I raise my glass and do the same.

Well Jon, I think I better call it a night. Unfortunately, I have to be up super early so I can get my work done and head back to Fresno tomorrow night. Yeah, I probably should get going to. I'll tell you what, you wait here while I go pay for dinner and then I'll walk you out, sound good? Oh no, I can't let you pay for me. I should pay for you, I mean you did help me today and show me a good time this evening. Get real Grace, I got this. And he strolled up to the bar, I see him take out his wallet and peel off a couple bills and give them to Mike. He waved his hand at change, and I see Mike grin. Then he stood there a minute, Mike handed him a pen and a napkin and jotted something down before walking back to the table. I stand up and grab my purse, ready? Yes ma'am, after you.

I turn back to the door and wave to Mike, thank you Mike. Dinner was so good. He waved back, no problem ma'am. I roll my eyes as I turn around and see Jon grinning like a fool. Ugh!

We stop in between the Jeep and his bike, you ok to drive he asks? Me, definitely, you? Yes ma'am. Oh, shut the fuck up with that already. Yes ma'am. I'm going to punch you Jon. He put his hands up, sorry Grace. But seriously, thank you for coming, I get a kick out of you. You're so funny and smart, it's nice. Thanks Jon and thank you for dinner and a fun evening. I'm glad I met you, it's weird but it feels kind of like we're old friends or maybe friends from a past life or something. I think so too, he says. Grace? Yeah? Here take my number, I think we should stay in touch. I mean since we're friends from a past life it would be a shame not to talk until the next life, right?? You're right Jon, it would be a shame indeed. I'll text you when I get back to the station, that way you'll have my number too. Perfect he said, then leaned in and kissed my cheek. Good night, Grace. Good night Jon, you be safe on that bike. Yes ma'am. Whack! Ouch! I told you I would punch you; I did warn you. Yes, you did Grace. Then I grabbed his arm and lifted up on my tip toes and kissed his cheek. Bye Jon. By Grace.

Chapter 5

In the Jeep on the way back, it struck me. We could be best friends. He is hot but there's something else there, I wonder if he feels it too. Like we truly are best friends from another time, I am never that comfortable with someone I just met. He makes me feel relaxed, like I can truly be myself. And odd thing is, I can't even imagine having sex with him... Maybe I am going crazy... I roll my windows halfway down and just enjoy the radio and the cool night breeze.

Pulling into the ranger station I notice the truck is still here, I wonder if there's a problem? I park next to the truck, grab my overnight bag off the back seat and go to the door. I try the handle, unlocked...hmm. I open the door and Hough is at the desk, he looks up. Grace, there you are. I was getting a little worried it's nearly ten thirty. I know, sorry. I stopped to grab dinner and I guess I lost track of time. I tried you on the radio a couple times, didn't get an answer so I figured I'd wait a bit to be sure you were safe. Hough, I'm so sorry. The radio was in the Jeep while I was in the bar, and I never thought to check in with you. I am truly sorry, forgive me?? Ah hell, no harm done. I'm just a worry wort sometimes, you going to be ok here tonight, he asks. I can stay if you think... I cut him off, put my hand up to wave him off. I'll be fine, I'm a big girl and I live alone anyway. I'll be fine, I'm going to grab a quick shower and then just crash. Ok Grace, but I'll wait to leave until you back from the shower. Just in case there's any stray wildlife out there feeling frisky tonight, just then he blushed and looked a little shocked at himself. Thank you, Hough, that would be great. Just let me grab a couple things from my bag and I'll be quick, fifteen minutes at the most. Take your time, no worries. I grab the whole bag and my phone and head out the door. I take a cursory look around, all clear. I go to the bathroom; the light is on. Hmm, Hough must have left it on for me, such a nice man. I lock the door and set my bag down, opening it I grab my toiletries bag, a towel, and my cell. I turn on the shower to let it heat up and fish the napkin out of my pocket.

Me: I text Jon, Good night Mr. Observation... thx again for dinner. P.S. this is Grace and finish with a wink emoji.

Jon: I kinda figured it was you Miss Melody, wink emoji.

Me: What does Miss Melody mean??

Jon: means I like the way you sing, wink emoji, microphone emoji.

Me: Awe, that's so sweet Jon. But don't expect me to do it again

Jon: Why not?

Me: That's a story for another time, I'm stepping into the shower, ttyl

Jon: Can't wait to hear it, ttyl

The shower is warm and relaxing, I quickly wash my hair and put some conditioner in so I can get a brush through it later. The wet mass hangs down past my shoulder blades when wet. I need a haircut, ugh!

I scrub my body, first with soap and then body wash. I think, jeez I should probably be on medication for this OCD thing... I rinse everything off and step out. I dry off as quickly as possible put on some cool cotton shorts and a tank top, this will do well...it is so warm tonight. I brush my teeth and quickly grab all my stuff. Opening the door, I look around carefully and when I am sure it's all clear, I quickly head back to the ranger station.

Hey Hough, thanks again for waiting. I appreciate it. No problem, Grace, you sure you'll be ok here alone. Absolutely, I'm beat and I wanna be up early so I can get to the seven remaining sites and get all the samples by late afternoon. I wanna make it back to Fresno tomorrow evening. Well, that's ambitious, I'll be in by noon but my partner Ranger Markem, Todd that is will be here in the morning around 7am if you need anything. And Grace, don't hesitate to call in the night if you need anything. Numbers are on the desk by the phone. Thanks Hough, you're a peach. Alright then, good night. Night Hough. Lock up behind me Grace. Will do. I lock the door and take my stuff to the back room, dropping it just inside the door.

I flop on the bed; I am so tired. Buzz, buzz... It's a text message.

Jon: you all settled in for the night?

Me: yes, you?

Jon: yup, so tell me

Me: tell you what?

Jon: duh...why you don't sing very often. Even though you are sooooo good

Me: jeez, really... it's late

Jon: I've got all night

UGHHHH!

Me: Fine, I don't like everyone looking at me. When I was little, I would sing and people would stare...it creeps me out. Ok now you know.

Jon: what! Of course, they stare Grace, they are in shock at how good you are.

Me: smh, whatever

Jon: whatever yourself, I just call it like I hear it Miss melody, wink emoji

Me: Fine, whatever

Jon: Truth time...

Me: ???

Jon: Truth is, it's weird... you could be my best friend and I barely know you

I pause, I don't know what to say. I'm sort of shocked that he said exactly what I've been thinking. How is that even possible...

Jon: You still there? Did I scare you off?

Me: No, you didn't scare me, you shocked me a little to be honest.

Jon: shocked, as in a bad way? I'm sorry

Me: No in a good way, I guess. I was thinking the same thing. You seem like an old friend, it's weird. I feel this connection and we just met. It's such an odd sensation.

Jon: whoa, I mean...really?

Me: truly...yes

Jon: what do you think it means?

Me: idk... maybe it means we were friends in a former life or that we were destined to be friends in this one. Do you believe in that sort of thing? If not, I'm sure I sound like a lunatic.

Jon: well...... jk. I actually do believe in that sort of thing. Like cosmic energy and karma, and aliens wink emoji

Me: Me too! Jon, I think you might be becoming my new best friend

Jon: Miss Melody, I feel the same way. I'm going to say something that might make you mad...

Me: Oh no... what now?

Jon: Well... at first, I thought to myself, she's hot maybe we'll hook up. Sorry, it's a guy thing. But now it's like no way, I see the potential for so much more with us. An epic friendship, like we're kindred spirits or something. Too much??

Me: Not possible

Jon:??

Me: You can't be having my exact same thoughts...

Jon: really?? You thought I was hot, and we'd hook up? My, my, my, Miss Melody

Me: UGH! Why not, because I'm a girl??

Jon: Correction, you're a woman, and a hot one. But I meant, I just thought...no way someone like you would even look at someone like me, much less think about me like that.

Me: Why?

Jon: come on, look at you. You're so smart and successful. I'm just a construction worker, who barely made it through high school.

Me: Jon, you are SOO HOT! That's the first priority in Hookup 101. But getting to know you was even better, and I agree.

Jon: agree to what?

Jon: and thank you

Me: you're welcome, and I agree to no hookup. I think this new friendship is way better.

Jon: I'm glad, the "regular girls" would never understand...smh

Me: good thing, I'm not a regular girl wink emoji

Jon: No ma'am, you are not

Me: ugh!

Jon: jk...

Me: it's getting late, and I have a long day tomorrow, I should get some sleep.

Jon: I have enjoyed this, Grace; I have a feeling about us... I want to stay in touch with you if that's ok.

Me: you better! It's not every day you meet a best friend from a past life

Jon: true, then it's official. We're new best friends for life, I'll message you tomorrow. Be safe out there tramping through the woods.

Me: Agreed, it's official. And don't worry about me... I can take care of myself, but thanks anyway. Good night, Jon

Jon: Goodnight, Miss Melody

Miss Melody, too funny. I stretch out on the narrow twin size bed and burrow down into the pillow. Comfy enough, I close my eyes. I feel happy, like in a way I can't explain. Jon, I say his name like he's there... and then I drift off to sleep.

Chapter 6

A sound wakes me, knock knock. Yes? You decent? What? Oh yeah, come in.

It's the other Ranger, what's his name...I can't remember. Hi Grace, I'm Ranger Todd Markem. Call me Todd. Well, good morning, Todd. What time is it? It's just after seven. Oh, I shrug as I sit up and try to wake myself. Thanks for waking me, I need to get started. Is there by chance any coffee? I'm a bear without a cup in the morning. Yes ma'am, I was just about to brew a fresh pot. I grin, ma'am... Thank you Todd, I'll just head to the restroom and get changed for the day. Sounds good Grace, I'll get the coffee on while you do that.

I hear him lowly whistling as I head out the door and to the bathroom. Strolling over with my bag in hand, I look around and notice how lovely everything looks today. So bright and fresh. The flowers are blooming in shades of red and pink, yellow, blue, and so much green. The Forrest is alive today, I am alive today. I stop walking and it hits me, it's me. I'm what's different today, this realization stuns me for a minute. I feel totally and completely alive. Suddenly I snap back to reality. Pee. Yes, I need to pee. I hurry to the bathroom and lock myself in. When I am done peeing, I grab my bag and look for my toothbrush. Dressed and ready for the day I emerge, but the strange feeling is still there. I am alive. It's like a revelation.

Opening the door to the station I smell the coffee and my stomach flips. Mmmmm, that's what I'm talking about. Thank you, Todd! He turns around to display a box containing a dozen donuts. Todd, I could hug you right now! This is wonderful. Well, we don't get too many guests out here, gotta treat em right, especially when they're doing us a favor like you are. Awe Todd, that's very sweet. And I am starving, you're joining me, right? Yes ma'am, I surely am. I turn to the coffee pot rolling my eyes and think, I guess I'd better get used to that already. Want me to pour you a cup Todd? That would be great Grace. How do you take it? Black with two sugars please. Coming up, I pour his and then mine. Mine of course is loaded with cream and sugar, a blonde they call it.

Come sit over here Grace he says and points to a chair on the side of the desk, sit and eat before you head out. These roads are too bumpy to take an open coffee with you. I know, yesterday I was driving around feeling like popcorn bouncing all around. Yep, that sounds about right he said with a chuckle.

So, Todd, how long have you been a ranger? I ask as I sit and grab a glazed donut stuffing almost half into my mouth like a pig. Oh, about five years now. I guess you were hungry he says as I stuff the remaining piece in my mouth. I laugh and choke a little at the same time and reach for the coffee to wash it down. Clearing my throat I say, sorry. Not very lady like I know, but I am so hungry. That's alright, have another. Don't mind if I do Todd and thank you again. No problem, Grace. So, you thinking to get all this done today? Yes, I got the furthest two done yesterday and have 7 more sites today. Should be fine if I don't encounter any distractions, I say and secretly think how well yesterday's distraction worked out. Well Grace, if you find out you need the bed again tonight it's yours, Hough said he gave you the code so you're all set. I shouldn't but thank you Todd. I better get going, I'll just make up that bed and grab my bag. I dash in straighten the bed quickly and stack the pillow on top. Luckily, I already shoved everything into my bag, so I am ready to go.

Alright, I'm headed out Todd. I have the radio if I need anything and thanks again. Be safe Grace, I'll be here if you need anything.

I head out to my trusty Jeep to start the day, and it truly is a lovely day. I'm smiling and I feel so light. Pulling up to the first stop on my list, I grab my gear and head out to get the job done.

As the day winds on, I'm on pace to finish on time. At the last stop I realize that the two donuts are all I've had to eat all day. Jon is right, the thought of a protein bar is so gross right now. I need real food and it hits me, Betty's. I can grab a bite on the way back to Fresno, perfect. Last sample collected and labeled I make my way back to the Jeep. I happen to glance at my reflection in the glass, hot?? Not today that's for sure. No makeup, ball cap and dirt on my face... I shake my head, oh well the dirt is the only thing I can fix now. Stashing the samples, I rifle through my bag for a towel and wipe as much off my face as I can. Spotting my hairbrush, I grab that and remove the cap to see if I can tame the beast. Brushing vigorously, I do what I can, and honestly, it's not too bad even if it is a little wild. That done, I jump behind the wheel and speed off to Betty's.

I pull up to Betty's and park in the same spot as last night, jump out with my purse in hand and head for the door. I open the door and see a mostly empty bar, just a couple guys at a table and one woman at the end of the bar. Mike sees me and waves, back again so soon. Yes sir, I have another hamburger on my mind I say with a grin. I'll get the order right in, are fries ok? Absolutely, and a water with... he interrupts me, let me guess two shots of tequila. You got it Mike.

I hop up on the second stool from the end and wait, I pull out my phone and text Jon.

Me: Guess where I am?

Jon: ??? Betty's??

Me: How could you know that?

I start looking around, but I don't see him anywhere.

Jon: Maybe I'm psychic...

Me: yeah, right lol

Just then the door opens and the last bits of light from the day shine in through the door. And there he is, just standing there. Jeans and construction boots, an AC/DC t shirt. I smile and come off the stool to greet him. What are you doing here? He looks at me and says I could ask you the same thing Miss Melody with a wink. Touché Mr. Observation. Hungry he asks, starving I already ordered a burger wanna join me?

Absolutely, at the bar he asks. Sure, why not... it's closer to the tequila I quip with an exaggerated wink, and he laughs. Hey Mike, Jon calls out...well looks who's here again, two days in a row. Why Jon you must be sweet on Miss Grace here. Shut up he says with an annoyed tone, you're like an old woman looking for gossip. Maybe I am but tell me this, am I wrong?

Jon paused for a moment and said in a more earnest tone, no Mike. I don't think you are. But it's not at all what you think. And he jumps up beside me and says, I'll have what she's having. I just grin and think, he gets me.

Ok Mike says, a hamburger and tequila coming right up. One eyebrow raised Jon looks at me, why Miss Melody tequila two nights in a row...what a lush you are. Bite me, I say sarcastically but the grin in my eyes gives me away and I laugh despite my attempt at keeping a straight face.

Looking at him I ask, so what are you doing here? I assumed you were headed back to Reno. I am, tomorrow. You didn't ask and you know what they when you assume something??? I square my shoulders at him with a straight face and say well you're already an ass, so I figured I'd join you. That was it, we both cracked up and couldn't stop laughing. Mike came over with four shots and two glasses of water, looking at us like we are lunatics...what's so funny, he asks? Jon tries to compose himself and manages to say, oh nothing just Miss Melody's smart-ass mouth. I sober instantly and look at him, I think he notices because he meets my eyes, and the humor starts to drain from his face. Whose Miss Melody, Mike asks? I look at him and dryly say, it's nobody, our friend here is just being an ass. Looking quizzically between the two of us, Mike sighs and says ah well, that is true enough but somehow, I'm just not sure that's the whole truth and then he turns and goes into the kitchen.

Jon don't call me that in front of people. Why not, it's just an endearment and nothing to be embarrassed about. Well, it is to me, I told you how I feel about singing.

Look Grace, you did tell me, but I don't understand why it still bothers you. You are so confident and outgoing. That can't be the whole reason. And anyway, I think it has a nice ring to it and you can tell people it's because you're named after a famous singer. So, tell me the real reason or live with it, he said but with true kindness in his voice.

Fine, I'll live with it then. He looks at me quizzically for a moment, head tilted to the side like he's searching my eyes for some hidden truth. What are you looking at? You Grace, I'm looking at you. It's like I can see a whole other world in those big green eyes. They're hazel actually, I say. Well, I can't explain it, it's like I'm mesmerized or something. Well, quit it, it's weird and they're just eyes I say looking into his blue grey eyes that look almost like polished steel. We are suspended there for just a moment before we both look away. In unison we say, that was weird and look at each other again.

We are quiet for long moments before Mike comes back with our food. It snaps me back to reality and I pick up my shot, Jon sees me and does the same. I say cheers to destiny and down the shot before he can say anything. Placing the glass upside down on the bar I reach for some fries and begin eating. John does the same and we continue to eat quietly for several minutes. I wonder what he is thinking and if this can honestly be happening. Could I have actually found my best friend soul mate? Is that even a thing? I have no idea, but I do know that this person, Jon was sent to me for a reason. Now I just have to find out why...

Glancing in my direction Jon clears his throat, I look over as he is about to speak. How's your dinner Grace? I think, is that what he really wants to talk about? But I say, it's very good, yours? Great as always. More silence. I grab my second shot and say, cheers to you and cheers to me and cheers to new friends. I pause as he raises his glass and clinks it to mine, then we both throw back the shots setting the glasses upside down on the bar in unison.

Are we going to talk about this thing between us? What do you mean? Come on Grace, you know there is something sort of magic going on here... I take a deep breath and let it out, I know there is. I feel it deeply, it's almost electric. I glance around and say, let's go sit over there and point to a table in the corner. Ok, are you all done? Yes, I'm stuffed and you? Yea I'm done, want another drink? Sure, grab me a Corona. Perfect, I'll meet you over there. I walk over to the table I had indicated and pull out a chair to sit and wait for him to come over.

He makes his way over to me carrying two Coronas with limes, kindred spirits indeed I suppose. Setting them both on the table he pulls out his chair and sits. I don't know where to start or what to say Grace, I just really feel we should talk because I have never met anyone like you before. Like never! You seem to have this thing that pulls me to you, and not in a sexual way but more of this intense feeling that I was meant to meet you and that the universe has some big plan for us. I know I must sound like a crazy fool, a total loon but I swear I am not bullshitting you, Grace.

Mouth hanging open, I am stunned speechless. I don't think I could conjure a cohesive thought to speak if I tried. My mind is racing and whirling in a dozen different directions. He's just looking at me like he knows exactly what I'm thinking. I'm quiet for long moments before I begin to form some of the words, I want to say... Jon, I manage to say in a voice barely over a whisper. I start to speak but stutter a little, ah, er I mean I feel exactly the same way. I manage to say this and watch as his face forms into a bright realization and I know that in this moment we are indeed meant to have met and that there is a reason we have to discover.

So, what do we do now, he asks? I don't know, this is definitely not a situation I've been in before. I know, me neither. Maybe we should just spend more time together, get to know each other better and see if some mythical, magical... Whatever kind of reason jumps out at us. Ok, that does make a lot of sense. But where? I'm in Reno, you're in Fresno. It's not that far but also far enough to be pretty inconvenient Grace. Agreed, well, how about next weekend? You could come to Fresno, or I could come to Reno... We could meet in the middle somewhere. I don't know?? That could work, I don't usually work weekends and can take a little extra time off here and there if I need to. So can I, plus my boss, Terry owes me big time for sending me up here this weekend to work. But come to think of it, truthfully, I feel like maybe I'm the one who owes him. Without him, I might never have met you and somehow that feels like it would be a tragedy. I know what you mean, I'm glad I met you to Grace. This is such a trip; my boys would be ragging on me so bad if they knew about any of this. Great guys, I mean they really are true friends and we're a tight group but this... they would never understand. They'd probably laugh me straight to the nut house.

Ha! My friends would be no better, except for maybe Lisa. She's my best friend and next-door neighbor. I met her a few years ago when I bought my condo. Lisa's a hoot, you'll get a kick outta her. She's feisty as all hell! She's in real estate but don't be fooled by that, she's a real party animal and definitely a man eater.

She sounds fun. My friends are all good guys if a little rough around the edges. Will and Eddie are my roommates, Eddie is a serious kind of guy but very genuine a great guy to have in your corner. Will is the "baby" of our group, he's 23 and thinks he's hilarious. He's funny enough and a cool guy. Chicks love him and he's always looking for one or has two or three at a time, you just never know. Laughing I say, maybe we should introduce him to Lisa. Right! Sounds like maybe we should he replies laughing. And there's Rob, he's always coming up with some big plan or get rich quick scheme, solid guy though. Finally, there's Preacher or Colin, we call him preacher because he was raised real religious and he used to be in the army. He's no goody goody but he does try to keep us all as down to earth as possible. The five of us are as close as brothers, hell we are brothers. Been through a lot together, any one of us would walk through hell for the others.

Wow, I say. That's pretty amazing to have five friends that close as an adult. I mean I have a lot of friends, but none that close except for maybe Lisa. My family is all back in Florida, so I only see them once or twice a year at most. I envy you Jon.

Well now you have me Grace, and when I say that I mean it. You can count on me, no matter what and I know when my boys meet you, they'll adopt you too.

That sounds wonderful. You know what, I'm going to take some vacation days and come to Reno. I've never been, I can book a room then I can poke around and explore when you're working and hang out when you have time. Maybe you'll introduce me to your boys. How does that sound?

Looking at me he says, a room? You mean you're not going to stay with me?

Umm, uhh...well... you have roommates, don't you? You can't possibly have room for me, right?

Grace, I'll make room. In fact, you can have mine and I'll take the couch. Oh no, I couldn't let you do that. Why don't I take the couch? Get over it Grace, I'm-not having you sleep on my couch. You'll stay with me and take my room; I'll take the couch and I'll hear no more discussion about it he says very matter of factly.

Well then, I guess that's settled but you'll have to let me make dinner for you all one night to say thank you and I'll hear no more discussion on the matter.

You'll get no argument out of me; I just hope you can cook. Well Jon, I'll guess you'll just have to wait and see.

Chapter 7

Hello, Hi Lisa it's me are you busy? Not really, what's up? So, get this, I met a guy. But not how you're thinking though. Well, what then? Who did you meet?

His name is Jon and I think he's my soul mate, but not in a romantic way if you know what I mean.

I have absolutely no idea what you mean Grace. You sound weird are you sure you didn't eat some funny berries or "magic" mushrooms out there in the Forrest?

No, I didn't eat mushrooms in the forest, jeez Lisa! I can't even explain what I mean, it's the weirdest thing ever. I pull up to the first site and there he is in the woods, with some other guys. Everyone leaves but him, and all of the sudden it's like we're best friends. I mean, I followed him to a bar, and we spent hours talking about ourselves and getting to know each other. Then we texted for hours after that, we even have nicknames for each other already. Crazy town, right?

Umm, are you sure this isn't like love at first sight or some shit like that? Sounds pretty romantic to me Grace.

That's just it, at first, I was like oooohhh he's so hot and I thought maybe.... but then I got to know him and it's definitely not, I can't even imaging kissing him much less having sex with him. When we look into each other's eyes it's like cosmic, there's just something there. A pull to each other, like we were meant to meet. Now I know you must be thinking I'm crazy, hell even I think I must be losing it.

I have never known you to be crazy Grace, for some reason I believe you. Maybe it's the passion in your voice or maybe I'm just caught up in the mystery of it but either way it sounds amazing. So, what's next? Are you going to see him again?

Well, as a matter of fact I am. I'm actually going to Reno to see him this week. I just have to go in and talk to Terry about taking some time off work. And don't freak out but I'll be staying with him and his roommates for a few days.

Are you sure about this Grace, Reno isn't just around the corner and what do you really know about this guy? I'm not sure this idea is safe. What about his roommates, what if they aren't good guys? You could be walking into a trap; I don't think I like this.

Look, I have already considered all of this. And you are right, it isn't a smart thing to do...normally. But Lisa, I swear to you, I feel it in my bones that this is the right thing to do. And I promise I will give you the address and names, I'll call you every day and check in. You can alert the police in Reno if I don't.

I don't know, maybe I should go with you, and we should stay in a hotel. You could meet him in a public place. I mean if he's so hot maybe I should come, you're not romantically interested but I might be.

I giggle, you know that's not the worst idea and he does have a roommate that I think could be perfect for you. How about this, I'll go alone and if anything feels weird, I will turn around immediately and come back home. You can come next time or maybe I'll invite them here. Don't worry, I'm a smart girl, I won't do anything dangerous.

Oh sure, like I believe that Gracie. Laughing she says, fine! You win, but you have to call every day and answer anytime I call.

Deal! So, how was your weekend? I listen to her ramble on about this party and that guy for a while and then notice I am only a half hour from home now.

Hey Lisa, sorry to interrupt you but I'm almost to the turn off for home. I'll come over for breakfast and we can get all caught up. Sound good?

Yawning she says, perfect. I'm getting sleepy, it's been a long fun weekend.

Well, I am sure we'll both sleep in tomorrow, so I won't come over too early. I'll bring mimosas.

Absolutely perfect, I'll have fruit and muffins. We'll have a patio picnic and get all caught up.

See you then, sleep tight.

Home, a feeling of relief floods over me as I walk into my condo and drop my bags by the front door. I kick off my boots and pad into my bedroom, oomph I exclaim as I sit down on the bed and begin to undress in preparation for a shower. All showered and ready for bed I crawl under the covers and snuggle into my pillows. I reach for my cell phone to text Jon, it's almost automatic like it's the most normal and routine thing to do. This is so weird.

Me: I made it home safe, and I've settled in bed for the night.

Jon: that's good, I can't wait to get home tomorrow and relax too.

Me: Let me know when you get home. Oh, and I told my friend Lisa all about you. She thinks I might be crazy, but she believed me and is very happy for us.

Jon: That's good, I may not confide everything to my friends at first. They will likely razz me forever lol

Me: whatever you want is cool with me. I'm going to crash now, that long drive drained all my energy. But I wanted to say goodnight first

Jon: Good night, Miss Melody, sweet dreams.

I put my phone on charge and close my eyes, a huge smile on my face.

I awaken feeling refreshed, looking at the clock I am surprised to see it's only eight forty-five am. Feels like I slept longer. I get up and start the coffee, stretching all my muscles while I wait. Taking my coffee to my room I decide I have plenty of time to check a few emails and get dressed before heading over to Lisa's.

I grab the OJ and champagne, slip on my flip flops and stroll over to Lisa's. The blinds are open, so I know she's up.

Knock knock, I say rather than do as I let myself in, she always leaves the door unlocked for me, bless her as my hands are both full.

Hey girlie, bring that right over here and let's mix up the mimosas. I'm ready for one now. I have all the food ready she states as she grabs two trays laden with goodies and takes them out to the patio. I see the glass pitcher she's left out and two glasses. I pour the OJ first and then top it off with the champagne, using a long spoon to give it a quick stir. Pitcher in one hand and the glasses in the other I head out to the patio and sit down opposite Lisa and pour us both a glass. Handing her one I raise mine and say here's to great friends! She looks back and says and cheers to the cocktails they share. We clink glasses and both melt into a fit of giggles.

After a long leisurely breakfast that turns into brunch, a couple hours of chatting and telling each other all the details of our weekends we decide we'd both love a good long nap.

We say our goodbyes and promise to talk later. I head back to my house and go straight to my bed.

Mmmm this feels so good, I glance at the clock. Wow it's already quarter to two, I snuggle myself back into bed and drift off to sleep.

I awaken to my phone chiming that I have a text message waiting. I reach for my phone, four fifteen... It's Jon, and that makes me smile. I pull up the messages and see one from my mom too.

Jon: I'm home, how's your Sunday going?

Me: Lazy lol

Jon: lucky

Me: yup, slept in, had brunch with Lisa and then a long nap. Feels pretty good

Jon: I told the guys we were going to have company and who it was. They think I've lost it, but they are excited to meet you. They probably think you'll be nuts and it'll be good fun to see what happens.

Me: Can you blame them? If they told you the same thing, what would you think?

Jon: probably the same thing, you're right of course.

Me: Ah well, I guess we'll show them huh. I really am nuts lol just kidding, they'll love me...everyone does. Wink emoji

Jon: true true... go back to your nap, I need to get situated for work tomorrow. I'll text you tonight before bed.

Me: sounds good ttyl

Mom: Haven't heard from you in nearly a week Grace... don't ignore your mother, it's rude. And I love you

Me: I'm not ignoring you mom. I had an assignment up in Yosemite this weekend and it was late when I got home. How are you? Is dad, ok? And Janis? And I love you too

Mom: Everyone is fine, just wondering when you're coming home for a visit. We're looking at getting the house on Sanibel Island again for vacation this summer. If we coordinate dates maybe you can make it.

Me: Oh mom, I'm not sure of dates yet. I've been busy with work. I might not make it this year for the family trip.

Mom: But Gracie, you always make it home for family vacations. Isn't there anything you can do?

Me: I'll try mom, but I've made it for 35 summer vacations, it won't kill anybody if I miss one...ok? I'm sorry and I will try, I promise. Plus, it's always all couples and kids and I get stuck babysitting.

Mom: You love the kids, and you could be a couple if you would just settle down already. So many nice guys and you're beautiful my darling, aren't you ready yet?

Me: Mom I am not talking about this again; I do not want to be married and have babies. O.K. I have told you this a million times, it's not in the cards for me.

Mom: whatever you say dear, I just think you might regret it one day. And I worry about you being so far away and all alone.

Me: I am not alone; I have great friends and work and hobbies. I am fine, I'm more worried about you giving yourself high blood pressure worrying about me for no good reason. Dad understands, why can't you?

Mom: Let's not talk about this, please try to come home if you can. We miss you and love you.

Me: I promise I will try; I miss you too mom.

Mom: I love you darling, let me know. I'll send you the dates that the house is available just in case.

Me: Sounds perfect mom, I love you too and tell dad hello and I love him.

Mom: I will, bye

Me: I'm still in bed, and I think I'm going to stay here until tomorrow lol

Lisa: I'm at the gym... but going back to bed when I get home ttyl

Me: you're an animal, ttyl

I roll back over, phone still in my hand and drift back off. When I next open my eyes it is fully dark. I click my phone on and see that it is after ten. Wow, I must be exhausted. I see a couple messages from Jon over an hour ago.

Jon: I'm settling down, five am comes early.

Jon: You must still be sleeping, lazy bones lol

Me: Sorry, I just woke up again... I am absolutely being lazy today. Get some sleep and we'll chat tomorrow.

Jon: sounds good, sleep well Miss Melody

Me: Good night, Mr. Observation

Monday morning dawns, and it's a cloudy day. Looks like it will rain, I muse on my way to work. I pull in and park in my usual spot, Hi Grace I hear and whirl around to see Jenny.

Good morning, Jenny, how are you today?

Oh, pretty good considering it's Monday and she laughs at that.

Why are the weekends never long enough?? I actually have to go let Terry know I will need to take some extra time off.

Why? Is everything ok? It's not your family back home, is it?

No, no everyone is fine. There's just something kinda personal I need to take care of soon. Nothing bad, in fact it might be good...I guess time will tell.

Oooohhh... that's intriguing Grace. Why don't you tell me all about it over a cup of coffee??

Nice Try Jenny, but no. Not talking about this yet.

You're so secretive all of a sudden, and there's this glow about you... I think a man must be involved.

Oh Jenny, you are so silly I say while secretly smiling at just how on the money she is.

Knock, knock.

Come in, oh hi Grace. How did the weekend go? Get all the samples we need?

Absolutely, plus a few extra where it looked like it might be needed. But that's not why I'm here, I need to talk to you.

Ok, what's on your mind?

I'm going to need some time off. I need to take care of a few things and it's going to take me out of town for a bit.

Are you ok? Your family? How much time are you thinking about?

I'm good and the family too. I honestly don't know how much time, maybe a week to start with.

We can do a week, when do you need to go?

Well, that's just it, tomorrow or the next day would be best.

That's kinda short notice Grace...But I think we can swing it. Will you be available by phone if we need to get in touch with you?

Thank you, Terry. I will be available at times, and I'll stay in touch. I plan to work today and part of tomorrow to get everything here situated to be off. I don't want to leave anyone in a lurch if I can avoid it.

Much appreciated Grace, you know how much we depend on you around here.

Thank you, Terry, I appreciate that. Guess I'll go get to work and get everything shored up before I head out.

I grab my phone to text Jon.

Me: I took some time off work; I think I'll head that way on Wednesday if that works for you

Jon: that's perfect, I have to work but I could possibly take Friday off

Me: You don't have to do that, maybe I'll just mosey around Reno and see what's what

Jon: You sure, I'm not usually home until about 5pm

Me: Oh definitely, I love adventure. We can meet back at the house in time to figure out dinner

Jon: Ok, if, you're sure. I'll make sure my room is all cleaned up for you Wednesday night

Me: Perfect, I don't need anything fancy. I'll probably get there between 6-7 pm, will that work?

Jon: that works great, can't wait to see you

Me: Me too, it already feels like it's been forever lol

Jon: I know what you mean. See you soon

Me: Hey girlie! Stop by after work, you can help me pack

Lisa: of course...as long as you're providing the wine

Me: as long as you've known me, have you ever known me not to have the wine ready??

Lisa: you're right...of course

Me: see you then

Standing in my closet trying to decide what to pack I hear Lisa come in the door.

I'm in here sweetie, trying to decide what to pack.

Well, hello, you've got a nice little mess going on here don't you

I know, and I have no idea what I want to pack...it probably doesn't even matter. We're really only going to be hanging out so maybe just t-shirts??

No way, you can make a little more effort than that, I mean there's no need to be fancy, but you can make a little effort Grace. Seriously, she says shaking her head just a bit.

I know, I know... So, what do you suggest??

Well, I am thinking some casual things that can be dressed up a little just in case. Let me take a look.

An hour later I have a suitcase neatly packed with enough clothes for a week and a few pieces to pump up some looks just in case and an overnight bag loaded down with my toiletries, hair products and a small assortment of makeup just in case I feel like putting any on.

Now we need wine Lisa declares and marches off to the kitchen in search of some.

Agreed, let's get a bottle and relax, we've earned it.

So, Miss Grace, when are you leaving?

Wednesday, I am going into the office for a half day tomorrow and then I have a few   .
errands to run before I go. This way when I wake up Wednesday, I don't have anything to do but load the car and hit the road.

Sounds like a solid plan, are you nervous?

You know what Lisa? Oddly enough, I'm not nervous one bit about seeing Jon. It's his friends that worry me...they'll probably think I'm some nut bag just looking to hook up with a hot younger guy... ugh...

No, they won't, at least not as soon as they get to know you. No one who knows you could ever think anything bad about you.

I love you Lisa, you're so amazing. You always know just what to say to make me feel better.

Chapter 8

Wednesday morning dawns with the odd summer rain, luckily, it's nothing bad or that would deter my trip. I am so excited, literally giddy. Like a child on Christmas morning. I am looking in the mirror and taking extra care this morning with how I look. I have washed and dried my hair and opted to put some nice large beach waves in it with my hair wand. I applied a little serum to make it bouncy and shiny, I like the effect, it's very polished without looking like I tried too hard. Makeup, here I went a little overboard, but it looks great. A sweet eye with tones of mauve and browns, lots of shine and contour. Looks very classy and fresh at the same time. I am wearing a very cute pair of cut up capri jeans, an adorable flowing white tank that cuts in a low V-neck and has straps across the back. I finish it off with a pair of brown Birkenstock's and some rose gold earrings and a bracelet. I got a manicure and a pedicure yesterday in a gorgeous shade of peachy nude and I think it actually compliments my whole look perfectly. Looking in the mirror I think, WOW I can't remember the last time I looked this good. It's so refreshing to feel this invigorated about anything.

I am all packed with the excellent outfit choices Lisa helped me pick out and another bag with toiletries and necessities. I grab my cross-body shoulder bag with the fringe, it was a little expensive, but I love it so much and it's absolutely my style. I guess you could say my style is "bohemian" at least according to all the magazines and stores but honestly to me it's just great clothes that truly feel good.

I drag my bags and myself out to my Jeep, the rain has stopped, and I am glad. I would love to take the top off but just in case I think I'll leave it up. I load up my bags and climb in, I punch in the address Jon gave me and grab my phone to text him.

Me: About to pull out of the driveway, I'll see you in about 5 hours

Jon: Awesome, can't wait

I press start on the GPS and glance at the time, just after 12:00. Perfect timing, with a stop for gas and the restroom I should make it before 6pm. Here I go!

I listen to my favorite tunes and the drive is uneventful, when I stopped for gas, I was able to grab a bite and use the restroom, so I am good to go for this last 20 minutes of the drive. It's 5:15, I'm making excellent time, so I decide to take a quick detour. I look for the closest liquor store to grab something to bring. I mean it would be terribly rude to show up empty handed.

I pull into the parking lot and grab my purse to head in. I'm just wandering around thinking about what anyone might like. I grab some silver tequila, the good stuff and then some bourbon and rum...who knows what they like. I think a case of Corona couldn't hurt either. I look like a total lush with all this but hey, who cares anyway. At the checkout I see some limes and grab a half dozen just to be safe.

Loaded and back on my way, I text Jon.

Me: ETA 15 minutes

Jon: perfect, I just got out of the shower, so I'll keep an eye out for you and help with your bag.

Me: You're a peach, see you soon

I pull into the driveway of the little ranch style house, it's plain but neatly kept on the outside. Exactly what you'd expect for a bachelor pad.

I give a little toot of the horn and jump out. Jon is coming out the door and he looks as cute as ever...damn why can't I be sexually attracted to him. Ugh.

Hey Grace, how was the drive. Uneventful, but smooth...can't complain. How are you doing? Good day at work? Meh, it's construction, so a thrill a minute you know.

Well, I'm here now and I could use a little help. I stopped off for a thank you gift for putting me up and got a little crazy. Awe Grace, you didn't need to do that. Well, wait till you see what I brought before saying that, I say with a giggle.

We walk to the back of the Jeep, and he sees the liquor store bags. Nice! Looks like we're having a party.

Well, not on my account but a few drinks won't hurt us. No, they won't he says with a wink.

At the door I see two men standing there watching us, Jon yells over, give me a hand and quit staring like a couple of creepers. The younger of the two bounces over to us with a huge grin on his face. You must be Will; I say and extend my hand. Yes, ma'am I am he says with a twinkle in his eyes and a big toothy smile, dimples popping on both sides. Oh, jeez I exclaim! He looks at me and I say, I'm Grace and it's nice to meet you sir. That shakes him a little and he looks at me quizzically. Uh sir?? What don't you like to be called sir? No one has ever called me sir before, makes me feel so old. Ahh, I see, kinda like how I feel when people call me ma'am.

He has the decency to flush red at this and I give him my most radiant smile in hopes of easing his embarrassment. It works and we both chuckle. Well then Grace, let me help you out. Thank you Will, that would be lovely.

Jon is looking at us both with mischief in his adorable blue eyes. Looking in the Jeep, Will whistles and exclaims whew... Grace you're my kinda house guest. I do what I can Will, I do what I can.

Laughing as we go, the three of us collect my bags and the liquor store loot just as the other roommate finally shows up. He's more serious and I don't know what to make of him. But at last, he gives me a small smile and says welcome Grace, I'm Eddie. It's nice to meet you Eddie, thank you for allowing me to stay with you. No problem he says, any friend of Jon's is welcome here.

This way to my room Grace, I'll let you get settled then we can discuss where to have dinner. That's perfect, Will could you take the drinks to the kitchen or wherever you guys keep that sort of stuff? Yes m.... Uh absolutely Grace! Thanks again, looks like a sweet selection. I roll my bag into Jon's room and look around. I notice he has taken care to tidy up and seems like he even dusted. Very nice. He sets my small bag down and I turn to his open arms and give him a quick hug. I've missed you Miss Melody. And I have missed you Mr. Observation. We part and he proceeds to tell me where the bathroom is and luckily, it's right in the room. Apparently, he drew the master bedroom when they moved in. This is just great Jon, I'll keep it clean and don't hesitate to come and go as you need, I really appreciate you having me.

It's no problem, Grace, I am very excited to have you here. I think Will may already be in love with you. OMG he is not, it's a Mrs. Robinson crush, that's all. Well, I already told him hands off, I mean unless you want something to happen? Oh no Jon, he's sweet but not my type at all. I like your roommates, at least what I can tell so far. Let's just keep it all friendly, ok? Sounds good to me, I'd hate to have to wipe his tears when you broke his tender heart, he said laughing. I roll my eyes and threaten to slug his arm. Me, a heart breaker? Yeah right! Oh, I think you've likely broken your share of hearts Grace... Not even close. Well maybe one or two I say and turn to set my stuff out of the way. Alright then, just meet me in the living room when you're ready. Will do, I say!

I tidy my bags away and make a quick trip to use the bathroom. While washing my hands I check the mirror and notice I'm still looking good, so I stroll out to the living room to see what the plans for the evening are. On the way I grab my phone and quickly text Lisa.

Me: I'm here and settled, nice place and I'm fine. No worries

Lisa: That's good, be safe and don't drink anything you don't make

Me: oh Lord! Yes dear, I promise

Upon arriving in the living room all three guys are there and immediately stand up. Will says, where would you like to sit Grace? Doesn't matter to me, I'm fine anywhere. I choose a spot on the sofa between Eddie and Will and look over at Jon as he sits on the recliner. So...anybody hungry? I'd love to buy you all dinner.

Will smiles and Jon and Eddie just look at me... What? I look a bit self-conscious I imagine. Grace, we're taking you out tonight since you promised us a home cooked meal tomorrow. Oh ok, well then, I'm ready whenever you are.

Is there anywhere you would like to go? Nah, I'm fine with anything. Nothing fancy for me. Well perfect then, we know a great place we go all the time. We can have some good food and drinks and shoot pool if you'd like Jon says. Sounds perfect.

The guys all get up, so I do as well, let me just grab my purse I say as I dash into Jon's room. I grab it and head for the door. I'll drive Eddie says and we head for a large black extended cab truck. Nice truck I say, and I see the hint of pride in his eyes as he says thanks Grace. I yell SHOTGUN and beat the guys to the front seat. What Will exclaims! I was clearly in sight of the vehicle when I called it and I got here first. So, what are you complaining about? I'm clearly within the guidelines for shotgun. His face looks wounded, and Jon and Eddie are laughing hysterically. She's right Will and you know it, Eddie says.

I know but I just thought she'd sit in back with Jon. Get over it, dude, she beat you says Jon as he gives me a high five and we all climb in.

Awe Will, I'm sorry buddy...You snooze you loose I say. This causes another round of laughing and this time Will joins in.

Jon says, Grace a couple of other friends are joining us there. Seems like everyone wants to meet you. Sorry, hope you don't feel overwhelmed by everybody all at once.

Me... Nah., I love people, the more the merrier. I'm excited to meet everyone too, I've never met so many guys all at once though. Usually when I go out it's one or two at a time I say and laugh. I'll be fine, I say and smile.

We're almost there Eddie says as we pull up to a nice-looking bar and grille. He parks and before I can open my own door, there is Will opening it for me. Thank you Will, very gentlemanly of you. He beams and takes me by the hand to pull me along. I hear Jon and Eddie behind me laughing and as I glance back, they both just shrug.

He opens the door for me and as we step in, I see a group of three guys standing by a large table and they wave us over. Following Will's lead, we head over with Jon and Eddie right behind us.

Everyone, this is Grace. Grace this is Rob, Preacher and Les. Nice to meet you all.

Jon comes up beside me and says, Les is our boss at Cobalt Construction and I told you about Rob and Preacher or Colin. I look at him, yes you did thanks Jon. They all gather around me and some even hug me and welcome me to the "family".

I'm so happy to meet you all, Jon says you're all great guys and his family. That we are Preacher says, and very glad to meet you. It's nice to put a face to this mysterious woman Jon keeps talking about. I flush a little but say, well I'm glad to be here. Anybody want a drink? I could definitely use a drink after the long drive today. Hell yeah! Rob says and offers me his arm, I take it and we stroll up to the bar. Jon and Will are right behind us, and I get the feeling they are both angling to stand next to me. I roll my eyes and inwardly think... I should have some fun with this, oh yes and I think I will.

Jon wins and stands next to me at the bar, can I get you the usual Grace? I look at him and wink, why yes Jon I think that's a great idea. Everyone orders and we stroll back over to our table. I sit down and Jon sits on my right, Preacher snags the seat to my left and leans over to whisper; I'll sit here and save you the hassle of fighting the boys off all night. I lean close and whisper; you're a life saver Colin and we exchange smiles.

The drinks arrive and are passed around. I raise a shot and say: here's to new friends! A resounding collective cheer is voiced and glasses clink all around. I throw back my shot and turn the glass upside down. I forego the lime and smile at everyone. I feel eyes on me and then Eddie says out of nowhere, a woman after my own heart. I half laugh, half choke at that and everyone else joins in the laughter. Jon leans over, you've won over Eddie I see... That was the only wild card in the group and you managed to overcome that within the first hour. You are a wonder Miss Melody. I smile at him and wink... I do what I can Mr. Observation.

I turn my attention back to the table as an adorable little waitress strolls over with a smile on her face as she takes in this good-looking group of men. She looks to be about 20 years old and has a very hot body. A mass of blonde curls piled on her head and a ton of makeup on and an obviously fake and bake tan. I don't blame her for grinning, they are all pretty good looking with the exception of Les... who isn't all that bad just not what I consider hot.

Hey ya'll, she says. I'm Lindsey and I'll be your server tonight. I see you already have some drinks can I get you more or would you like to go ahead and order?

Well hello Lindsey, I'm Will. You new around here, he asks?

Yup, started two days ago she says as her eyes are roaming the group. Will smiles at her and says well Lindsey, welcome you'll be seeing a lot of us around here. We're regulars you see. I think we're ready to order, he looks over at me and says Grace, ladies first.

I look up at her and smile, hello I say. I'd like a cheeseburger all the way and fries, with mustard on the side. She writes it down and nods turning her attention to Jon. Upon looking at him closely she says and for you? Ogling him openly she is flirting with him and reaches over to point out something on the menu. I look at Colin and roll my eyes. He smiles and shrugs, it's always like this when we are out with Casanova over there... Really? I say and shrug. Good thing I'm not interested in him that way or I'd likely be super jealous. He looks at me oddly for a moment and says you're not into Jon? I whip my head back and level my eyes at him, no I am not. We are friends but it's not romantic in any way. Didn't he tell you that? He flushes a little red but says, yes he told us but none of us believed him. I guess we should have. I can see by the way he interacts with you and the waitress that he was telling the truth. I guess it's just odd to see Jon with a friend who's a girl and not a "girlfriend". I think you're the first as far as I know.

Huh... well, I don't know but he's pretty much my first good friend that's a guy. So, does that mean you're available? Why Colin, are flirting with me? I say with a mischievous grin. Not that I wouldn't be interested Grace for many reasons, but I'd never cross friends and women. That's just a recipe for disaster. I was asking more for the other guys; they would likely not hesitate if given the chance. I'll keep that in mind Preacher, but while I am single and available, I'm really not looking for anything or anyone. I'm kind of a lone wolf in the ways of relationships. I can't really see myself settling down or tied down to any one place or person... know what I mean? Grace, I honestly have no idea, he says with a chuckle. I would love to find "the one", settle down and have a family. Ahh you're one of those "Vanilla" types. Vanilla?? You know, family, kids...same thing everyday type of stuff...no excitement. Grace, I don't necessarily think those things are without excitement, maybe just a different kind of excitement. But I get what you mean and it's not for everyone.

I smile at him, well I'm glad you understand. I wish my mother could. She still thinks I'll get married and have babies and shit like that. I keep telling her it's never going to happen. My dad is fully supportive of my choices, he gets me. That's good he says, and you're lucky, it sounds like you have a family who really cares. Oh, I do, my family is the best, I see them as often as I can get back home to Florida and they'd be here in a minute if I needed them. But that's the thing you see, I don't need them like that. I love them and want them in my life, but sometimes I think they'd like me to come home and be close forever. For me, that would be something akin to a slow death... How do you mean Grace? Well, I crave adventure and I have a need to see new things and go new places. I like helping people, that's why I'm an Environmental Engineer. I hope to be in somewhere South America or Africa within a year or so. See what kind of good I can do.

Speechless for. Moment, Preacher clears his throat and says, those are very good goals Grace. I think you're just the kind of person who'll do it too. Thanks, I hope so, things haven't gone exactly the way I imagined they would yet, but I am determined to make them happen.

Just then the food begins to show up, our waitress Lindsey comes bearing a tray along with two others who seems to have jumped in to help out with the large order. It looks like a mountain of food, and I realize I am so hungry. Everyone is served and Preacher lifts his glass and says, cheers to our new friend and the old ones we love. Here here's and clinks all around, we all take a drink and begin to dig in. The food is good, it's no Betty's diner but it'll do. We're all chatting lightly and eating when I hear someone announce karaoke starting in 15 minutes. I look at Jon and he shrugs, it's just what they do here on Wednesdays he says. We usually listen while we eat and once in a while the kid or Preacher will get up there and sing a ditty. I look at him skeptically but say nothing and return to my food. I drink my next shot and order another round for everyone, giving Lindsey my credit card to start a tab. She takes it, looking at me like she can't believe I can afford it, but I just give her a small smile and she turns to go.

She's back with the drinks shortly and everyone thanks me, I wave it off and say enjoy. We all have another toast to friends, and I take both my shots back-to-back. Jon looks at me and says, you doing ok Grace? Me, oh for sure. I'm having a great time. I really like your friends; they all seem great.

They are he says, and it seems like they all like you as well. That's four shots in an hour though... you sure you can handle it? I roll my eyes and say, shots champion remember? Yeah yeah, I do...I was just checking. Thanks, but I'm good.

Chapter 9

I hear the singing begin as Lindsey comes back and starts to clear the table. She brings a binder that is full of song choices and tells the group, just take your choice up to the MC if you wanna sing. Will grabs the book and flips through some pages. I look at Jon and say, I guess he's going to sing. Is he any good? He's ok Jon says, Preacher is better, but neither could hold a candle to you. For some reason this remark doesn't embarrass me, and I smile at him. Preacher grabs the book and I glance at it while he flips through the pages. You sing Grace? He asks.

Me? Not really, I have on occasion but not often. Is that a fact? Well then, I think you and I should sing a duet, we can drown each other out, what do you say? Oh, I don't know. I probably won't but thanks for the offer. He gives me a grin and says, have another shot I'm putting us down for Islands in the Stream. You can't go wrong with a little Kenny Rodgers and Dolly Parton he says. I flush a little red but say nothing. I am thinking in my head, I can just sing quietly, and it'll be no big deal...his voice will drown mine out for sure. I give him a weak smile and he head's over to put us on the list. I see Will follow him and assume he's doing the same. Jon puts his hand on mine and says, you know you don't have to sing if you don't want to. I take another shot and turn to meet his eyes. I know I don't but what the heck, it's an easy song and I'm sure no one will hear me over Preacher anyway. You're sure? You can tell him no if you want to, Preacher will never make a fuss.

I'm sure, it'll be fine, it's not a power ballad or anything. Ok, he says, then I guess I'm glad. I'd love to hear you again, he looks left then right and sees no one is looking or seems to be listening and whispers Miss Melody and gives me a wink. The remark gives me an odd sense of pride and encouragement. I find I like it. It's almost like with Jon backing me up, I can do anything. I must be drunk I think and wave to Lindsey to line me up a couple more. I quickly down my fifth shot before she arrives with numbers six and seven. I sip my water and look around. Lindsey is openly staring at Jon, and I think he's noticed. I wave her over again and strike up a conversation. She looks at me oddly for a moment and then smiles a little. You from around here I ask? She says yes, she's from Reno and lives pretty close by with a couple of roommates she met when she was in junior college. Nice, what did you major in? The smile fades from her face and she looks down for the briefest moment before looking at me levelly and saying I decided it wasn't for me, so I left after the first semester. No sense wasting money. I don't know what to say to this, so I just smile and say, makes sense to me. I tell her my name is Grace and that I'm here visiting my friend Jon for a few days. I touch Jon's arm and say Jon, this is Lindsey, Lindsey, Jon. Then I stand up and stroll over to where the guys are standing closer to the karaoke stage leaving Jon and Lindsey alone to get acquainted. When I look back, I catch Lindsey's eye and smile. She returns with a slight smile and a nod then turns her full attention back to Jon. They seem to be hitting it off from what I can tell and continue talking for a few minutes until she heads over to check on some of her tables. She continues to circle back to him whenever she can and I notice she gives him a slip of paper, presumably her phone number and I smile to myself. Preacher comes over to me and says we're up next Grace, you ready? I shrug and say sure. He takes my hand, and we walk over. As the young lady on stage finishes singing a sweet little country song, everyone claps, and they announce us. Up next is a regular of ours Preacher, singing a duet with Grace...we take our microphones, and the music begins. As the words roll across the monitor we begin to sing in unison and with a small adjustment we blend our melody together and it becomes very harmonious. I begin to relax; this is going well and who doesn't like a good old fashioned sing along. I'm tapping my foot and getting into the rhythm, so is Preacher and we actually make a good duet. I'm totally relaxed which is odd for me and I don't even think about what I'm doing. I just sing and move to the music, Preacher is doing the same but keeping an eye on me for cues, at least I think that's what he's doing, and we move through the song together. It's his solo and he sounds great, we blend back together before my solo and I don't even think about it. I just sing and it feels good. As we wrap up the song everyone cheers loudly, and I look at Preacher then at Jon who is standing in front of the stage with a dreamy look on his face. We take a silly bow and leave the stage, heading back over to our table and our drinks. Rob is sitting there, and he stands as I approach, wow Grace that was awesome you have a beautiful voice. Thank you I say and sit down reaching for my water and begin slowly sipping.

Jon sits next to me and then he and Preacher both exclaim at how good I was, and I say how good Preacher was and it seems like he blushes just a little. We did great I say, and then look to Jon for that encouragement I know will be there. He doesn't disappoint. He looks almost proud, and he takes my hand for a brief moment and squeezes, leaning over he says I knew you could do it Miss Melody. I squeeze back and let go changing the subject. So, I saw little Miss Barbie give you her number, I assume your little chat went well. He grins and says yeah, it did. She seems nice I guess, definitely not a love match or anything but she could be fun to hang out with. Oh, I see... I say and wink like a "regular" girl and he flushes. Oh, jeez Grace, you ever gonna let that one go? I laugh, not on your life buddy, it's just too easy. But she did seem nice, a little bitchy at first but I bet she relaxes after a while. Yea she did, I think she thought we were "together". I told her we were very good friends but not romantic, that made her happy, I think. I laugh and exclaim, men! You just don't get it. Get what? Women I say... Jon, she likes you, obviously... and she thought I was competition, so when you told her I wasn't she got all happy. Now she'll try to get her hooks into you. What? How do you know that? Because I'm a woman and I have women friends that's how I know. It's in the handbook I say with a chuckle and roll my eyes. Let me guess, she asked what you were doing after her shift right? Yes, she did, but... Look I get it, she's young and hot and so are you. I say go for it. If you wanna go home with her it won't bother me at all. Grace, I am not doing that. I wouldn't leave you while you're visiting and I have work tomorrow, remember? Ok, but don't miss out because of me, ok. I won't believe me, he says.

Hey, I know what, wait right here I'll be back. I get up and stroll over to the bar area. I see Lindsey and start talking to her, I see Jon watching and I assume he thinks I'm making plans for him or something because he stands up and starts to head our way. I quickly tell Lindsey that I am cooking for the guy's tomorrow night and that she should come have dinner if she's not working. She looks at me smiling and I think she likes this idea. Just then Jon steps up and looks at me, oh Jon glad you're here I say. I was just telling our new friend Lindsey that I am cooking dinner tomorrow night and that she should come by if she's not busy. She quickly interjects, I'm not busy at all, sounds like fun. Jon turns to her and says, of course come by. I'll text you the address. I say, how's 6:30 work? Both agree and I smile feeling very pleased with myself. I turn back to the table and say I'll see you tomorrow, Lindsey, bring your appetite. Back at the table I notice she and Jon are still talking. They are cute. He heads back my way and is shaking his head but smiling so I know I've gotten away with it.

That was very sneaky Miss Melody... I know but hey the more the merrier right, and you might just get lucky I say winking at him. He grabs his last shot and I grab mine. He says, here's to getting lucky, in every way. I smile and clink my glass to his. I down my shot. I like that, I do feel lucky, very lucky Jon.

I hear my name and turn to see Preacher waving me over to the stage. Up next is Grace, she'll be singing alone this time so let's give her a big round of applause. I stand up and head that way, I'm shaking my finger at Preacher, but I smile, and he says not my idea. Rob over there said he wanted to hear you sing his moms favorite song. I glance at him, and he smiles and raises his beer to me. I look back at Jon and he's cheering me on. Oh, what the hell, I might as well. I climb up on stage and grab the microphone. As the music starts, I recognize the melody and think... oh fuck! Not just a ballad but a classic, I quickly clear my throat and sing the first line: at last...my love has come along... everyone erupts in cheers and I continue, giving it my all. I sing every line and note the best I can. I nail the runs and hold the long notes. I feel as though it's going well and at this point everyone seems to be watching and smiling. As I close out the song, I hit one last powerful note followed by a soft one and the music stops. Everyone is clapping and whistling, I get a standing ovation and I am blown away. I head off the stage and there are the guys, waiting. Jon's arms are outstretched, and I jump into them. He swings me around and as he puts me down, they all crowd around. Rob grabs my shoulders and I see a tear in his eye. Thank you, Grace, my mom would have loved that. It was wonderful, and he hugs me quickly.

Thank you everyone, I say and begin trying to make my way to the table. I sit down and they all begin to follow suit. Really fantastic Preacher says you were awesome says Will. All around the table they echo agreements. I thank them again. Preacher says ok boys I think I better settle up and head home it's 9:45 and 5am comes awful early. I look at my watch and realize it is getting late. Maybe we should all call it a night; you all have to work and I have exploring and shopping to do. I stand up and wave over to Lindsey, I catch her attention and she waves back. I make the check symbol and give her a thumbs up. I hope she knows that means tonight is on me and she heads to the bar to check us out. I see the guys giving her the same check signal and she nods back. She comes over with the black folder that has the receipts and my credit card she puts it down and hands me a pen. I glance at the total, $395.71... not bad for 7 people and I realize. I haven't seen that Les guys since we ate...odd but oh well. I tip $75 and sign the slip handing it back to Lindsey. The guys look around puzzled and Lindsey says, it's on the lady with a smile. I see her peek at the slip as she walks back, and she stops as she sees the tip. She glances back and I nod with a wink. That gives her a little pep in her step, and I stand. Thank you, gentlemen, for a wonderful evening. I had a great time and I looking forward to seeing you all again tomorrow night for a home cooked meal. They all smile and say they'll be there, but Jon has half a scowl on his face. He says, I told you I was buying your dinner Grace. Well, you were too late Jon, I clearly called it first and beat you to it. I smile at that, and he tries not to, but he does too. Will says, she's right Jon. She did beat you to it. We all chuckle at Jon in a good-natured way and his scowl fades. He shakes his head, Grace, Grace, Grace, whatever am I gonna do with you? I shrug, I don't know but I guess we'll find out and I wink, heading for the door. As soon as I open the door, I look at the truck and say SHOTGUN. We all peel off in laughter, even Will and we head home.

We pull up to the house and head inside, I go straight for the bathroom. I have got to pee so bad, jeez I guess that's what eight shots of tequila will do to you. I finish up quickly so Jon can go as well, and he takes his turn. He quickly changes into pajamas, and I get mine out opting to shower first.

I'm gonna grab a quick shower, wanna wait for me so we can chat a little before bed?

Sounds good, I'll give you some privacy just holler when you're ready. Ok, sounds good I respond and head for the shower. I decide not to wash my hair since it looks so good, and I don't want wet head for bed.

I shower and quickly dry off and dress in my pajamas, which are really just a small pair of cotton shorts in grey and a light blue camisole. I brush my teeth and head for the door, stepping into the living room I nod at Jon, and he says to Eddie See you in the morning. Eddie looks at us and nods back.

Jon comes in and heads to the bathroom, just gonna brush my teeth, be right out. I sit down on the bed then decide to get up and pull the covers down. I usually only use a sheet unless it's cold. The linens smell fresh, I like it and climb in. I lay on my side facing the bathroom. Jon comes out and I tell him have a seat, I won't bite.

He does and we begin talking. I really like your friends Jon; and I had a great time. I kinda think your friend Rob might like me... Oh he most definitely does; I think you won all their hearts tonight, Grace. But Rob can be a little intense, a totally great guy and I love him like a brother but be careful. Jon, I'm not interested like that, I mean he is cute, but I don't think I could date one of your friends. I love you too much, in a different way but still...it wouldn't seem right. I'm starting to see them like brothers or cousins... something like that anyway. You know I wouldn't mind if you did date one of them, as long as we stayed best friends. I won't but never worry, I'm pretty sure we're going to be best friends for life I say. That makes me happy Grace. I've missed you and I am so proud of you for tonight. I know you don't like singing for people, but you did it and you rocked! Thanks, I guess you just give me some magical confidence I never had before. With you beside me I feel like I can do anything. Grace, you can do anything, I have never met anyone like you in my life. You're kind of amazing. You're not so bad yourself Jon and I know what you mean. I hope we discover what brought us together but even if we don't, I'm sure glad we found each other.

We chatter on for a while and then I feel myself dozing off. He stands to go, and I say, this is silly. We are both adults and this is a big bed... why don't you just sleep here; I don't mind, and I sleep like the dead, so you won't bother me if you snore. You sure? Because I don't mind the sofa. Oh please, I sat on that thing for 10 minutes and thought no way can he be comfortable on that all night. If you're sure then I accept, my bed is actually pretty awesome. I got it last year, it's one of the Tempurpedic ones that costs a bundle but hey a good night's sleep is well worth it. I know what you mean, I paid a fortune for my bed and Lisa, and I went to about 10 different places to find the one I wanted.

He climbed in next to me, it's a queen size bed so there's plenty of room. I turn on my side facing him, and he does the same. I look at him for a minute and then say, I think I want to try something. You game? Ummm what do you have in mind? Oh, get your mind out of the gutter...jeez. I sit up and he does too. I tell him close your eyes, and don't worry.

He complies and I slowly lean over and press my lips to his, I press a little more firmly and reach my tongue out to lick his lips, they part, and I slide my tongue inside. It touches his for a brief moment and I slowly pull away. We look at each other for a minute, then start laughing. I fall back over onto my back, and he does too. Well now I guess I know for sure I say through my laughter, and he says yup. As we start to settle down, I hear a voice say, trying to sleep in here. I yell sorry and look at Jon.

Well, hey, at least we can't say we didn't try. I just wanted to be sure what my gut was telling me was right. Yup, we were both right. But I'm glad you kissed me, Grace. Now I'll never wonder, you know. Exactly, well I am tired. What do you say we turn out the lights and get some sleep? Yes, Ma'am he says, and I slug him in the arm before clicking off the lamp. Good night, Jon, good night, Grace.

Before I know it, I hear Jon in the bathroom, it's still fully dark and I roll over and click the lamp. He steps out, sorry Grace I didn't want to wake you. That's ok, I'll go right back to sleep. Ok good he says and steps back into the bathroom.

I'll be home after 5, I left you a key on the counter by the coffee pot. Feel free to have anything you want.

Thanks, I'm gonna do some exploring today and then come back and make dinner.

Sounds good darlin, go back to sleep and have a good day. I'm on my cell if you need me.

Thanks Jon I say and roll back over asleep in a matter of moments.

When I awaken again it's daylight, I look at my phone and it's 8:20. Perfect, that gives me plenty of time to be lazy and still go exploring. I text Lisa,

Me: good morning, dear, I survived the night lol

Lisa: I'm glad, having fun??

Me: oh yes, I even sang karaoke

Lisa: were you drunk?

Me: nope, it was fun too. These guys are very nice, I really like them all

Lisa: really, any good ones for me???

Me: might be, depends on what you want out of them lol. No breaking any hearts here

Lisa: Buzz kill

Me: sorry

Lisa: I'm sure... Ok back to work. Talk later?

Me: yes ma'am

Chapter 10

I grab a very quick shower; my hair still looks great so I decide a touch up will do. I shave my legs and underarms so I can wear shorts today. I pick an adorable pair of army green shorts that come just a little above mid-thigh and think, glad I've had some sun lately. The top is a striped tank with a braided racer back and it's not too tight. I love the coral and teal colors. I opt for my white vans and no-show socks since I'll be doing some walking today. I pair the cute necklace that Lisa picked out and some braided bracelets I got while in Mexico on vacation a couple of years ago. I touch up my beach waves and opt to put my hair in a high ponytail leaving just a few wisps out around my face. This looks good. I go for minimal make up with a glowing bronzer on my cheeks. Peach lips and shimmering taupe eyeshadow. Perfectly sun kissed look. This will definitely do. I grab my bag and the key from the counter and head out the door.

Climbing in the Jeep I realize, I have no idea where I'm going. What a loser, I guess I should have asked what there is to do around here. I grab my phone and look up shopping near me. It pops up a few ideas including a mall and I decide that will work nicely. GPS on, I point the Jeep in the direction of the mall in hopes of a little retail therapy.

I park and head in, the AC is nice, I see the food court and decide to grab a chicken sandwich. I snack on that and look at the map to see what stores there are. I notice plenty to choose from and head out to see what bargains I can find.

I spend a few hours browsing around department stores and smaller shops, I grab some really cute shorts and a few tops. They're nice but not what I'm really looking for, I want something that wows me. I pass the Pac Sun and stop in, a new swimsuit sounds good. I try on about ten before I find an amazing one piece that is perfectly high cut on the hips and low cut at the cleavage. Even better is that it's backless with just a couple of thin strips across the back, it's white and fits like a dream. Perfect. I pick a couple more to go along with it and head for the check out. I need to wrap this up and get to the grocery store to pick up the food for dinner tonight.

At the grocery store I browse the meat section and decide I want to make some hearty comfort food that the guys will love. An amazing dish my momma used to make, skillet beef stew over homemade mashed potatoes with fresh green beans on the side. I grab some celery and onions to go with the beef, butter, flour, beef stock and all the seasonings I need to make it savory and delicious. I grab golden potatoes and heavy cream for the potatoes as well as two loaves of soft French bread. I should have looked at what they have at the house for cooking, but since I didn't, I decide to buy an extra large skillet with lid and a two pots for the potatoes and green beans. I spot a nice set of white Cornell serving platters and dishes and decide they will do nicely. A breadbasket, knives, glasses and set of silverware round out what I need to set a passable table. I grab some red wine, iced tea and a bouquet of flowers before heading to the checkout line. Loading the groceries into the back of the Jeep I can feel my excitement building. It's just a simple dinner but for some reason I can't help feeling it's a pivotal point in this new friendship with Jon.

Back at the house, I am chopping, peeling, and dicing away. The music is turned up and some classic rock is swirling all around me, making me feel energized and full of electricity.

I find a plain blue tablecloth in the drawer and a glass container that will hold the flowers well enough. I set the table with the freshly washed dishes, silverware, and glasses. It looks nice and I am quite pleased with myself. Back in the kitchen I am braising the beef tips I cut from the huge roast I bought, adding in the onions and diced celery. Once they are all perfect, I use the pan dripping to make an amazingly flavored gravy, then add it all back into the skillet with a few spices and cover with the lid so it can spend the next couple of hours getting tender and juicy. I move on to the potatoes and green beans and pass the time just cooking and daydreaming about where life might lead me.

Before I know it, the guys are coming in the door and exclaiming about the amazing smells coming from the kitchen. I welcome them all and let them know dinner will be about an hour. Perfect Jon says, that will give us all time to shower and for the others to get here. Well good, it's great when a plan comes together. Ya'll have a good day? I ask. Yes's all around and they disperse to their respective rooms to get cleaned up.

A couple knocks and in walks Preacher with Rob close behind. I walk over and give them both a quick hug and tell them dinner is almost ready. Preacher says, darlin that smells incredible. Then Rob comes close and says, she sings and cooks. A woman after my own heart and gives me a telling wink. We lock eyes for a brief moment then the doorbell rings. I tear my eyes away and say, I'll get it. When I open the door, it's Lindsey standing on the other side with a six back of Heineken. Am I early, no no, I say and take her by the hand bringing her inside. The guys have all migrated to the living room except Rob who seems to be hanging back. I walk past him with Lindsey and take her into the living room with the others. I say to everyone that we'll eat in about fifteen minutes and head back to the kitchen. I'll help, Lindsey calls after me and follows me in. I'm glad to have the help, can you slice the bread I've had warming in the oven? Sure thing, she says and sets herself to the task. Grace, she says. Yes Lindsey? Well, I'm a bit nervous, I mean I'm not so used to being around so many men at one time. Oh, well me neither really, I say, but at least we have each other. Plus, these guys are all pretty harmless, at least in reference to our safety I say with a wink. Lindsey smiles and says, but what about the safety of our hearts? That stops me for a minute, and I look at her thoughtfully. You really like Jon don't you hun? Yes, he's really sweet and kind. There aren't many guys like him. That's true enough I say and lean a little closer to her, Jon is my best friend, and he is one of a kind. So be good to him or you'll have to deal with me missy, but I say it with a friendly smile, and it seems to ease her a little.

We carry all the food to the table in the serving dishes and place them in the center of the table. Jon brings in an extra folding chair to add to the six already there and we are ready to sit down and enjoy the meal.

Everything looks amazing Grace; I didn't know we had any of this stuff Jon says. Well, you didn't exactly have most of it, but I picked up a few things when I was out today.

Awe Grace, you didn't need to do that. These knuckle heads would be just fine eating off paper plates and from the pots. Are you kidding me! There was no way I was going to serve my mother's famous beef tips and mash from the pot, plus I wanted it to be nice. My way of saying thank you for putting me up and welcoming me into your little family at least for a little while. It means a lot to me and I'm so happy to be here.

Preacher speaks up now and says, we are so happy you are here Grace and now you are part of our family as well.

Here, here! Says Will raising a glass, and I glance around feeling so full of joy at being a member of this oddball group.

Jon is next and he says, I am so glad I met you Grace and I thank you for this amazing meal. And here's to Lindsey, welcome and thank you for joining us. Lindsey is blushing to her roots and her eyes are gleaming with admiration as she looks at Jon. I glance around the table and notice that everyone else is also noticing this. Eddie is rolling his eyes and Preacher is trying to stifle a laugh.

I clear my throat and say to everyone, dig in. Everyone is dishing out their food and passing around the platters and bowls.

Wine, we have wine I say and dash to the kitchen bringing back two bottles of red that I've had breathing in the kitchen. I set them on the table, help yourselves everyone. There's also some Heineken in the kitchen that Lindsey brought. We settle in to eating and I am pleased with all the praise over dinner. This is so good; Lindsey says as she dips her bread into the gravy. Good thing I don't eat like this too often or I would be so fat. Oh, I'm sorry Grace, I didn't mean any offense by that. None taken hun, I'm glad you like it. I don't cook like this very often for that very same reason. We both giggle and Will says, women! Why are y'all always so worried about your weight? I like a girl with some meat on her bones myself. This only makes us laugh more and he shakes his head. Preacher says to Will, boy don't you know anything? You can't say things like that to ladies. Why not, it's the truth? Oh brother, several of them say in unison. Alright, alright, I say. Will it's fine but they're right. We women don't usually like to be told things like that. For me though, I agree. I also like women with some curves better than a stick for sure. Suddenly six sets of eyes are on me. What did I say? You like women, Jon says. I roll my eyes at them all, jeez people grow up. Of course, I like women, I also happen to like men...very much. And yes, before you ask, I have been with a woman, and I did like it. But to be honest I prefer a man, ok? Heads shake and I roll my eyes again laughing. Are you telling me that not one of you has ever looked at a guy and thought he was hot? Or even thought about kissing a guy? Again, all heads shake in a firm no. Well then, I guess I'm the only one who is evolved enough to know that sometimes gender isn't that important. Apparently, Will mutters and stuffs more food into his mouth obviously uncomfortable with the topic. Grow up Rob says, it's the 21st century. Agreed chimes in Eddie.

Alright, let's change the subject Jon says and asks Lindsey to tell everyone a little about herself.

Well, she starts, I'm 24 and I've lived in Reno my whole life. I went to college for a couple of months, but I decided to take some time off and try to figure out what I want to do. I share an apartment with a couple of my friends, and we love hanging out at the pool, shopping, and going to parties.

Well, that sounds like fun. Have you decided what you want to do next I ask? Not really sure yet, for now I think I might just travel a little. My friends and I are talking about going skiing in Colorado this winter and possibly a trip over to Cali before the summer is up to catch some sun and surf.

WOW, I say that sounds like fun! You must make a lot in tips Will says, and Lindsey just looks at him. If you must know, my parents like to treat me to nice things sometimes. They pay for the trips so I can focus on my priorities. What does that mean, Will asks? WILL! Jon says and he looks at him like he doesn't understand what he said wrong.

Eddie punches Will in the shoulder and says, brother you got a lot to learn about women and politeness. Will looks down and has the decency to flush, sorry Lindsey. I didn't mean to offend you. It's fine she says although not too nicely.

I think we need more wine I say and fill up my glass, offering the bottle to anyone who wants some.

Well, this is getting uncomfortable, Preacher chimes in as he stands up. This was so wonderful Grace, a real treat but I should get going I have to be up early for work. Oh no, do you have to go? Yeah, I think I better. Well, I'm so glad you came, I hope I'll see you again before I leave. When are you leaving? Not really sure yet, tomorrow is Friday so at least a couple days. Well then, I will definitely see you again before then. Perfect I say as I stand and head around to give him a hug. He wraps me in his arms and gives me a big squeeze. After he leaves, I sit back down and see that it looks like everyone is done, can I get anyone anything else?

Heads shake and Rob states that he is so stuffed. Why don't y'all head to the living room to relax while I clean all this up and I'll join you in a little bit. Rob stands and takes the plate from my hand; you did the cooking, so we'll do the cleaning. Absolutely Eddie says in agreement, and they nudge Will who reluctantly agrees and begins to help clear the table. Alright then, thank you all very much.

Jon, Lindsey, and I venture into the living room, and she immediately grabs a spot on the sofa right next to Jon. I choose a chair opposite and sit down to relax, whew what a day. You tired? Jon asks. Oh, not much I reply, it's still early and I might grab my iPad and check some emails. Oh ok, he says, and Lindsey looks at me like I should leave. I'll be back in a little bit; I'm going to wash up and check those emails. Ok he says and turns his attention to Lindsey. I watch as I am leaving and notice they seem really into each other. I'm not jealous at all but I start to wonder if I should clear out of his room so he can have privacy with her if he wants it. For now, I decide to just grab a shower and check those emails.

When I come back out only Jon and Rob are in the living room. Where did everyone go? Will and Eddie headed to their rooms, and I told Lindsey it was getting late, and I had work tomorrow. Oh Jon, you didn't have to send her away. I was going to offer to move to the couch if you wanted her to stay.

No way Grace, you're my guest and I want to spend all my time with you. This makes me smile but I notice just a hint of something in Rob's eyes when he hears this. Well, here I am, wet hair and all. I'm sure I'm quite a sight. I think you look great, Rob says, and we both look at him. Thank you, Rob, I say and offer him my best smile. Jon just chuckles and I sit down. So, I say, and can't think of what to add.

So, Jon says. It is getting a little late and he's looking at Rob as he says this. Rob looks a little uncomfortable but gets to his feet and stretches, it is a little late and I think I should head on home.

I stand and walk to him, touching his upper arm I say thank you so much for coming to dinner. I hope you enjoyed it. I did very much Grace, his eyes gleaming and a smile tugging at the corners of his mouth. You're a wonderful cook, it was a pleasure. Then he takes my hand and kisses my fingers, I hope I'll see you soon he says and turns to leave.

When the door closes, I flop back onto the chair and look at Jon, we both erupt into laughter. I have never seen him act that way, I think you have cast a spell on him Grace. Oh please, I haven't done anything. He's just being friendly. Yeah right! Will walks in, what's so funny in here? Jon looks over at him, it's seeming like Rob is sweet on Grace. No way! Really? Oh yes Jon says. Get real I say rolling my eyes and shaking my head. No way, we just met. He kissed her hand and told her she looked great. Oh God Will exclaims; he must have a crush on you. Both are laughing now, and I say, so what if he does. It's no big deal, he's a nice guy. Looking at me quizzically Jon asks, Grace do you like Rob? What? No, well I don't know. I mean I barely know him. Glances are exchanged and I flush with embarrassment. Will starts singing, Rob and Gracie sitting in a tree k.i.s.s.i.n.g... Jon gives him a friendly arm punch and all I can say is grow up Will.

I turn and head for the bedroom, this is all just too much. But do I like him, I think to myself. Hmm? He's tall, good looking and very sweet. Oh God, he's another Mark. Or is he? There does seem to be something else there, something I haven't seen yet. Jon walks in and snaps my attention back to reality. Grace, are you ok? I hope our teasing didn't upset you. I look him in the eyes and give him a small smile, absolutely not. Truth is, I don't know if I like Rob. I really don't know him well enough to tell. Plus, I have so much going on in my life right now and so many plans that it's probably not a good idea to get involved with anyone just now.

Ok Grace, but just so you know Rob is a great guy and he would treat you right. Thanks, I'll keep that in mind. So, let's talk about something else. Deal, he says.

Well, I have some good news. Oh yeah, what's that? I'm working a half day tomorrow and then coming home to hang out with you. That's great! Anything specific in mind? Nah, I just figured we could hang out and talk, get to know each other better. Just some quality time alone you know. Sounds good, I didn't have any plans. Although I did buy an amazing new swimsuit today, thought I might find somewhere to do a little swimming and catch some sun. But your idea sounds much better anyway.

Well now that you mention it, there was some talk of a quick trip down to Tahoe this weekend. We could extend it and stay Saturday night if you wanted to. Really, I ask? Sure, why not, does that sound like fun. Absolutely, but why do you need to go to Tahoe?

He looked away for a moment, just something for my boss. Not important. I turn my head to the side and look at him, I can tell he's withholding something. Don't look at me like that Grace, I really can't tell you. Why, is it bad? Do you have to work? Not exactly, I just have to meet with some folks for my boss and then I'll be free to enjoy the weekend.

Jon, you can level with me you know that right? I promise I would never judge you. I can tell you're only giving me half the truth, and I have no right to ask but if you wanted to talk to me, it would be ok. Thanks Grace, I promise if I need to talk, you'll be the first one I come to.

Ok, well that's good. I want you to trust me. I feel like I can trust you and it's nice. I rarely have that. Awe Gracie, I'm glad and I trust you too. I promise. Wanna lay down and get comfy? Yes, I do, cooking and shopping really wears me out I say with a chuckle.

We climb in and settle into the pillows, ahhh. This feels so good. Yes, it does. Have I told you how glad I am that you came to visit? Awe Jon, I'm so glad too. It's been wonderful and I feel like I'm really getting to know you better, and of course your friends have been dazzled by me I say laughing. You're right, we've all been thoroughly dazzled. Watch it now, you'll give me a big ego I say playfully.

Alright then, how about we get some sleep and talk tomorrow? Perfect. I snuggle up close to him and he drapes his arm around me. I feel so peaceful with him like this, I sigh in such contentment. Sleep finds me quickly and I do not stir until Jon's alarm is going off.

Chapter 11

I roll over and peek out of my eyes to see Jon sitting up and stretching, I whisper good morning. Morning Grace, you should go back to sleep. Definitely I say, after you leave. Sorry I keep waking you. It's no problem at all, I'm used to getting up early...just not this early I say with a small chuckle. I should be home around 12-1, just as soon as I wrap up. Sounds good, I think I'll just hang around the house until you get home. Sounds good sweetheart, he says and heads for the bathroom.

I roll over and look up for Jon and realize the sun is up and I must have dozed off while he was in the bathroom. Oh well... I grab my phone and see it's already nearly 9:30 so I sit up, stretch it out and head for the bathroom. I decide to shower and dress. After that's done, I head to the kitchen to grab some much-needed coffee and sit on the recliner to enjoy it while I check in with Lisa.

Me: good morning sunshine!

Lisa: well hello stranger

Me: how's it going?

Lisa: pretty good here, better question is how's it going there in the land of hunks??

Me: oh jeez...land of hunks is a bit of a stretch but it's going great. I hosted dinner last night and it was awesome

Lisa: oh really, that's nice

Me: and even better Jon took a half day to hang out today and tomorrow we are going to Tahoe for the weekend.

Lisa: Tahoe? Really, sounds fun. Why Tahoe?

Me: Jon has to do something for his boss but said after that he's free so we can make a weekend out of it

Lisa: Just the two of you?????

Me: I don't know... I'll have to ask

Lisa: do I smell a budding romance??

Me: Get real Lisa! I told you it's not like that

Lisa: hmmm? Seems weird to me, but ok Grace if you say so

Me: I do say so, and anyways if sleeping in a bed together hasn't sparked a romance nothing will

Lisa: you're sleeping together?

Me: yes, sleeping and nothing else. I even kissed him just to test the theory and nothing

Lisa: what a shame, especially since he's so hot according to you

Me: he is hot, but I don't see him that way. He's just a friend

Lisa: well, that's just boring, but hey I gotta show a house in ten minutes so I'll call you later

Me: sounds good, and good luck on the sale

That done I decide to check in with my mom, I get the usual speech about family blah blah blah... Then decide I need more coffee and head for the kitchen. While there I grab a banana and head back to the comfy recliner.

After drinking my coffee, checking a few emails and Facebook I decide to take a peek at the rest of the house. I look inside Will's room and as suspected it's a hot mess. So, I go across the hall and look in Eddie's room, not too bad I see. It is a bachelor pad I think so I can't expect too much. I look in the bathroom and notice at least it's clean. There's an odd door at the end of the hall, I turn the handle, but it's locked. Hmm?? Wonder what's in there, maybe a closet or the basement. I decide it's none of my business and stroll back to the comfy recliner to wait for Jon.

I'm sitting in the chair watching various funny videos on my phone when I hear the key in the door. I look up and Jon is coming in, hey Grace. Hi Jon, how was work dear? We both chuckle and he says, alright I guess, how was your morning? Well, you can see it I say giggling, coffee, chair, and social media crap. Sounds exciting he says. I am going to clean up and change, are you hungry? I could eat I say. Me too, you wanna go out or order in? I'm fine with either, what do you want to do? He looks at me and says, jeez...women! Can you ever decide anything about a meal? I look right back at him and say NOPE! We both laugh and I say, heads we go out and tails we order in deal? Deal he says? I pick my phone up and say Siri, flip a coin. Siri says, "it's tails". Tails it is he says with a roll of his eyes. I'm getting in the shower, while I'm in there you can decide if you want pizza, subs, or Chinese cause that's all that delivers around here. Ok, let me just ask Siri, I say with a mocking laugh. He rolls his eyes and tosses a pillow from the sofa at me. What was that for I say, then remark, I told you I couldn't decide what to eat. He ducks into his room as I throw the pillow back and he shouts subs then, I'll order when I get out but there's a menu in the last drawer in the kitchen. Ok, I say and head to get it. I browse the menu and decide a turkey club sounds great.

Jon comes out all clean and dressed in a t shirt and basketball shorts, he asks what I want and then orders lunch. So, what do you wanna do I ask? Relax if that's ok. Fine by me I say and sit back in the recliner while he lounges on the sofa.

Before I know it, the food arrives, and he jumps up to get it. We decide to just have a sofa picnic and sit down to eat. So wanna watch tv or listen to music I ask. Sure, if you want to, he says. Ok, I say and grab the remote. Flipping through the channels I see that Goodfellas is on, Oooohhh I love this movie. Me too he says, and we settle in to watch.

Before I know it, I'm looking up to see the credits rolling and Jon asleep next to me on the sofa. I touch his cheek and his eyes open, hello sleepy head. He looks up and realizes he has fallen asleep. Oh no, sorry Grace I missed the movie. No big deal, Jon, I dozed off too...somewhere after Henry got out of prison, I think.

We sit up and stretch. I'm looking forward to tomorrow. I forgot to ask if we were going alone or is someone else going to. Well, the whole gang is going actually he says. We all have to meet with someone for Les and Rusty, our boss, and his brother. But I will drop you at the hotel first so you can lounge by the pool, we won't be too long and then we can all grab food or whatever you want to do. Are you sure I say? I mean if I need to go with you I can. Nah, no need he says. I don't say anything else because I can tell he wants to change the subject. Just then the door opens, and Will comes barreling in with Eddie right behind him. Hi guys I say and jump up to greet them. Hey yourself says Will and Eddie gives me nod before saying I call first shower. Will pouts a little and I say, he called it first Will. We all chuckle and I offer to grab him a drink as consolation. A beer would be great he says. Coming up I say and look at Jon who gives a nod as well, indicating he'd like one too. I grab three beers and we all sit down while Eddie grabs a shower.

So, who's up for a night out Will asks? Jon looks at me and I shrug, sure I'm always down. What do you have in mind? Nothing fancy we can head back to our spot if you'd like, it's Friday so there's always a lot going on and I think that Lindsey girl will be working he says with an exaggerated wink at Jon. Jon just rolls his eyes at him. So, Tahoe, I say and Will looks at Jon quizzically before Jon says oh yeah, Grace is coming and we'll stay over until Sunday. I told her that we'll drop her at the hotel so she can swim or catch some rays while we go to our meeting and then we're free for fun. Well alright Will says, sounds like a great plan to me, and I'll pick up a nice chick down there. I look at Will, I just bet you will darling, and I bat my eyelashes at him in a super flirty way. We have a good chuckle and I say, well if we're going out, I think I better get dressed. You look fine to me Will says. Jon nods in agreement but I look down at my shorts and tank and say, umm no I will not be leaving the house like this. Suit yourself they both say, and I just shake my head and go into Jon's room to freshen up. I look in my bag and find and amazing pair of ripped jeans that fit oh so good and a very low-cut tank top that is super cute. I grab a pair of sandals and the coordinating jewelry that Lisa picked out and head to the bathroom to fix my hair and makeup. I decide I'll wear a little bit more dramatic makeup and decide I'll straighten my wild hair. When straight it hangs halfway down my back, it's so silky after I put a little product in it that it shines in the mirror lights. Perfect I think to myself and add a little more mascara for an exaggerated eye look. Just about ready, I stand and look myself up and down in the mirror, not too shabby Grace, not too shabby at all. I turn and see the black lacy bra was perfect under the top as it shows just enough to be a little racy. I guess this will have to do, I open the door into Jon's room, and he looks up from tying his shoes and freezes, staring at me oddly. What I say? Is something wrong? Do I look bad? Bad? He says, no Grace you look way too hot to be going out with a bunch of guys like us. I let out my breath and shake my head, whatever! I am not hot, and you are all great guys and very easy on the eyes yourselves. Ok he says, but I better keep an eye on you tonight. Men will be all over you, looking like that. Oh Jon, you're such a tease I say and walk past him into the living room where Will and Eddie are waiting. Both look up at me and I say, sorry if I kept you waiting. Will stutters, uh um no problem, Gr gr Grace. Are you ok, I ask? Eddie whistles and says, damn our Gracie is HOT!! Jon says, told you so. I just sigh and say, whatever, can we go now. Sure thing, Jon says and as soon as we step outside, I yell shotgun! Will says, you don't even know what car we're taking. Doesn't matter, I'm in clear view of all of them from here I say, and we all laugh. She got you there, little buddy says Eddie, and I'll drive again. Perfect I say and head for the very nice truck.

As soon as we walk into the bar, I notice eyes begin to travel my way. I must be looking good I think myself and smile while I straighten my shoulders and walk proudly in. I spot Lindsey and wave; she waves back and heads over to us.

Hey girlie, looking good she says. Thanks Linds, which section is yours, we'll sit there I say and give a conspiratorial wink. Right this way, follow me she says and the four of us head her way. She places us at a very large table which is good as I assume the other guys will be joining us shortly.

What can I get you all to drink she says? I reply requesting a double shot of Patron Silver and a glass of water. Everyone else requests a beer to start. Coming right us she says as she turns to head for the bar.

So fellas, will the rest of the guys be joining us tonight? Jon turns and says, yes. They should be here any minute. Great I say!

A few moments later I see Preacher walk in with Rob and Les. I say to Jon, they're here. He turns and we wave them over.

Shew wee Preacher says as he approaches the table and looks at me, you look dam fine tonight Ms. Grace. Why thank you kind sir, I reply and give him a most genuine smile. I nod to Rob, and he nods back politely giving me a small yet sweet smile. Hi Les, I say as I notice him blatantly staring at me, slack jaw and all.

Preacher notices Les and gives him an elbow to the side to break the spell he seems to be under. I look and notice the others are all giving him dirty looks too.

He recovers after a moment and says, yeah, uh hi. Good to see you again, really good in fact. To which I reply, uh gee thanks Les and quickly turn the conversation to dinner. So, is everyone hungry? I know I'm famished. We all settle in at the table just in time as Lindsey is approaching with the drinks. The additions all order a beer, and she hustles away to grab them.

So how was work today gentlemen? I say to fill the silence while we wait. Les pipes up first, it was good, a long hot day of work he says. Will looks at him and laughs, when do you ever work Les? The others chuckle and Les replies, I'm the boss remember...everything you do is my work. Will whistles, dang man if that's the case I don't know how you manage to stand up at the end of the day. Les just grins and says, it is a wonder. We all laugh at that and settle into easy chit chat as we wait for Lindsey.

Lindsey is back with the remaining drinks and menus. We each take one, glance at them and promptly lower them ready to order. They all know the menu by heart and I'm simpler, I just know what I like. We all giver her our orders and I say to her to add another round as well. Sure thing, sweetie she replies while not even bothering to take her eyes off Jon. I just grin and when she leaves, I say to Jon in the most sickly-sweet southern accent I can manage, boy she sure does have a Texas sized crush on you partner. Everyone erupts into laughter and Jon actually flushes. My my, Mr. Observation, do I detect a flush on your face? Oh yeah, I do, you're sweet on her too, aren't ya? Everyone is listening as Jon says, she's ok, I guess. I punch him playfully on the shoulder and say Liar! He just grins and rubs his shoulder pretending I hurt him.

Ok, ok Preacher says, let's all give lover boy a break. Ms. Grace would you like to dance? I agree and Preacher leads me out onto the dance floor. It's a nice upbeat country song and we take off in a steady two step.

So, why you looking so good tonight? If you don't mind me asking, he says. Well Preacher, it' like this...sometimes a girl just wants to look pretty for a change.

Grace, I've never seen you not looking gorgeous. In fact I don't think you could look anything but pretty if you tried. Awe Preacher, thank you that is very sweet but don't be fooled. Catch me after 10 hours of sweating in the heat, digging in the dirt or muck taking samples and you'd see how far from pretty I can get; I say and laugh. Real gross at times.

Doubt it he says, I think if you rolled yourself in mud and seaweed, you'd still be beautiful and those boys would all still worship you.

Well, I do appreciate the compliment and your wonderful opinions of me, I say and smile so warmly at him. You know what I think? What he says? I think we're becoming great friends; I truly believe you are a wonderful person Preacher.

Well, he says, I don't know about wonderful. I'm no saint for sure, got all my own issues but I do try to be as good as I can whenever possible. That's all any of us can ever do, really, I reply. Yup he says and we continue the dance quietly until the song ends and head back to the table.

As I begin to sit, Eddie says I call the next dance Grace. I smile at him and say, of course Eddie. He promptly stands and I walk over to him. He takes my hand and leads me back out to the dance floor. This one turns out to be a bit slower and so we fall into a half waltz, half two step of sorts and I just let him lead me.

You look very beautiful tonight, Grace. Thank you, Eddie, you're looking pretty good yourself I say with a smile. He smiles brightly at that and holds me a little closer as we continue the dance. So, Eddie, tell me something about yourself I really haven't gotten to know you well yet. He looks down at me, me being so much shorter and says what do you want to know?

I don't know, where are you from? Reno, he replies. Any family around here? Moms in an assisted living facility, my dad passed away several years back and my sister moved to Colorado after college.

I'm sorry about your dad I say and give a small smile. Is your mom very ill? Thanks he replies, and moms not too ill, it's just hard for her to get around and she needs help with all the day to day stuff. We were never super close, but I visit when I can.

Well at least she's close, my family is mostly all in Florida where I'm from. I only go back to visit once or twice a year.

You ever think of starting a family here Grace? Oh no I think, here comes that same old question... Well, Eddie, here's the thing, I begin. I decided long ago that I'm not really interested in having a traditional family. I don't really see myself settling down for the whole husband and kids, minivan, and soccer mom routine. I mean it's great for people that want that but it's just not me. It's why I can never seem to keep a boyfriend. They say that's what they want until it isn't, and then try to change me.

He seems to relax after I answer the question and smiles down at me. I'm very glad to hear you say that Grace. Oh yeah, I ask? Yes, I never wanted kids either. I had a few girlfriends try to convince me and even one who tried to trap me. I had a vasectomy two years ago, I figured I would just take all the risk and worry out of the equation.

WOW I say that's definitely a made up your mind kinda move. How old are you now Eddie? 29 he replies.

Oh Jeez! I say, you realize I am 35. And? he says. So what Grace, age doesn't mean anything, it's just a number. Yeah, a number a lot closer to 40 than yours, I retort. He shakes his head and laughs, women! I chuckle back at him, and he pulls me closer and begins to sway slowly to the new song. This is so nice I think to myself. Eddie leans in close and rests his head on the top of mine and I can feel his breath in my hair. Very nice I think and tighten my grip a little. We finish the dance and as it ends, I say, I think we should go back to the table I'm sure the food is ready by now. He pulls back and looks down at me, anything you want Grace, and we turn back for the table.

We sit back in our seats; the food is already there along with the second round of drinks. Glad you two could join us Rob says aloud, and we all begin to eat.

A moment later, Jon leans over and whispers to me, now who's flushed Miss Melody? I absentmindedly touch my cheek and it feels warm. So what if I am, I reply and we both grin.

I reach for my glass and say, I propose a toast here's to friendship and the great weekend we'll have in Tahoe! Here, here, and clinks all around.

As the night goes on, I dance with pretty much everyone except Les. Thank goodness that weirdo had to go after dinner. I dance with Eddie two more times and can tell he is really into me. I decide that I want to be cautious, he is Jon's friend and roommate. Jon is my best friend soul mate or whatever and I don't want to do anything to risk what we have. Plus I can tell Rob may not like it that much...I wonder if he really does have a crush on me... hmmm?? Something to think about, maybe I'll ask Jon what to do.

Chapter 12

Back at home, I say goodnight to Will. Jon seeing that Eddie wants to talk to me alone, says he's gonna grab a shower before bed and heads into his room closing the door.

We're alone in the living room, and I'm actually a little nervous although I don't know why. Grace? Eddie says. Hmm yes, I reply coming back to reality. Wanna sit for a minute he asks? Sure I say and we head over to the sofa and sit side by side.

I had a really nice time dancing and talking with you this evening I say. He looks at me and says, I did too. I think you're pretty amazing Grace. I smile and look up into his big brown eyes, with a wisp of hair hanging over them. I reach up and move the hair away from his eyes with my fingers. He's looking back at me intently and I know he is going to kiss me. Should I stop this or let him, I think, but before I can come to a decision his lips are on mine and he's moving them over mine softly but intently.

This is very nice I think as I lean into the kiss and part my lips for him. Soon the kiss turns into a full on make out session, his hands in my hair, mine on his shoulders and neck. WOW, he sure knows how to kiss I think, though forming thoughts is becoming increasingly difficult. The kiss goes on a little longer than expected so I gently pull back and look at him. That was very nice I say, and he shakes his head in the affirmative while never breaking eye contact. Maybe we should go to bed I say and see his eyes flash in surprise. I meant maybe we should call it a night, not...well... I didn't mean sex. Ugh I sigh. I am making a mess of this, and I grin. I just meant, it's getting late and it's too soon to take this farther. And if we keep doing this, I will lose my good sense and take this too far.

He looks at me for another moment before saying, I think you're right Grace. But can I ask you something? Of course you can, you can ask me anything Eddie.

You and Jon, there's nothing romantic there is there? I take his hand, no Eddie there's nothing romantic going on. We are close, I even kissed him once to see if my gut feeling was right about us. Nothing, no sparks at all. We're very good friends, it's hard to explain but from the moment we met we both just knew we were meant to find each other but only as friends. Trust me, we have no romantic feelings at all. And what about Rob? I pause for a moment, never breaking eye contact. No, nothing there either at least not on my side.

I can tell he has doubts by the way he looks, but he doesn't voice them. He just looks at me and says, ok Grace I am glad. I really like you and I'd like us to get to know each other better if that's something you would like too. I squeeze his hand and shake my head yes. I would like that too, but just so you know I won't do anything to jeopardize my friendship with Jon. Good he says and we both stand. He gives me another kiss before he turns to leave. Good night, Grace. Good night, Eddie, I say and turn to head into Jon's room.

He is sitting on his bed when I walk in, he looks up and says, well?? Well what? I say and sit to remove my shoes.

You know what Grace. Oh that, I say and turn to look at him. Eddie just wanted to say goodnight and ask me if I wanted to get to know him better and see where things go. Really? Whoah Grace! That's big, what did you say to him? Well, after he thoroughly kissed me goodnight, I said that I would like that. But that I wouldn't do anything that would harm our friendship. He also asked if I was into Rob, I told him I wasn't but now I'm worried because I think Rob might be into me a little. What a mess!

Jon is looking at me in surprise, his mouth gaping open. I reach over and put a finger under his jaw to close his mouth, you'll catch flies like that I say and laugh. You're so funny he says rolling his eyes. He kissed you. Yes, he did, and he asked if you and I had any "romantic" feelings for each other. Oh jeez, he says. Don't worry, I told him we didn't and that I even kissed you to be sure.

Grace, you told him that. Yes, I did, why is that bad? Not bad really, but guys don't wanna hear that stuff. Well, you know me Jon... I don't like lies or secrets, so he'll just have to get over it. Oh and did you know he had a vasectomy? Yes, I knew, but I'm surprised he told you that. Wow he must really like you. What's not to like? I say and stand headed for the bathroom, I think I'll grab a shower too. Ok Grace. And Grace, there's nothing not to like about you. I smile back and give him a wink before closing the bathroom door.

Shower done and jammies on, I crawl into bed beside Jon and curl up on his shoulder. I'm glad you invited me here Jon, thanks for being such a great friend to me. He hugs me with one arm, and I snuggle in close, I'm glad you came and that we are friends. But what do I do about Rob? Nothing he says, you didn't lead him on in any way, did you? No, I didn't. I swear I did not. He gave me some compliments and kissed my hand but nothing else. Then I think it's fine Grace. You shouldn't worry. Ok, if you're sure, because you are all friends and I refuse to get in the middle of that. Just relax darlin, it'll be fine. They're both big boys. Now go to sleep, we have a fun day planned for tomorrow. Yes sir! I reply teasingly and roll over to go to sleep. Sighing contentedly.

Jon is shaking my shoulder to wake me up, rise and shine he says. We need to get up and get ready to head out. There's coffee in the kitchen, want some? Yes, please I say and begin to sit up and stretch. I grab my bag and start digging for clothes. I find a really cute bohemian maxi dress and decide to wear that with my new white swimsuit underneath. I grab some sandals and a floppy hat to complete the look.

Jon walks in with a steaming cup of coffee for me, and I smile appreciatively and take it from him. I deeply breathe in the aroma and take a sip, perfect I exclaim.

So I know you're dropping me off at the hotel before your meeting, but what about after? What are the plans, so I know what to take with me?

Well, after some pool time, I figured dinner and drinks. Then back to the hotel, as for tomorrow I have no idea so bring just something casual he says.

Perfect, I wore my swimsuit under my clothes today and I'll bring a change for tomorrow and something to sleep in. It'll all fit in my backpack. Viola!!

A girl after my own heart, a light packer he says laughing. My bag is already packed and by the door as soon as you're ready we'll head out.

Sounds good, it won't take me longer than 10 minutes I say and dash into the bathroom to brush my teeth and tame the mane. I opt for only some lip gloss and throw my toiletries bag into my backpack. I don the swimsuit and dress quickly then add my hat and sandals. I toss clean pajamas and underwear in the bag and add shorts and a tank for tomorrow plus a spare swimsuit, just in case. I grab my sneakers just in case and throw them in. Done! I get my purse and cell phone and head for the door.

Everyone is waiting for me, even Preacher and Rob. Good morning I say to all. I'm ready whenever you all are.

Jon takes my bag and says Rob is driving since his big SUV seats 8. Awesome I say and as soon as I step outside, I yell SHOTGUN! Rob and Preacher just look at us as Will, Eddie, Jon, and I all peel off in laughter. Inside joke I guess, Preacher says, and we all load up.

I'm ready for an adventure, how about you guys? Hell yeah! Will says and this time we all laugh.

The drive is only about an hour, and we stop at a diner for breakfast on the way. We pull into the hotel, it's small but looks pretty decent. We go into the lobby to check in, Jon has reserved 3 double rooms. I take the key to our room and say goodbye to the guys as they leave for their meeting. I head to the room; I open the door and see it's a standard room with two double beds. No frills but it's clean and will do nicely for an evening. I drop my bag on one of the beds and check the AC. It's set on 75 so I drop it down to 70. I grab the key and my sunscreen and head down to the lobby to look for a magazine to read by the pool. I find a couple choices and settle for the recent issue of National Geographic. By the pool I find a chair in the sun and remove my dress and sandals. I leave my hat on and apply sunscreen all over. I sit down and begin flipping through the magazine. I grab my phone and snap one of those cheesy selfies that show half your body with the pool in the image and send it to Jon.

Me: "pool mode" lol

Jon: Nice! Enjoy

Me: Thanks, be careful...see ya soon

Jon: Absolutely

I get back to the magazine, reading articles for a while before I decide to turn over and get some sun on the backside. It's a warm clear day, not a cloud in site. The sun feels so good on my skin. I am so relaxed I start to nod off after about twenty minutes, so I decide a swim is needed and head to the pool.

The guys pull up to the meeting spot and get out, Les and Rusty are already there. Les comes over, thanks for being on time guys. No problem, Jon says, they on their way? Yup, should be here soon but Rusty wanted to talk to us first.

Jon walks over to Rusty with Les and Preacher, the guys a couple steps behind. Hey Rusty, he says, you wanted to talk to us? Yup, I wanna be sure we are all on the same page before they get here. Okay, so what's the plan Preacher asks.

Well it's like this, they want us to burn a house for the insurance money, our take is 40%. How is that worth the time, Jon asks. I know what you're thinking boys but this ain't no regular house, it's more like a mansion. Worth a little north of 8 million dollars.

Preacher whistles and Jon just says whoa, the guys are all looking at each other in disbelief.

So let me get this straight, Preacher says. We just burn down this house and get 40% of 8 million dollars?

No, no, no, Rusty says, we burn down this house and get 40% of 25 million dollars. That's 10 million dollars boys... Of which you all will receive 1 million each and the rest is for me.

Whistles all round, are heard and the guys are all looking at each other. Preaches says, Rusty give us a minute to discuss this. Sure Preach, he says but we all know this is gonna happen, he says with a dead look in his eyes that clearly says he will brook no refusal.

The guys step away to talk Will looks at the each of them and says, we're not seriously thinking about not doing this are we fellas?

I don't know says Preacher, all that money means this is a lot trickier than we think. And dangerous says Eddie.

Exactly Rob and Jon say almost in unison. Something doesn't seem right here, Jon says. Why get a group of guys that are lower-level criminals like us for such a big job?

Just then Les interjects from out of nowhere because that's what makes it so perfect, don't you see? No one would ever suspect you or us. We have never dabbled in anything like this. Rusty and I have been known to move stolen goods from time to time, you guys don't even have records at all. I'm sure by working for us, it might be suspected that you could be involved with our "dirty" side of the business but there has never been any proof of that. I mean we employ over 40 guys in construction, so they would all be suspect too. You see that's why we or you all would never be suspected of anything like arson.

That is true Preacher says, but do we even know how to commit arson? And if we did, do we know how to not get caught?

Don't worry about that boys, I've done this before and I'll be helping. Wait, Rob says, you have done this before?

Sure have, twice to be specific. Both times arson wasn't even suspected, that's how good I am. But see, here's the thing with this job. It will take all six of us, this ain't no little bitty place. It's a bonafide mansion. Ten thousand square feet, so we'll have to plan it carefully and then execute it all together. That's why we brought you guys in on it and why we're paying so much.

Well, I'm in Will says and all eyes swing to him in unison. Little buddy, that's good but it's all or nothing Les says. See I need a tight crew, a group I can count on and one that can count on each other. It's the only way it works, so it's all or nothing. And you heard Rusty...you can't really say no.

Preacher takes a deep breath and looks at the guys one at a time, each nods in confirmation when he looks at them. He them walks over to Rusty and puts out his hand to shake in agreement. That's real good Preach, real good Rusty exclaims. Now when they get here, I'll do the talking. This shouldn't take long at all.

Just then a black SUV pulls up, here we go Rusty says and walks over. Let's hang back just a little Preach says to the guys, close enough to hear but not so close it's uncomfortable. And let's keep our mouths shut and looks at Will directly when he says this but says it with a slight grin and they all turn their attention to the SUV and edge a little closer.

Two men step out of the SUV from the back seat, one looks to be a guard and the other the boss possibly. Mitch? Rusty asks and the "boss" steps forward. I am Mitch to you he says, just then Rusty glances back at the guys and gives them a look to remind them to stay quiet.

Rusty steps forward and so does Mitch, they extend hands to shake in greeting and Rusty says calls me Tom.

Good, so Tom here is the deal. We need this done on the third Friday in July, the house will be empty, and the owner will be at a function with many people as witnesses. You will have approximately 5 hours to start and complete the job. The neighbors are not close so no one will see you, also the staff does not live in the house so it will be empty. It must appear to be faulty wiring, the company that built this house has already had a similar situation occur and it was ruled as faulty wiring. At that Preacher and Jon look at each other knowing what he means. He means that they burned another house built by the same construction company for the insurance money and will likely do more. Highly insured houses...

He goes on to say that the risk will be low as long as the job is done right. The insurance company will think it was the same faulty wiring when they investigate, and the money should come sometime between 1-3 months if all goes well.

Fine Rusty says, we will handle the job and you will handle the payment. I want half up front, call it a security deposit for the job if you will. In cash.

Mitch looks at him for a moment and then says; agreed. I will deliver the cash the day of the job, to you here in Tahoe. That puts me far away from anything you understand.

That works for me Rusty says and they shake hands again, then he hands him a card. Use this number to confirm with me, it's a burner. I assume I don't need to tell you to call from one also. Absolutely not, I know the drill. Then Mitch turned to the SUV and got in, followed by his associate and they quickly drove away.

Well boys, looks like we need to prepare for the job it's almost July now. Looks that way Preacher says and then adds, now let's talk money. We would also like half up front, as a good will gesture you understand. Rusty doesn't say anything for a moment and seems to be pondering this. Finally he replies fine, you'll get it on that Friday when you show up for the job. Les will give it to you right before, and I'm sure I don't need to tell you that trying to rip me off would be a very bad idea.

Of course you don't Rusty, we would never do that Jon says. But as you said, it's a gesture of good will and it keeps everyone honest. Now, we're going to enjoy our weekend. We'll expect Les to have a plan worked out to share with us on Monday, does that work for you? Works for me, and don't look so worried boys we're all gonna be rich in less than a month.

On the way back to the hotel I look at Preacher and say, what do you think? Honestly Jon, I'm not sure. On the surface it seems ok, I want to get a good look at this plan and make sure there's as minimal risk as they're saying. Do some digging and be sure this is all as we're being told. And I ain't doing nothing without $500K in all of our hands up front.

Agreed was murmured all around. I also think we need a backup plan Will says. Whatcha mean Preacher asks.

It's like this, I know ya'll think I'm just a young guy who doesn't take anything too serious but the way I figure it, we need a plan in case things aren't as simple as they say or if something goes wrong. I don't know about you guys, but I don't plan on going to jail for some strangers.

Makes sense Jon says, I think we'll come up with an escape plan just in case something happens. Good idea Will.

Chapter 13

Back at the hotel Grace has dozed off in the lounge chair by the pool when the guys walk up.

Uuuhhumm! Jon clears his throat and Grace begins to stir.

I sit up straight and shake off the sleepiness while looking around to center myself.

You know it's not a good idea to fall asleep in the sun like that Jon says. I know, I was reading a magazine the next thing I know here y'all are waking me up.

Well since we are here, who wants to grab a drink Will says. Sounds good I reply, let me just take a quick dip and cool off. Have you all checked in yet?

Not yet, let's do that now boys and we can change before meeting at the little tiki bar over there. Sounds good Preach, Jon says, and he winks at me. We'll be back down in a few so go have that swim.

Looking HOT ma'am Will says and winks with an over exaggeration and Eddie punches him in the arm playfully before pulling him along. Rob looks at them both with something akin to aggravation in his eyes. Oh boy I think, but they're gone, and I am hot so to the pool, I think.

While the guy's head in to check in and drop their bags I head over to the pool and dip my foot in to check the temperature, deciding it's nice I dive in and swim the length under water emerging at the other side.

I roll on my back and float a couple minutes, this is nice, I think. I hear my name and see the guys are back and in shorts and t-shirts. I swim to the edge and Jon reaches a hand to help me out.

I grab my towel and dry off then reach for my sun dress to throw on over my swimsuit, slip on my sandals and leave the rest on my chair for now.

Ready? Eddie asks and I smile back at him, yup! Let's go, who wants a margarita? Yes, please Will says and we all chuckle and head to the tiki bar.

We order drinks and sit at a table under a large umbrella, just the 6 of us relaxing. It's late afternoon already so the sun is starting to shift west in the sky. It's a beautiful day I remark out loud to no one in particular. Eddie, who is sitting next to me looks over and smiles, then leans in and quietly says, almost as beautiful as you. I smile at that and look at him through my lashes, and think he really is the nicest guy.

I hear Jon clear his throat, he's sitting on my right side, and I glance over at him to see him rolling his eyes at Preacher across the table. Rob seems to be looking down, maybe a little uncomfortable. I say nothing and look back at Eddie who is still looking only at me.

We sit around talking and drinking for an hour and a half at least before Will says, I'm starving! We planning to eat sometime or are y'all just trying to kill me from starvation. At that, I realize I'm hungry too. I second that I say aloud, and everyone jumps up. Preacher says, you should have said something sweetheart we can go eat anytime. There's a great bar and grille not too far from here where we can continue the fun.

That sounds nice, do I have time to change? Absolutely he says and looks at his watch. It's about 5:30 now, why don't we meet in the lobby at 6? Will that work Grace?

Works for me, I can be quick if you don't care how I look I say laughing. I hear chuckles but Eddie leans in and says you'd be gorgeous in a hefty sack. To which I laugh out loud, and everyone looks at us. I hold up my hand and say never mind to everyone and lean to Eddie and say thank you while giving him my best smile.

We disperse to get ready, I head to my room, which I am sharing with Jon. I head straight for the shower to rinse off, I scrub quickly and wash the chlorine out of my hair. I'm nicely bronzed from the sun, so I forego makeup and just opt for moisturizer and lip gloss. I step out into the room towel around me and let Jon grab a shower.

I go into my bag and grab shorts and a t-shirt, under garments on I put on my outfit and grab my flip flops. A quick brush through my wet hair and I decide, it's a bun kinda night...definitely a bun night and wrap my hair on the top of my head and secure it with an elastic. Jon comes out fully dressed in shorts, t-shirt, and flip flops. We look each other up and down and laugh...great minds I say and grab my purse as we head out the door with five minutes to spare.

In the lobby Preacher and Rob are already there, so we head over to wait with them. And here I thought it's you we'd be waiting on Rob says with a grin. Nope I say, told you I'm fast when I need to be. He seems to give me a small smile but then looks away.

We stand here chit chatting for a few minutes about nothing in particular when Will and Eddie show up. The kid wanted to primp in case he finds a girl Eddie says out loud and we all laugh. Hey, you never know...I'm a catch and this'll be a whole new crop of ladies to choose from.

Crop of ladies I say rolling my eyes, jeez... You are a hot mess Will. Hey, don't hate the player... I interrupt him there, Will if you say don't hate the player, hate the game I will definitely punch you. He looks affronted for a minute before I start laughing and playfully punch his arm. He throws his arm around my shoulder, you're like the sister I never had Gracie. Oh yea? Yes ma'am, the hot sister, I pull away and say EWE! Too far, now it's just weird I say, and we are all laughing as we walk out. Just call it like I see it he remarks in a good natured way.

At the bar and grille we find a large table and place orders for drinks and food. Smells good at least I say, I am so hungry it really doesn't matter if the food sucks. I am sitting between Eddie and Jon again, with Preacher directly across the table looking back and forth between the 3 of us and Rob sitting at the end of the table.

So I ask what are we doing tomorrow, adventure or just heading home? Well I figured we go out to the lake before heading home, have you ever been Jon asks?

No I haven't but I've seen pictures and it looks so majestic, the water clear and all those rocks...looks like paradise.

Eddie speaks up now, I say we show her some waterfalls and then take a swim. Let her see just how beautiful it is.

Everyone agrees, I am so excited I say and smile. Dinner comes along with more drinks, and we all talk about tomorrow and this and that while relaxing.

When do you have to head back to Fresno Eddie asks? Well, I'm not sure, I told my boss a week or so, but I haven't exactly decided. I could stay a couple more days if I'm not an imposition. Of course you're no imposition Eddie says, and I look at him, thank you Eddie but what about Jon? It is his room I have commandeered. You know I want you to stay Grace, he says, and everyone seems to agree.

Well if you're all sure, then I'll stay. But I will have to head back this week at some point I say, but in my head, I am thinking do I really have to? I will miss this and them so much, it's like I finally have real friends. I mean Lisa is my best friend, like a sister really but this feels so very different. We order and eat, chatting a little as we do.

Grace. I hear my name and it snaps me back to reality. Yes Jon? Where'd you go there darlin? Oh just lost in thought, its nothing. What's up? I asked if you were ready to go? Oh yes, absolutely we need to get sleep for our big adventure tomorrow. I agree to let them buy my dinner and we head back to the hotel.

At the hotel I say good night to everyone as they head up, Eddie is standing beside me, and I give Jon a look that says I will be up soon and he turns to go as well.

I look up at Eddie and smile, so nice, I think. He immediately leans down and kisses me, after a minute I pull back and suggest we step outside onto the patio where there aren't so many people and lot of quiet places to sit and talk. We step out and find a seat off to the side. We sit and I reach for his hand, he leans down to kiss me again. It's really a great kiss and it makes me think all sorts of dirty thoughts. I touch his chest and then his neck with my hand, as he reached around and rubs his hand up and down my back his other hand on my leg. He pulls back and gazes into my eyes, oh Gracie can you really be real? You're so amazing, I can't believe I am this lucky. I grab his neck and pull his lips back to mine; I deepen the kiss thrusting my tongue into his mouth and sweeping it around slowly. I hear him groan as he joins me in the same, our tongues meeting, our hands moving over each other. It feels like the kiss will last forever, and it's so good I want it to. I feel his hands move to my breasts, his thumb is slowly running back and forth over my hard nipple. I break the kiss by throwing my head back with a soft moan it feels so good. He immediately has his lips on my neck, dragging his tongue from the base of my throat up to my chin. I shudder involuntarily and feel myself get wet between my legs. Oh my God I think, if I don't stop this, we will wind up doing it right here. Oooohhh what do I do I think? But I know that I must stop this, at least for tonight. This is something we need to explore privately, definitely not outside on the hotel patio.

I pull away slowly, Eddie we have to stop. We can't do this here; I really want to believe me I do but we should really wait until we can be alone. He looks into my eyes, you're right my sweet Grace. You are not the type of girl who wants a quickie in the shadows, you deserve the best and that's what I want to give you. Always.

Oh Eddie, you are so wonderful. Thank you for understanding. I'd like to continue this when we can be private if that's ok. Of course it is sweetheart, I want that too. Now we had better go up before I don't have enough will power to stop.

We stand and straighten ourselves before heading in. At the door to my room, I say good night and kiss him one more time. A slow sweet kiss, then I go in and close the door leaning against the inside for a moment.

Chapter 14

Well, well, well, Miss Melody, you're looking mightily flushed there... Oh Jon, hush! I say teasing. I am a grown up and I can kiss whomever I want. True, you can. So tell me what happened...on second thought, don't.

Good, because I wasn't gonna. I grab my jammies and head to the bathroom to change and brush my teeth as much as cool myself down from that amazing make out session. Whew! I haven't been that turned on in a long, long time. Can I really like this guy that much, I think? Time will tell, I guess.

In the room I flop down on my bed as Jon is relaxing on his. So Grace, tell me something, are you and Eddie like a thing now? Oh I don't know...maybe. It certainly seems like it's headed in that direction but it's too soon to really know for sure. I don't want to rush anything, I mean you know what direction I want to take in life, and I want to be sure I don't hurt anyone in the process, especially Eddie.

He is very quiet, and I look at him, you ok Jon?

Me? oh yeah just a lot on my mind. Well spill it then, what's going on? He looks at me thoughtfully for a minute before saying, not sure it's something we should talk about Gracie. I mean, it's a work thing with the guys and it's sort of confidential.

Confidential? In construction? What's going on, you know you can trust me with anything. Are you in some kind of trouble? I wait...

I really can't discuss it, I'm sorry. I don't like seeing you worried like this Jon, maybe I can help you work it out. No judgement, I promise.

Oh Gracie, I'd tell you if I could. I really would, I promise.

Ok, well maybe then just give an overview like not the specifics just what kind of problem and maybe I can help out with some advice. I mean, I am pretty smart you know.

I know you are darlin, it's just really a tough situation. Well, try me, you might be surprised.

I have no doubt you can help, but I'm sort of embarrassed and I don't want you to be disappointed or not want to be my friend anymore, that would kill me.

Jon, look at me. There is NOTHING you could say or do that would make me turn away from being your friend. You know as well as I do that what we have found in each other is rare. What if the reason we were brought together is for me to help in this situation? How do we know, maybe I'm supposed to be here for this...?

Ugh I don't know; I suppose it is possible. Ok then, just give me a little something and see what I can do to help.

Well, you see the guys and I kinda have a side business. We work for Les and his brother Rusty at the construction company but... he trails off.

But what Jon?? What kind of side business? Is it illegal? Like drugs or guns?? No, no, nothing like that, exactly...

What does that mean? Like it's illegal but just not those exact things?

Yes. It is illegal, well we've moved stolen goods in the past. Nothing too major, small amounts at a time. We usually just transport or store them until they're sold.

Well that's not too bad, I mean stealing is bad but you're not physically hurting anyone. It certainly doesn't change my opinion of you.

Yeah, but what they want us to do next might...

So it's worse than moving stolen goods?

Much worse, and more dangerous.

Jon, what do you mean by dangerous? Are you and the guys in danger?

Actually yes, we could be. I'm a little worried we're in over our heads with this job.

Ok buddy, maybe it's time you tell me the whole story. I'll just worry myself to death if you don't and maybe it's not as bad as you think.

Oh it's every bit as bad as I think... but you're right, I may as well tell you at this point. But Gracie, you have to swear you won't tell anyone. I mean no one not even the other guys can know that you know.

Ok, I swear. I won't tell anyone. I promise Jon. I sit up and crisscross my legs, raptly listening as he begins to tell me everything...

So you know what we have done in the past for Les and Rusty. Now they want the 5 of us and Les to do this job. It's arson Grace, freaking arson. Apparently Les has done it before and this guy we're working for is going to pay $10 Million dollars for us to do it.

Holy shit! Really? $10 million dollars? What the hell kinda arson pays that much money?

Apparently, some guy owns a mansion worth like $8 million dollars, but he has it insured for $25 million and we get 40% of the insurance take. Half goes to Rusty and Les and each of us gets $1 million.

My mouth is just hanging open as he says this...but he goes on.

So the deal is we have to make it look like the fire is caused by faulty wiring, Rusty will be in Reno and the guy who owns the house will be at some big event with lots of witnesses. No one will be at his house and his messenger said the neighbors are not close, so we won't be seen coming or going. We get paid half up front and the rest when the insurance comes thru. Apparently, they have done this before to a house built by the same company with no issues, so it will just look like the company does shoddy work.

Whoa baby! That's a hell of a plan Jon. Are you serious?

Unfortunately, yes, and I forgot to mention that we can't say no...

Can't say no? Like something bad would happen if you did?

Yup. exactly like that, Grace.

I breathe deeply and sigh. That does sounds like a problem. So let's think about this. You are definitely doing this job. So, what we need to do is make sure you don't get hurt or caught.

We? He says, what do you mean we?

You can't seriously think I'm letting you do this without my help?? You're nuts if that's what you think. Jon I am an environmental engineer, I also minored in business so I can help.

Listen, you need to be sure you have a solid plan to accomplish the actual arson. I'm no expert at that but you should test it somehow. Like on a model or something. I don't know but to be sure it will work.

Then you need to make sure you do not deposit that money and don't accept any bills over twenties. Also, you'll want to make sure there are no security cameras or if there are that the tape is replaced with a tape showing nothing. Those things usually back up to the cloud and if they are disabled it will look suspicious, oh and don't google anything on the internet they can totally trace that stuff. Maybe even wear all black and ski masks or something. And gloves, definitely gloves, no fingerprints or DNA can be left anywhere.

Ok, ok, slow down CSI... how do you know all of this?

I told you, I'm really smart...and I have read a few crime novels I say laughing. A few dozen.

Look, I won't say I love this idea but since it's happening, I want to help you. You can tell the guys these are your ideas, that way no one will know that I know.

Grace, he says and comes to sit next to me. Why are you helping me with this? I wouldn't blame you if you ran out of here and never looked back. This doesn't seem like anything you would be a part of.

I sigh deeply, I really don't know why. I just know that walking away from you is not an option. And let's remember, I am only helping you plan the crime not execute it.

I love you Grace, I really do. Thank you, I think you really have helped.

I love you too, and I'm not done helping yet. Can you remember all this, or do you need to take notes?

I can remember it.

Perfect, so tell me everything you know about the plan. We talked late into the night and by the time we fell asleep we had a solid plan to get away with it.

Morning was shining thru the drapes when I heard Jon in the bathroom, so I sit up and stretch. All of last night comes flooding back to me in an instant and I flush with the weight of what I know is coming.

I grab my bag and dig out my yellow bikini and a pair of Bermuda shorts and a tank, this will work, I think. If I need to pee, it's easier than a one piece. Jon comes out of the bathroom wearing a pair of swim shorts and nothing else.

Good morning darlin, did I wake you? Yes, but that's ok, I'm excited to start the day.

I head into the bathroom myself, relieved and freshened up I step out and begin repacking my bag.

I opt for sneakers and a ball cap today; I apply sunscreen all over just to be safe. Hungry I ask?

Yes actually, wanna see what they have in the lobby while we wait for everyone else.

Sure, I reply and we head down to the lobby. When we get there the guys are already there, raiding the continental breakfast, so we join them.

A little fuel in our stomachs and we're ready to hit the road. Tahoe Baby! I exclaim as we prepare to pull out of the hotel parking lot onto the road. It's not a long drive, and I am so excited. As we pull up to an area sort of off the main road, I see a beautiful waterfall and rocks, it's so gorgeous.

Ok Miss Melody, Jon says as Rob pulls the SUV to a stop, let's get out and look around. Really? I ask, we can explore.

Absolutely! Preacher and Jon say in unison, causing us all to chuckle. We all hop out and head over to the edge of the lake. Eddie walks up next to me and drapes his arm around my shoulder, it feels nice, so I lean in a little and we stand there just enjoying the view.

I see the other guys take a couple steps away, but I don't care, it just feels so nice standing here like this. Someone here, for me, romantically, it's just been so long since I have felt anything remotely like this.

I grab my phone and snap a few pictures of the falls. Eddie, I say looking up at his sweet face. Yes Grace? If everyone wasn't looking, I would kiss you. He leans down and whispers into my ear, and I would let you. It gives me shivers to feel his warm breath on my neck and ear, I extend my neck to him and sigh.

Uhhhumm, we hear a throat clear and look to where our friends are standing a few feet away. Jon speaks up first, sorry to interrupt you two but we should continue on so we can do some swimming.

Yes, let's do that! It's so hot and the water looks amazing. Alright then, let's load up and drive over to the best swimming area.

As we pull up, I realize why they call it the best spot, holy crap it's amazingly beautiful. Almost majestic in its perfection, the water is so clear you can see all the way to the bottom. There are these rocks everywhere in different shapes and colors just shining up from the bottom.

I look around at these people, these guys, these wonderful friends I have made, and I feel lucky. Cosmically lucky in this moment, next to this place that defies my wildest dreams of what true beauty is.

Let's go swimming, I say as I jump out of the SUV and begin to remove the clothes, I am wearing over my bikini.

Well alright, I hear from Jon, and everyone follows suit to join me.

I toss my towel on the bank and step into the water. It's so clear I can see everything, it's cool but not cold which is very refreshing on this hot day.

I walk in up to my knees; I look around and decide to wade left toward some small rocks. I want to see them up close. I'm about 20 or 30 feet from the guys at this point but I don't care, I can't get enough of these experiences. I am in awe of this place, these people, and this experience. I can't believe I've been missing this, this...what?? I think and ponder on it, what exactly is it that I'm missing? I can't quite put my finger on it, it's something though. I know that for sure. I keep looking around and feeling everything, then all of a sudden it hits me, LIFE! That's it, that's what I've been missing. My life. I'm 35 years old and I've only accomplished a small portion of what I want. True I am an environmental engineer, but I am not using it the way I wanted to. I never wanted to be married or have kids, but I do want love. I want a partner, someone who values me as I am, and someone I value for who they are. I do have friends, amazing friends. Lisa and these guys are like family and that makes me grateful.

Grace! Grace! My head snaps up at the sound of my name and just like that I am pulled back to reality.

I turn to look and call back. It's Eddie coming towards me and that makes me smile.

Hey darling, I was calling you, where did you go? Oh sorry Eddie, I guess I was lost in thought or daydreaming. What's up?

Not much, just wanted to see if you wanna swim with me. Of course, I love swimming. I grew up in Florida and I would race my sister and cousins all the time growing up.

Race, huh?? Is that a challenge, he says with a sexy smirk?

Of course, I say, let's race to those rocks over there. Looks like about a hundred yards or so, you up for that?

As soon as he says yes, I turn and immediately dive into the water and begin swimming as hard and fast as I can. I'm gliding through the water so easily, stroke and breathe, over and over. I can sense him closing the distance, so I change my strategy and switch to swimming under water. This will help as there is less resistance and will make me much faster.

Before I know it, I am at the final destination, and I bounce up to the top of the water drawing in a deep breath of air just in time to see Eddie come in first loser. I am so excited

I yell a whoop in victory and Eddie grabs me around the waist and kisses me full on the mouth, lake water and all.

I hear the guys cheering for me in the distance, obviously they figured out that we were racing I say as I tear my lips from his.

Looks like it he says then begins to kiss me again. I surrender wrapping my arms around his neck and giving in fully to the kiss.

He is turning me on so much, I begin to let myself feel it and think about where this could be going with us. I mean we don't have to get married but having a boyfriend might be nice.

I break the kiss and look up at him, I think I really like you, Eddie. At least what I know of you so far. He smiles back at me and the twinkle in his eyes is so damn adorable.

Well then Miss Grace, maybe we should get to know each other better. I already like everything I know about you, and I think you can tell I would like to take this thing between us further.

I do know that, and I agree, I also want to see where it goes as long as we still agree on a few things.

Such as?

Such as, I do not intend to be a wife and mother. And I don't intend to settle in one place forever.

Grace honey, on those things we definitely share the same opinions. I can't see the point in marriage and kids are not in the cards for me. What I want is a partner someone to love and respect. Someone to have adventures with me, someone to love. Know what I mean?

Yes, I do. That's just it...I know exactly what you mean. I feel a hole where that is missing in my life. Don't get me wrong, I'm fine with how things are. I do very well in fact, but it would be nice...ya know?

I do sweetheart, I really do. Why don't we go out on a real date or just hang out if you prefer, see if what this is starting to feel like is real.

We could do that Eddie; I would like that very much.

Whistles sound from a bit away and we swing our heads in that direction. Hey, you love birds, come over and swim with us before we have to leave.

I turn and look at Eddie smiling, that's our cue then lover boy. He grins back, that's lover man if you don't mind. We both laugh at that and turn to swim over to where our friends are.

Well now, glad ya'll could join us before we have to leave Jon says. Then I swim over and put my hands on his shoulders and dunk him under the water. He bobs up and sputters, we're all laughing, and the horse play begins in earnest. About five minutes of hard playing and we're all pretty worn out.

I call out as loud as I can sputtering water, truce please! I'm drowning here people.

Ok, ok, let's all head back Preacher calls out. Good grief I feel old says Will and we all chuckle more at that. Come on ya'll, there's towels in the truck Rob says and leads us back.

At the truck we are all breathing a little heaving and panting as we dry off. I grab my clothes and slip the top on and pull my bikini top out from under it. The top is just long enough that I slip off the bottoms and my shorts on without anyone seeing a thing. There, I'm dry and dressed viola. The guys are all doing the same, soon we're all ready to go.

Chapter 15

In the truck headed back, I'm looking out the window head laid back against the seat. Just thinking about how wonderful this week has been, how amazing these people are.

Thank you all so much, this has been such a good week I say out load. Tears begin to roll down my cheeks silently. Rob looks over and I think he sees me, but he looks away, back at the road again and says nothing. I breathe deeply and exhale.

Jon leans up and says quietly, you ok Grace? I turn and look into his beautiful kind eyes. I am my friend, just doing a little thinking, I guess.

What about? I hear Will say so I turn to look at him and see all four guys are looking at me and seem to be listening eagerly. Waiting for me to say something.

I take a deep breath and look at them all for a moment. I, well I guess I am thinking about my life. What I mean is, how my life got so derailed from where I wanted it to go and how lucky I feel to have found you all. I know you all don't know me well, but I'm the kind of person who dreams of adventure, seeing different places and helping where I can. That's why I became an environmental engineer. Somewhere along the way I got sucked into a corporate job, yes, it's environmental and we do good work but it's not where my heart is.

Where is your heart? Will asks me quietly.

I am not sure Will, I always wanted to use my degree and my skills to help people. I wanted to go to Africa or South America, to places where I could help them get clean water, grow healthy food. But I wound up in Fresno of all places, spending more than half of my time in an office wearing skirts and silk instead of out actually doing the work. I bought a condo and make a lot of money; I have friends and fun but there is still something missing. It wasn't until I met Jon and then all of you that I started to see that. To really remember what I've always wanted. I was planning to go in a year or so, but I'm thinking maybe I should move that up. I just don't know, I need to think about it, make sure my family will be ok and that I don't leave my job in a lurch.

My mother, I say with a chuckle. Now she will have a cow when I tell her, a literal cow. She has these grandiose dreams that I will come to my senses and settle down to a vanilla life with a vanilla man have little vanilla babies, ideally back in Florida down the street from her. I hear quiet laughing from the back, and it makes me smile.

You laugh but you don't know my mother. My sister is the same, only my dad ever really understood me or accepted that I knew what I wanted for myself. He gets me, I think it's because he was a lot like me before he met my mom at Woodstock.

Woodstock? Preacher asks? Yup, they met in the mud listening to amazing music, dancing around naked probably I say with a shudder. Everyone chuckles at that.

Maybe I'm just being silly or fanciful, I could be completely wrong about everything but somehow it just feels wrong to give up on my dreams.

You can't give up, never do that Grace. Oh Jon, you're so sweet but what if I've got it all wrong. Everything I dream of could be a mistake

Grace listen, dreams are never mistakes. Sometimes we have to experience life to find our place, where we belong. If you don't try, that won't happen for you and that would be a shame. I hear these wise words from Rob, and I think wow of all the group I least expect it from him.

The words are so kind, and I smile and say thank you Rob.

He's right I hear Preacher say, damn right Will says. Jon just touches my arm, and we don't have to say words to understand each other. I look at Eddie now, he's been pretty quiet. And you? I say to him, what do you think?

I don't know Grace; he says and looks right into my eyes almost as if he's pleading with me not to leave him. My eyes widen a fraction at the realization of what he seems to be conveying to me.

Grace, he finally says almost in a whisper breaking the silence. I care about you, but I wouldn't want you to sacrifice your dreams. I smile at his words, but I realize it's suddenly very quiet and everyone has heard what he's said. Still I keep my eyes on his and I give a slight nod.

I lean back in my seat and return to looking out the window. So much to think about, I close my eyes and drift off to sleep.

Before I know it, Jon is shaking my arm to wake me, we're home Grace. I stir and open my eyes, realizing what he's said I sit up straight and look around before getting out.

I guess I fell asleep, you could have woken me. Nah, why do that he says. You looked tired and the rides not too long. Are you still tired, do you want a nap?

No, I think I want a shower and then food. It's late afternoon and we didn't grab lunch.

I'm sorry Jon says, we thought about it, but you looked so peaceful sleeping we decided to push through.

That's fine, really. We can just order some dinner if you want, or I could cook. It's really no trouble at all.

Nah, let's just order pizza and relax. We all have work tomorrow and there's no point going shopping and making a mess. Does everyone agree, he asks the group.

Works for me Will says and Eddie shakes his head in agreement. I need to head home and get ready for the week I hear Rob say and look to Preacher to see if he will stay.

Well, I should probably go too, long week ahead and all plus I wanna get cleaned up too.

Sound like a plan Jon says, I turn to Rob and say thank you for a nice weekend and your kind words. I appreciate it. He smiles back and nods before turning to go.

We grab the bags and head in, I go straight to the shower. Leaning against the wall the water running over me, I think again just how lucky I feel and how hopeful I am of the direction my life is beginning to take. For the first time in a long time I feel such hope and excitement for what is to come next.

All dried off and dressed I head out to the living room where Eddie is out of the shower and waiting on the sofa. I sit next to him, and he takes my hand, feel better?

Yes, I feel a lot better. You? Yes ma'am, there's nothing like being clean and comfortable he says with a grin, his damp hair hanging across his forehead in an adorable way.

So damn cute, I think. Too cute really, I muse but dismiss it, he's not even as cute as Jon but there is just something about him.

What are you thinking Miss Grace? Huh, oh not much just thinking how cute you are, all damp hair and sexy grins.

He blushes at this, and it makes me giggle, not for long as he leans in to kiss me. I lean into it and savor how sweet it is.

Mmmhmmmm, uhhhumm. Will is there clearing his throat, hey there lovebirds, did anyone order the pizza. I laugh but Eddie shoots him a dirty look, some privacy would be nice here.

Me? Will asks, I live here too. If you want privacy, you do have a bedroom with a door. I freeze as he looks at me as if asking me do I want to go to his room. I give a slight shake of my head but it's enough for him to know that's not an option right at this minute.

I look over at Will, he's just grinning like a fool. I shake my head at him and say grow up. We all laugh at this for a moment before we ear the doorbell. Pizza's here I say and head to the door.

I put the pizzas on the kitchen counter and grab paper plates and some paper towels. Will, Eddie and Jon are standing right behind me waiting. Ladies first Will says, and I say thank you kind sir and grab two slices and get out of the way.

Sitting in the living room eating pizza it feels so much like a home, like I belong here. I love it, I just smile and eat my pizza.

Jon flips on the TV and settles on a good old 80's movie. We all just watch and eat, before we know it, it's after ten pm. Wow, I didn't realize it was getting so late, you guys have to be up so early. I want you all to know I really appreciate you having me here with you and taking me to Tahoe this weekend, I haven't had so much fun in a long while. It's been so nice to relax and think. I appreciate how well you've all accepted me; this is all starting to feel like family to me.

Awe Grace, you're just like a sister to me not sure Eddie feels the same Will says laughing and it makes me laugh too.

Jon just rolls his eyes, but Eddie says grow up dude. This makes us all laugh.

Listen Grace, you are always welcome here. You are my best friend and I love you. You have been such a gift to me, you are part of our family. If you ever need anything I am here for you and I'm sure Eddie and Will feel the same way. They affirm they do, and I fall into Jon's arms for a hug, Will joins in and Eddie does too. I'm weeping at this point from all the acceptance and love I feel for this new family I've found.

The hug breaks up and I wipe my eyes dry. Why the tears Miss Grace?

Oh Will, they're definitely happy tears. It's hard to explain but not many people have ever just accepted me for who I am, and it makes me very grateful.

Alright well good, no sad tears then. So, I guess I'll head to bed. Good night Will I say and give him a hug.

I look at Jon and he perceives I need a minute with Eddie, so he also says good night and heads to his room.

I take Eddie by the hand and lead him to his room, once inside I shut the door and take his hand. Are you ok? I kinda got an odd vibe from you in the truck on the way home today.

I'm ok Grace, it's just that when you started talking about chasing your dreams in Africa or South America, it made me realize you could leave and go far away for a long time. It scared me little if I'm being completely honest. We're just starting out in this, whatever it is. Relationship I guess, it's more than a friendship for sure and I'm not one to just keep things casual. I don't do that. If I'm in it, you can count on that.

Oh Eddie, I didn't mean I would leave forever or never visit. I'm sorry, I guess it must have seemed like I was dropping a bomb on you. I forget that only Jon knows about these big dreams I have. I've had them for so long I just didn't think. I do care about you and I'm not being casual about us either. I want us to get to know each other and see if we are as compatible as it seems we are.

I want that too sweetie, would you like to sit and talk for a while? Yes, I think I would. Let me tell you about this big dream of mine so you can better understand me, is that ok?

Yes, I'd like to hear it. Well, it all started when I was a teenager... I talk and talk for what seems like forever going over all the details of high school environmental projects, my years at Berkeley and how I wound up working at PCE. I give the overview of details of my friendship with Jon and how it came to be figuring all the details might be a little weird for him to hear. But I don't leave out anything important. By the time I am done, he is looking at me so intently that I worry I've said too much.

I'm quiet now and waiting for him to say something in response.

Eddie? Did I say too much? Oh Grace, no you didn't I've just never heard anyone speak with such passion about anything. You really feel so strongly about this don't you? I really do, does that bother you?

No, it's doesn't bother me sweetheart, it's kind of amazing actually. It's just that it makes me like you even more, and when you leave it will be very hard.

When I leave? I say it out loud and it's like it makes it so official, I am really going. Yes, I will go Eddie, but that doesn't mean I'll be gone forever, and we can visit each other. I mean I would definitely visit you and the guys.

I would visit you to Grace, maybe even stay a while and help out if I could. You would do that? What about work and your commitment to the guys?

Grace, if you care about someone, you want to be with them and it's not like you'll just be vacationing. You'll be helping people that really need your help, that's inspiring.

I throw my arms around his neck and practically jump into his lap. I kiss him hard on the lips and find myself grinning like a fool. I pull back and look into his mysterious and sexy brown eyes that seem to hold so much depth in them. For a moment we are frozen just looking at each other before I feel his hand go to the back of my neck and pull my lips to his. He kisses me so deeply and passionately that it's hard for me to think coherently. I let myself embrace the kiss and fall right over the edge of passion and common sense.

We're wrapped up in each other, exploring with kisses and hands. His hands are on my back and shoulders, mine are on his neck and hair, grabbing handfuls.

I'm so hot I feel it all the way to my toes, on his lap like I am I can feel how excited he is. I decide in that instant that I want this to happen, no, I need this to happen.

I pull back from the kiss and look him in the eyes letting him know that I am ready, oh so ready.

I push him back on the bed, his legs still over the side and looking down at him I realize just how much I do like him. I immediately come down on him, bringing my lips to his once again in a searing kiss making sure there is no doubt of my intentions.

In an instant his arms are around me and he's flipped me onto my back, never breaking the kiss. Whoa! I think, oh yeah this is gonna be good.

I trace my hands all over his back and reach for the hem of his shirt, I tug it up and off. Then I reach for the waistband of his shorts and attempt to pull them down. He doesn't protest but gets up and takes them off then locks the door. I sit up on my knees to greet him as he comes back to the bed. I'm raking his body up and down with my eyes, and oh what a body it is. I guess construction is good exercise.

Oh Eddie, you're so beautiful I say in a throaty voice. Look at you, your body is incredible. He gives me a sly grin but says, Grace you a beautiful, enchanting in fact. I think you have me under your spell. While saying these wonderful things he's looking into my eyes so intently and lifting my shirt off at the same time. He pushes my shorts down to expose me completely then takes an appreciative look. My lovely Grace, you are magnificent.

At that I put my arms around his neck, and we fall into the bed together, hot kisses and roaming hands.

He's taking his time running his hands all over my body. Tracing his fingers up the inside of my legs, over my knees and up the thighs. He doesn't stop there; he moves over my mound twirling his fingers there for a moment and it makes me moan in appreciation. His hand slides up and over my belly reaching my breast, he slowly circles each nipple, and they harden instantly. I hear him making noises that sound like he's being tortured.

He leans down and begins to take the same path in reverse this time with his tongue. It feels like electric heat as he moves over me, so slowly it's making my body scream with excitement and longing. He maintains these ministrations for so long I think I'll go crazy. I'm so hot and wet, I want him desperately, but I reach out and begin to run my hand from his shoulder down his back and to his firm smooth rump. I squeeze each cheek then begin to slide my hands around his body and reach for his huge cock. My left hand reaches it and I grip it in my hand lightly. It's so large my fingers won't close around it and I gasp just a little, but I know he's heard me because he pushes up on his arms and looks down at me.

Grace, are you ok? Yes, everything is fine...better than fine.

Are you sure? Because we can stop if you want to, I don't want to rush you if you're not ready.

Oh my God, don't you dare stop Eddie! I want you so bad, I'm absolutely ready for you.

That was all it took for him to pounce, savagely kissing me and gripping me firmly on my hips. At this point I'm nearly breathless and my blood is at a fever pitch. I push him up and beg him, now please. I spread my legs wide and wrap them around his back in invitation for him to finally enter me.

Ok baby he says while positioning himself at the opening, then with one swift motion he plunges inside me, and the sensation makes me scream out involuntarily. He closes his mouth over mine absorbing the sounds as he begins to thrust in slowly but steadily over and over.

My legs tighten around his back, my hands are all over his shoulder and back squeezing tightly. I'm stretched tight with the size of him, but I'm so wet that movement is easy, and the sensations are blinding my thoughts so that all I can think of it the need building deep inside me. I grab his hips to try and speed his movements, I'm reaching my limit of endurance and need to find my release.

He growls deep in his throat and the sound is so primal, that I feel it all the way to my toes. I'm aching for release at this point. I pull his hips harder to me and begin to meet each thrust slamming our bodies together. I hear my name torn from his lips, Grace! That's all it takes, and I am sent over the edge, shattering in a hard release. It feels like electricity is bolting through my body, it is so intense. I ride the wave with him, locking my legs around him and digging my fingers into his shoulders.

Oh baby, that was so sweet I hear him say before I feel him increasing the rhythm of his thrusts and feel him find his release hot and deep inside me.

We're both panting heavily, he rolls to my side and pulls me into his arms my head laying on his chest. We lay there, heaving breaths and hearts pounding.

Oh my God Grace, you're a firecracker. The words come out of him in heavy breaths. You're not too shabby yourself I manage to say. I'm thoroughly satisfied, you definitely put it on me. WOW! I mean just WOW!

He chuckles a little and holds me tighter. I'm glad sweetheart, that was my plan all along.

Oh yeah? You have a plan, do you? What say you tell me all about this plan.

Now that would be telling Miss Grace, he says. No fair, you can't have a plan and not tell me about it.

It' no big secret that I like you, Grace. My plan is to drive you mad with incredible sex, treat you like the queen you are, and hope you fall madly in love with me.

Whew! Some plan you have there, sir. You're certainly off to a good start with the incredible sex. That was truly amazing.

You were amazing Grace, the way you let go and opened yourself up to me. It takes two to have amazing sex, I can only be as good as you are with me. So WE were amazing together.

I sigh, enjoying being in his arms and listening to his sweet words. I agree Eddie, we are amazing. I feel so good, I don't want to move but I need to get some water.

I'll grab it, hang tight. He pulls on his shorts then out the door. I hear him stop at the bathroom first, I assume to clean up. The door opens and he's back with a glass of water. I sit up and take it drinking half before handing it back. He sets it on his bureau before sitting back on the bed.

He takes my hand and kisses my palm softly. I smile at him lazily; I can't stay the night in here you know that right?

You could if you wanted to. I know I could, but I shouldn't, is more what I mean. I want to, don't get me wrong Eddie. It's just soon and this has been so wonderful but I'm not quite ready to be so out there in the open and spending the whole night in here would definitely signal to everyone what happened in here tonight.

Grace, are you saying you want to hide us? Absolutely not, I think the cats out of the bag at this point anyway. I just don't want to be that girl who swoops in and shacks up with some guy she just met. It's kinda trashy don't you think?

There isn't a trashy bone in your body Grace, and we can move at any pace you're comfortable with. You should know that I am in this, I don't just do this and move on. That's not the kinda guy I am, I want you Grace and I'm hoping you want the me too.

Oh Eddie, I do want you and I am enjoying this immensely. I just don't want to ruin it by rushing into anything. Silly I know since we just slept together but I mean, I don't want to force a full-on relationship so fast. We still have a lot to get to know about each other and I have a lot to figure out about my near future as well.

So please be patient with me and I promise I'll talk to you about everything as I'm figuring it all out. Will that do?

Yes, it will do. Just know that I'm here for you and I was serious when I said I'd go with you.

Thank you, and Eddie? Yes Grace? Tonight, truly has been incredible. I take his face in my hands and kiss him softly before standing up to find my clothes.

I'm going to go to bed, but I'll be here when you get home tomorrow, and we can talk more.

Ok sweetheart, sleep well he says, and I close the door behind me.

Chapter 16

I tiptoe down the hallway and quietly open the door to Jon's room. He's asleep in bed so I quietly go into the bathroom and clean up.

I make my way to the bed and slip in as easy as I can in hopes of not disturbing Jon, but as soon as my head hits the pillow, I hear my name. Grace?

Yes Jon? What time is it? Oh I don't know, not that late. He turns over and looks at me.

Oh boy...you two had sex, didn't you? What! I say, what makes you think that? Give it up Gracie, it's written all over your face, not to mention your hair. Oh jeez, I am truly mortified and pull the sheet up over my head in an attempt to hide.

Get over it, he says and pulls the sheet down. It's really no big deal, we all assumed it was gonna happen sooner or later the way you two were acting all weekend.

Ugh! But it's so embarrassing having you all know. It's like high school all over again.

Relax, I'm the only one who knows for sure. Well plus you and Eddie of course. Nobody cares as long as he treats you right. He did treat you well didn't he Grace? Because if he ever hurt you, friend or not I'd hurt him back.

Now you Relax, of course he didn't hurt me. Everything was good, but I'm not talking to you about the details.

Agreed! But are you ok? You seem to like him, and I know he likes you. Eddie never acts like this, and he never brings girls home like Will and I do.

Awe that's sweet, and yes, I'm absolutely ok. Just a little tired, let's talk tomorrow it's been a long weekend.

Sounds good sweetheart, good night, and sweet dreams he says making kissing sounds.

Ugh, I lightly punch his arm and roll over. Goodnight and grow up I say, but I laugh, and he does too.

Next thing I know there's light streaming in the window. I roll over and I am alone, sitting up I stretch and head for the bathroom.

I look at myself in the mirror, hmmm I look the same, but I feel so different. I feel good, light. Actually, I think what I'm feeling is refreshed. I guess great sex will make you feel that way. Ah hell, I like this feeling. Coffee, I need coffee.

I grab my phone on the way to the kitchen and send off a quick text to Lisa.

Me: morning sunshine

Lisa: Well good morning, I'm glad you're still alive

Me: don't be silly, you knew I had weekend plans

Lisa: So... how was Tahoe?

Me: it was so amazing, I have so much to tell you.

Lisa: you had sex, didn't you? You and Jon came to your senses

Me: NO! I DID NOT HAVE SEX WITH JON!!! I had sex with Eddie, amazing sex at that

Lisa: OMG, tell me everything. Was it good?

Me: Better than good, I have never had sex that good.

Lisa: WOW! So, I assume, size was no issue... wink emoji

Me: The size was NOT an issue if you catch my drift... He touched me everywhere and just right, like he knew my body better than I do.

Lisa: Really?? Sounds amazing, but do you like him?

Me: I really do, he's kind and funny and so hot! Plus, he sees life like I do, he doesn't want marriage or kids. He even said he'd go with me if I left.

Lisa: that's good but how do you know he's not just saying all this to trap you in a relationship?

Me: Well for one thing he had a vasectomy after a girl tried to trap him a few years back. Plus I just get a good vibe from him. He's got an honest face.

Lisa: an honest face...really, Grace?

Me: I know it sounds stupid, but when I look into his eyes we connect, and I feel he's being genuine.

Lisa: well I trust your judgement, but when are you coming home.

Me: I don't know...not for a couple days at least. And then I might not be staying...

Lisa: What?? Are you going back there?

Me: Maybe, but I'm thinking about going to South America for a year

Lisa: Are you kidding? Now? You said that was a couple years away...what about your job?

Me: relax, it's not like I'm leaving forever. But I feel like my life has been on hold too long already.

Lisa: WOW! You're my best friend, what will I do without you here?

Me: You'll be ok, I feel like the time is right. Being with these guys has showed me that I don't have to wait to start my life.

Lisa: I hate them

Me: No you don't, you don't even know them. And you will always be my bestie

Lisa: Oh don't get all rational on me, I'm pouting here.

Me: well, wrap up the pouty party, I have to go. I need coffee and a shower.

Lisa: Ok, I love you. Text me later.

Cup of coffee in hand I head back to the bedroom and turn the shower on. After my shower, I dress in comfy shorts and a tank top. I feel refreshed so I grab my laptop and a notepad and head out to the living room.

I choose the comfy chair and fire up the laptop, I start researching environmental work in South America. I'm looking into different agencies and groups, taking notes, and reading testimonials from past volunteers. I fill out a contact form for a company that has great reviews and shows they have had good results from their work.

Almost instantly my phone rings. It's a number I don't recognize but I answer anyway.

It turns out to be a representative from the company, asking to discuss my credentials and availability. We talk for about thirty minutes; I take his number and agree to think about it and call back within a couple days.

I lean back in the chair and let out a deep breath. So much to consider, what should I do. Can I do this? I grab my phone and call my mom.

Me: Hi mom it's me

Mom: hello darling, this is a treat hearing from you on a Monday during work hours.

Me: well I'm off today so I decided to call you and chat

Mom: What's wrong honey, you never just call to chat

Me: Nothing's wrong mom...jeez. I just wanted to talk to you about something I'm thinking about doing

Mom: Ok dear, what is it?

Me: First you have to promise to have an open mind and listen to me

Mom: oh boy, that bad huh?

Me: MOM! I'm serious, I won't tell you if you don't promise. I'm 35 and I can do what I want with my life, but your support would make me happy

Mom: Darling, I have always tried to support you. I don't always agree with or like your choices. I will listen to what you have to say and try to be open minded. Ok?

Me: Ok. Well, you know why I became an environmental engineer and what I've have always wanted to do with it.

Mom: yes, I do

Me: so I have been offered an opportunity to go down to South America, specifically Ecuador.

Mom: why?

Me: to work on wells and irrigation. Specifically, to help set up some farming for crop rotation. To help them grow more sustainable crops.

Mom: Ok, that doesn't sound so bad... when would you go? Is it safe?

Me: well, they'd like me to go as soon as possible. They have security measures in place already. A team has been there for the past two and a half years.

Mom: two and a half years...already? Gracie, how long would you be there?

Me: .... well mom, that's the thing, it's a year commitment.

Mom: A year! What? Gracie, are you crazy? A year in Ecuador? Why?

Me: Mom, you said you would be open and calm. I want to help people; I love what I do. I can do this.

Mom: dear, I know you can but can't someone else help? That's a long time, and it's really far away. I don't know about this.

Me: Mom, I am a grown woman. I know what I want to do, I know what I can do. I can do this; and it will make me happy. Can't you be happy for me?

Mom: Oh honey, I'm scared for you, and I would miss you. Are you absolutely sure about this?

Me: Yes mom, I am sure. I am doing this, but I want your support.

Mom: Oh Gracie... I know your dad is always so supportive, he gets behind these wild ideas you have. But I'm your mother, you're my baby. I don't know.

Me: Oh mom, I love you. I know it's hard, but I'm strong and responsible. Please give me your support in this.

Mom: Gracie, I'll always support you. It just scares me.

Me: Thank you mom, your support means so much to me. Having you in my corner is important to me. I know, I didn't turn out the way you wanted.

Mom: Stop right now young lady, I may have had other ideas for your life, but you are not a disappointment to me, and I have always been proud of you. You have great strength and independence. You are smart and beautiful. I love you Grace, maybe I'm even a little jealous of you.

Me: Jealous of me, You can't be serious, what for?

Mom: Because you're so confident and self-assured darling, you know what you want, and you never settle. You have such an adventurous spirit, I thought I would too...once upon a time. You're like wildfire, fast spreading and unstoppable. Not many people can live that way darling, but you do and it's who you are.

Me: Mom, do you regret the path you took in life?

Mom: Absolutely not, I wouldn't trade what I have for anything. Your father and you girls have been the best blessings I could have ever received.

Me: I love you mom; I want you to be happy too.

Mom: I am happy dear, I promise you. Now let's talk more about this big adventure of yours.

After about an hour on the phone, I hung up feeling like I know my mother so much better than I ever did. She thinks I'm like "wildfire", she's never told me anything like that before. It touches me so deeply to have her admiration.

I feel so encouraged to move forward now that I have my mom's blessing. I always thought she didn't understand me, but she really does. What a revelation.

Engrossed in my research, it takes me by surprise when the guys come in the door from work.

Wow! 5:30 already, I guess I lost track of time. I guess so Jon says spying my pile of notes and the laptop.

Hey darling, how was your day? Eddie says and leans down to kiss my forehead. Very good, I did a lot of research and talked to my mom for like an hour.

I was hoping to come home to dinner, some housewife you'd make. WILL! I yell, and Jon punches him on the arm while Eddie gives him a serious scowl. Relax everybody, jeez I was only kidding.

We all chuckle, but I exclaim "I am starving though" ...don't think I've had anything but coffee today. Why don't I take us to dinner or we could order in, I have some news to tell you all too.

Really? What kind of news? Well Eddie, good news I hope but let's talk over dinner if that's ok with everyone.

So what do we want to do fellas? Eat in or go out?

Will chimes in, let's go out, who's up for the Brass Tap? Sounds good to me, let me throw on some clothes while you all get cleaned up.

I'll call Rob and Preacher Eddie says. Oh Good I say and go up on my tip toes to kiss his cheek before heading to Jon's room to find clothes.

In the room Jon asks, so what's this big news? You'll just have to wait like everyone else I say laughing. Ugh, I think I have to go home soon...I'm almost completely out of clothes.

Oh no he says laughing and I throw a shoe at him, but he ducks, and it hits the wall by the bathroom door. Poking his head back out he says, my, my, Miss Melody, you have a little bit of a temper on you and promptly ducks back into the bathroom before I can throw something else.

I opt for light washed denim capri pants with very fashionable holes in them, a grey Beatles t-shirt tied at the waist and my converse. I grab a hairbrush and decide to put my hair up in a ballerina bun with just a few whisps left out to frame my face. Looking in the mirror above his dresser, I turn all directions and think this will do fine. I grab my makeup bag and apply some tinted moisturizer, bronzer on my cheeks and lip gloss. Hmmm, needs something... a little mascara, that will polish this look up. All that done I head back out to the living room to wait for everyone else.

I don't have to wait long before Will heads out ready to go and a few minutes later Jon as well.

We sit and chat, well actually I sit and dodge twenty questions about my "big news". Luckily Eddie showers pretty quickly and we are ready to head out.

As we get to the door, I look out and yell, shotgun. I laugh and say, that never gets old. You're encourage-able Jon says, shaking his head at me but with a huge smile on his face. And I wouldn't have you any other way.

That makes me smile and we load up and head out. When we walk in the door, I immediately see Lindsey is talking to Preacher at our table, Rob sitting beside him.

Well hello he says standing up a I approach, what took ya'll so long? Dude, there's four of us and two bathrooms Will says.

Likely excuse, Rob says grinning. I bet she was ready before the lot of you.

Yup I say and giggle taking my seat across from Preacher and Rob, Jon, and Eddie on either side of me.

I am so hungry I say to Lindsey, oh and hello. Sorry I'm being rude but really I am starving. She laughs and says, need a menu doll?

Nope just a cheeseburger all the way, fries, and mustard. Oh and a Corona, no tequila for me tonight.

Same, I hear from Jon, Rob, and Eddie. Will orders a quesadilla and Preach the hot wings.

Well ya'll made that easy enough, I'll be right back with your drinks, and I'll get that order in ASAP.

Jon looks at me and says, so??

So what??

Don't be daft Grace, the big news... The suspense is killing me here.

Me too I hear Eddie and Will say, while Preacher and Rob look at me quizzically.

Jon sees them and says, she announced she had big news to tell us at dinner. Ok then, Preacher says. Let's have it, Miss Grace.

With five sets of eyes on me I look around this table and twist my hands in my lap looking for the right words.

I feel Jon touch my arm, so supportively. Ok guys so you know what we talked about on the way back yesterday. I see heads nod, so I continue.

Well, I did a lot of research today. I mean a lot, and I spoke to rep from an organization that wants my help in setting up crop rotation in Ecuador. Well not actually planting the crops but testing the soil and planning what crops will be most successful.

All eyes are aptly watching me as I explain the process and what it all entails, then I get to the part about needing to go soon. I see Eddie look down and I feel bad for that. I don't want to hurt him, and I do have feelings for him, but I can't plan my life around him. Jon on the other hand is different, he seems to be gazing at me in wonder. Almost like amazement in a way, and that gives me confidence to continue.

Well? I say when I'm done talking and everyone is still silent.

Jon speaks up first, Gracie, I think it all sounds wonderful. You seem very excited, like it would make you happy to do this. For me your happiness is what matters.

Thank you, Jon, that means so much to me I say and smile warmly into his eyes.

I glance around the table; everyone is still quiet, but it doesn't feel like a bad thing. I think it sounds like a wonderful thing to do, Preacher states. I'm all for helping people.

Why would you wanna go there, Will asks? I mean isn't it hot and dangerous?

Well Will, hot yes. I believe it will be hot and humid, lots of insects they told me. Dangerous, not so much. They have security and it's not a bad place, it's a poor place with a lot of good people and probably a few bad ones.... like anywhere else really. But there I can help, really help them have sustainable food crops and environmentally safe growing practices.

Wow, I guess I never even thought of something like that. I just buy food and never consider how it gets here or where it comes from.

That's pretty common Will, it's very easy to do. We live in a place where we can buy anything we want or need. But these people have to live on what they can produce or grow mostly. I believe I can help.

Sounds like you've got it all figured our Grace, Rob chimes in and we all look to him as he's usually the quiet one in the group.

I think so Rob.

Well, I know we all wish you the best of luck. It's been so amazing getting to know you, I hope you'll stay a part of our lives.

I look at him thoughtfully for a moment, then around the table at this amazing yet so very diverse group of men and think again just how lucky I am. I assure you all, that I want to always be a part of your lives and for you all to be in mine. I'm going for a while, but I'll be in touch the whole time and I am coming back. I'll always come back no matter where I go. I promise. You are all so important to me and I love you all.

Ok, so now let's just drink and eat and be merry. No more talk about my leaving for tonight.

Jon leans in and quietly asks, when are you leaving? I mean for Fresno, not that I want you to go but I realize you'll have to go home first.

Soon, maybe tomorrow. He looks at me forlornly and gives a slight nod before turning back.

The food is arriving and I'm so happy for the distraction it provides. We eat in relative silence, everyone seeming to be lost in their own thoughts.

After I finish, Jon asks; Gracie, will you dance with me. I nod and stand, letting him lead me to the dance floor. It's a mid-tempo dance not too fast, so we begin to move around the dance floor in rhythm to the music.

Oh Gracie, what will I do without you for a whole year? How will I get through this job coming up without you?

Oh my God! I exclaim, I almost forgot about the "job" coming up. Did you all talk about a plan? Did you figure everything out?

Yes, we talked with Les today and went over all the specifics of how to actually do it. And I gave them all your ideas on how to not get caught. Everyone was very impressed, although I'm not sure anyone but Les and Will believed they were my ideas.

Oh no, did they question you about it? No, but I got some knowing looks, and they know we share a room and have plenty of time to talk.

I'm sorry Jon, I should have just kept my mouth shut. No, not at all Grace. I'm glad you didn't, how else would I know how to keep my boys and myself out of trouble? You may have saved us, no one else was saying anything about what we need to do make sure we don't leave fingerprints or evidence.

Well, I am glad I can help Jon. I want you all to be safe, I can't live without you.

Me either Grace, I don't really want to do it at all, but I definitely don't want to go to prison over it. I wish I was just going with you to South America instead, that would be so much better.

Jon, that's it! What's it? You should go with me. It's perfect don't you see? If you come with me, it would be your alibis. We could drive south and fly out of San Diego or even Albuquerque, that would put us on the road out of town and you nowhere near the crime.

What are you talking about? How would that even work? I can't be in two places at once.

Of course you can't but it could "look" like you were with me. I can leave a few hours before the job, then meet up with you guys and we continue on to catch our flight. If ever asked, I'll swear you were with me the whole time. This will work, it can really work.

I don't know Grace, South America for a year. I have work and the guys, I'm not sure I can just drop everything and leave.

You wouldn't actually have to, don't you see? You could go with me, work for a week or two and come back, just say it wasn't something you could do after all. Or something like that anyway. Oh crap, I don't know why I didn't think of it sooner... you could all come. Volunteer for a week or two and come back. You guys do stuff together all the time, no one would question that.

I don't know, maybe. I would need to talk to the guys about this. And that would confirm to them that I told you. I'm not sure they would like me dragging you into our business. And Les...he could never know.

Well, then just tell them it's your idea or you could tell them the truth. I think it will be ok Jon. And don't tell Les at all, just say you decided to go on vacation as an alibi or something. To put you far away from the crime.

Actually sweetheart, this could be perfect. Maybe we should talk to the guys together... you know in case they have any questions.

We could if you wanted, or you could talk to them after I leave tomorrow. Then you all come visit me this weekend at my place. That way it shows a pattern of us doing things together. I don't know, but maybe. But it would allow me to take you for the shots you'll need to get before going.

Shots? We'll need shots. Yes silly, you'd be going to remote areas near forests and jungles, there are dangerous diseases, insects and who knows what else out there. You need shots and training in CPR, snake bite care and emergency first aid.

Ok, this plan is sounding less appealing every second. That's a lot of craziness to go through for a week or two.

Yes, but it would show the world you were planning for it to be a whole year. You don't do all that just to turn and quit in a week or two. And it shows you had a pre-planned trip not a last-minute alibis. Think about it...

You're right, I'm sure. I will talk to the guys tomorrow, let's just enjoy tonight. This is our second song so let's go back to the table before it looks too suspicious.

Back at the table I take Eddie by the hand, and he stands. I pull him out onto the dance floor, I want to be sure he doesn't feel left out since I danced with Jon.

What were you and Jon talking about? The trip mostly I reply, which is the truth just not all of it. I feel bad for withholding but this is not the time or place for that discussion.

Just then we see Jon leading Lindsey out for a dance, so I take the opportunity to change the subject.

They look cute together don't you think? Sure, I guess they do he replies. I mean she is a little young for him long term but she's nice when you get to know her. Honestly Eddie, the first night I thought she might be a raging bitch but then I chatted with her and she's actually pretty sweet if a little naive.

Grace, I don't really care about Jon and Lindsey. I care about you and me, I want to know if this could turn into something real? I believe it can if you do too, then I'm happy to wait for you. I want you to have all your dreams come true.

Oh Eddie, thank you and yes, I can see this going somewhere too. I know it's a year, but I'll email you and call you whenever I can.

Ok then he says, let's make the most of our time together until you leave and then he leans in to kiss me and holds me a little closer.

On the way home from the bar, I sit next to Eddie, holding his hand and laying my head on his shoulder.

Tired? He asks. Yes actually, quite tired tonight. I guess it's all the excitement, I'll probably just head to bed. I need to head home tomorrow and start to make some preparations. He squeezes my hand and I know that wasn't what he wanted to hear. I promise I won't leave without seeing you again, I have work to get settled and my condo. I need to get back to adulting before I run off to save the world, I say and chuckle hoping to lighten his mood.

I walk with him into the house, and we stop in the living room. Kiss me good night I say, and he wraps his hands around my waist and pulls me close, kissing me hard on the lips. The kiss is lingering, and I feel his emotions in my skin. When he finally breaks the kiss, I open my drowsy eyes and smile up at him.

You are so beautiful Grace, promise you'll come back to me.

I promise. I look at him for a moment, then say good night and turn heading to Jon's bedroom.

Closing the door, I lean against it for a moment and notice Jon sitting on the bed already dressed for sleep. I pad over and sit next to him laying my head on his shoulder. He puts his arm around my shoulder and lays a soft kiss on the top of my head. I sigh audibly, just enjoying this connection that needs no words.

After a few minutes of being still just like this, I lift my head and look at this man who is my best friend. You're my best friend Jon, thank you for being you. I don't know any other way to say it.

I'm just glad you are you Miss Melody, he says with a grin.

Dressed and ready for bed I climb in next to Jon and lay my head on his chest, snuggling next to him.

I am so bone tired, making life changing decisions really takes it out of you. Will you still talk to the guys tomorrow?

Yes, we'll have plenty of time at work when we can talk with no one else around. I will tell them all about the plan you have in mind and then ask if they want to come to your place for the weekend. If they do, I'll see if we can leave work a little early Friday and drive down.

That would be good, we can have a late dinner. I have two spare rooms and a sofa, so you should all be fine to stay with me. That is if the guys want to come and don't think my plan is too crazy.

I think they might like it Grace, it has a lot of merit and may help everyone feel a little better about this job. We're all a little worried.

I fall asleep pondering all that has happened in the last weeks and all that is to come.

Chapter 17

I wake up early, today is the day the guys are coming. I have everything ready. The guest rooms and sofa will sleep 3 of the guys. The other 2 will stay with Lisa. It should be interesting to see who wants to be where after dinner this evening. I can't help but smile thinking of Lisa corrupting our sweet little Will.

It's 3:30 and the guys should be here any time, Lisa will be here just after 4. I've had a roast in the oven for about an hour now and everything will be ready for an early dinner. We need to get situated because tomorrow should prove interesting. We all have to get shots and go through the orientation for the volunteer program. The more I think about it, the better I like my plan. I just hope it all works and I can help my guys get through this "job" situation unharmed and unidentified.

My phone buzzes, it's a text from Jon.

Jon- we're here, just parking the truck

Grace- awesome, meet you at the door

I race to the door and swing it wide open, they're all piling out of the truck and grabbing their bags. Jon is the first one to me and he grabs me up and swings me around like a little girl. I love it and him, he's absolutely perfect. I've missed you Miss Melody! I've missed you to, more than I thought possible. Now put me down so I can hug all my guys.

One by one I welcome them into my home, Eddie comes in last. He hugs me and gives me a very sweet kiss. Leaning down he whispers, I hope you missed me a little too. I squeeze him a little tighter and say more than a little.

Stepping in and closing the door, I say welcome to my home. Please make yourselves comfortable. There's a bathroom around that corner and plenty of drinks in the fridge. Just drop your bags over in the corner and we'll work out the sleeping arrangements after dinner. It will be ready around 5 and Lisa should be here any minute.

Lisa comes in the back door without knocking as usual. She comes over to me in the kitchen and gives me a very sly look. So, where's my prey, she asks with a cackle.

Hey lady, glad you're here. They're in the living room, come on I'll introduce you.

We walk in and I say, hey guys this is Lisa. She smiles and Will immediately jumps up and comes to stand in front of her.

It's nice to meet you ma'am, he says with a huge cheesy grin. I roll my eyes and Preacher throws a pillow at him. Down boy, don't get all excited. Everyone laughs and Will's face turns a little red. Lisa is grinning but I can tell she's checking them all out.

Well gentlemen, it's so good to meet you all. Grace has told me all about you, but she didn't tell me just how handsome you all are... this should be a fun weekend.

Ok then, with that we'll be going to the kitchen I say and pull Lisa by the arm dragging her with me.

I look at her grinning, you're like a dog with a bone woman. Or a hungry woman with a man buffet in the next room she says, and we fall into a fit of laughter attracting attention from said buffet in the next room.

I wonder what's so funny Will asks the guys. They all look around at each other and then back at Will, YOU they say in unison and begin to laugh as well.

I call everyone for dinner, I have the leaf added to the table and a folding chair to make seven seats.

We'll be a little crowded but that's alright I say as I carry in the huge roast to add to the array of food already on the table.

Viola! I say and ask if anyone would like something else before I sit.

Nope come and sit they say. Eddie looks at me and says, this looks wonderful Grace. Thank you for going to all this trouble for us, we would have been happy with pizza or subs.

Speak for yourself Will says right before asking for the mashed potatoes. Everyone chuckles and we dig in, passing disses and enjoying dinner together.

Lisa is sitting between Will and Preacher, hmmm? I wonder how this will turn out.

Will is flirting heavily between bites and she seems interested and amused. Preacher is being his usual pleasant and witty self, she seems interested in him also but I spy her casting glances at Rob across the table. He, however, doesn't look interested in the least. I doubt she's his type anyway, I think he'd like more serious women.

I lean over and whisper to Jon, what do you make of that? Slightly nodding toward the scene across the table. He whispers back, should be an interesting weekend. I think she'd eat Will for breakfast, poor kid. I lean up and shoot him a disbelieving look before leaning back to say, you're probably right but I think he just might like that.

I turn and whisper to Eddie, this should prove fun to watch and he grins at me. Yup, I think we're in for quite the show.

After dinner the guys offer to clean the kitchen. I'm happy to let them, gives me a few minutes to talk to Lisa.

So, who do you like? She looks at me levelly and with a straight face and says all and none. I look at her oddly for a moment before laughing out loud and rolling my eyes at her.

Touché, better question is which one are you taking home tonight?

You said I get two she says with a sly smile.

Why you little hooch I say playfully, and we giggle again.

Honestly not sure hun, Will is as adorable as you said. Like an eager little puppy, but that Preacher is interesting also. And don't get me started on that sinfully handsome devil Rob. I mean, hunk central girl...whew!

I'd probably leave Rob off the list, he didn't look too interested Lisa...sorry.

Really, I wouldn't have guessed with the way he kept touching his foot to my legs.

WHAT?! I exclaim a little too loudly and Lisa shushes me quickly and drags me away further.

Everything ok? Jon says coming out of the kitchen with a dish towel draped over his shoulder.

Oh yes, we're fine, just chatting. Sorry if we disturbed you, I say and give him my serious go away look.

Ok then he says and winks before turning to go back to the kitchen.

I do have to say Grace, Eddie is a looker for sure, but that Jon is something else. I don't know how you could pass that up for anyone.

I chuckle and remind her that I didn't pass anything up, I kissed him remember? There wasn't a romantic connection there for us.

You're crazy she says just before the guys walk back into the living room.

Who wants a drink Lisa asks and heads over to the small bar I keep. I can mix up some cocktails or grab a few beers from the fridge. I'll take a beer I say and quickly all the guy's chime in the same. Alright she says and heads to the fridge. I'll help Will says and jumps up to follow her eagerly.

Preacher looks at me and says, I'll take a room here. That woman frightens me a little.

I look at him and say of course and give him a conspiratorial wink. Eddie and Jon just chuckle, they know how Preacher is regarding overly aggressive women.

Oddly Rob says nothing, he's not giving any indication if he's interested or not.

Here ya go Lisa says coming back with Will and 7 beers. We all chat for a bit, telling a little about ourselves and such.

I look around and all eyes are kinda on me so I say, we should decide who will be where tonight. I was thinking Jon, Eddie and Preacher would stay here and Will and Rob would bunk in with you Lisa.

How does that sound to everyone?

Fine by me, Will says and practically jumps up to grab his bag. I shoot Preacher a knowing look and get a slight nod in return.

Jon and Eddie both give me knowing looks. I glance a Rob and again he seems to have no preference.

Well ok then, I'll show you gentlemen to my place. Grace honey, what time for breakfast?

I thought we could go to the diner for breakfast on the way to the clinic. About 8am will work, our appointment is at 10 and that gives us plenty of time.

Perfect, we'll be up and over here by 8 then. Goodnight and nice to meet you all.

The three of them walk out and when the door closes, I lose it, falling on the couch in a fit of laughter. The guys join the laughing and start making bets on what will happen over at Lisa's.

Ten bucks says Rob snakes her away from Will says Eddie. No way Preacher says, he wouldn't do that to Will. He thinks of him like a little brother, and everyone could see he has his hopes up for the night.

Preacher's right, Jon says. I'm not so sure Eddie adds.

Well, I guess we'll find out tomorrow. For now, let me show you fellas upstairs and to the guest rooms.

Eddie takes my hand, will I be in a guest room? I look into his eyes, so much hope.

Yes sweetheart, but I'll be with you in there. Jon gave me run of his room and I'll do the same. But I'll be joining you shortly. With that he smiles, and I open the door next to my room. In here for you Preacher, it's a good bed and there's cable if you wanna watch something.

Sounds good darling he says and kisses my cheek before going in.

Bathroom is across the hall.

I open the door to the next room, in here Eddie. He goes in and I wink at him before turning and taking Jon across the hall to the master bedroom.

We walk in, make yourself comfy. The bathroom in right in here.

Nice place Gracie. Thanks, I like it. A bit big for just me but smaller places don't have good resale value.

We sit on the edge of the bed, and I look at him, he knows what I want to ask.

So, you're dying to know how they all reacted to the plan.

Duh! Of course I am. I mean they're all here, but you haven't told me how it all happened.

Well, I told them everything at work when we were all alone. They listened and I tried to tell them exactly like you planned it. Preacher said it was brilliant but that it worried him to involve you.

Eddie said he didn't want to involve you at all, but I reminded him that you pretty much always do what you want anyway.

Jeez Jon, I'm not a wayward teenager. I don't always do whatever I want, well not if it's too bad anyway.

He's giving me a don't act like I'm naive look. Ooh that face, don't give me that look mister inquisitive.

Fine, fine, I won't. Anyway, after we all talked about it and thought about it, we decided it was a better plan than the rest of us could come up with and decided it would work well.

I'm so glad Jon, I want to make sure you are all safe and ok.

Now then that's settled, I'll let you get down the hall to Eddie before he comes in here and drags you out like a caveman.

He would not, I exclaim.

He might Jon says, you have put a voodoo spell on him or something.

I roll my eyes and say, now that would be telling. I laugh all the way down the hall to Eddie's room.

I wake up in Eddies arms, he's still asleep. I look over at the clock, six thirty. I should get up and shower before everyone else is up, so I slip out of bed and down the hall to my room.

Too late, Jon is up and showered already.

I didn't think anyone else was up yet.

Just me and Preacher, he's already got coffee on downstairs.

Sweet! Let me just grab a shower and I'll join you downstairs for a cup.

Alright. Grace?

Yes, I say looking back from the bathroom door.

Are you good? He says with genuine concern.

Very, I say and close the door.

I rush to get cleaned up, don't wash my hair to save time. I have a very cute outfit already picked out also. I look at the finished product in the mirror...hmm this will do nicely.

I pop down the hall to be sure Eddie is up, I knock, and he says come in. He's already showered.

Headed down for coffee I say, wanna join us.

He grabs me up in an embrace, I'd join you anywhere Grace but I'd rather we stayed right here. Then he kisses me.

MMMM! That does sound appealing, very appealing but we have an appointment to keep, and everyone will be here in about 15 minutes.

Well that definitely isn't enough time to do what I have in mind, so I'll take a rain check.

I look at him and smile, you got it. He's smacks my backside as I head out of the room, and I giggle.

Downstairs they're on a second pot and I grab a cup before it's all gone.

Rob knocks on the back door and I let him in, good morning, Rob. Have a good night I ask with a twinkle in my eye.

He gives me a look I can't discern and says absolutely and you?

Very good, I say. Hmm I think, he's a sly one.

Jon whispers to me when Rob gets past, he'll never give it up. We'll have to find out from Will. I wink at him right before we hear Will and Lisa coming in.

I immediately pounce on them. Good morning you two, how'd you sleep?

They look at each other and Will flushes beet red. Lisa just smiles and says fine and you before strolling over to the coffee pot.

She's a cool cucumber alright! So, details from Will it'll be then...

Ok, let's all finish up our coffee and head out to breakfast. We need to eat before getting our shots and physicals.

Only breakfast for me Lisa says. I think you're all certifiable to be following Grace to Timbuktu for a year! I'll be right here comfortably waiting when you get back.

That's my Lisa I say, but I say it smiling at her.

That's right, I am who I am and I'm certainly not traipsing through a jungle for anyone. But I do think it's admirable and wish you all the best and you can call me if you need me to send care packages or call out the armed forces to come rescue you.

You're a peach of a friend, but I doubt we'll need the military to intervene I say.

We head to the diner for a quick breakfast, afterwards Lisa heads off to shop the day away and the rest of us head to the clinic.

In the truck I turn to Will and say, spill it. What happened with Lisa?

He looks all around for help but finds nothing but expectant eyes and knowing grins. He's turning a lovely shade of red.

I say again, spill it. Oh, quit worrying Will, we're all adults here. Just tell us, did you hook up with Lisa?

If you must know Grace, we had a very nice evening together. She's a nice lady.

Nice lady? I ask and look at him bewildered for a moment. Oh, I get it now, you're scared she'll find out if you tell us.

What! No, that's not it at all. I just don't want to kiss and tell.

Since when Eddie asks

Since now Will says, but he's turning more purple than red.

Whipped, I say.

Am not!

Yes, you are, if I know Lisa and I do she gave you the wildest night of your life and then told you to keep your mouth shut about the details.

Shuddering for a second, how did you know that?

I told you, I know Lisa better than anyone. Don't worry Will, I won't tell her you told me anything.

He breathes out a sigh of relief and leans over to me, thank you Grace. She's amazing but a little scary.

I just give him an all to knowing wink.

Chapter 18

At the clinic we have loads of paperwork to fill out. Medical histories, consent forms...the list goes on. It takes nearly an hour for us all to get it done. They call us back one at a time to see the doctor. The physical part is easy, we're all in pretty good shape and relatively young. Then come the shots, 6 in all. By the time it's done I feel like a pin cushion.

We've been here for hours, what would you all like to do now? We can go out or go back to my house, there's not a ton to do here but I'd be happy to show you around.

Can we go back to your house Eddie asks?

Of course, are you ok? You look a little flushed.

I'm ok, they did say the shots could make you feel a little flu like for a couple days. Maybe that's it. I'll just relax a while and be fine.

No problem, come on guys let's get him home and I'll order us lunch. Is everyone else feeling ok?

Looking at them all they give the affirmative that they all feel fine, so we head home.

We don't make it home in time for Eddie, he yells pull over and bolts out to puke on the side of the road.

I start to get out and he tells me to just wait, he'll be ok.

Makes sense, I guess. I probably wouldn't want anyone to see me like that either. When he's done, we quickly get home.

Eddie, sweetie why don't you just go lay down in bed for a while. I'll order you some soup or anything you like.

Soup sounds good he says, thank you Grace.

Of course, it's not a problem. They did tell us this happens to some people but I'm very sorry you don't feel well. Go up and lay down, I'll check on you in a bit.

Ok he says and kisses the top of my head quickly before he goes.

Ok boys, what shall we eat?

Anything is fine with us, Preacher says.

Ok then, how about deli takeout? I know a great place that delivers soups, salads and sandwiches. Oh, and some of the best pies and cupcakes.

Now that's what I'm talking about Will says while draping and arm around my shoulder.

Perfect then, I have a menu in the kitchen so you can choose and then I'll place the order.

After lunch I head upstairs to check on Eddie. He's lying in bed, so I tiptoe over and set the soup I brought up on the side table for him when he wakes up. As I turn to head for the door, I feel his hand take mine.

Well, hello you, how are you feeling?

Oh, I'll be alright now that you're here.

I brought you some soup, think you can eat a little something?

Yeah, that actually sounds pretty good. How long was I out?

Only about an hour and a half. You definitely look a little better, not as pale for sure.

That's good, I guess those shots just hit me hard, but I'll be alright once I get some food and a shower.

That's good sweetie. Why don't I let you take care of all that and then you can come downstairs with the rest of us. We do need to talk about this "plan" I say in air quotes. That makes him smirk but only for a second.

Listen Grace, I know I agreed to this plan, but I'm not so sure I like you getting involved.

I give him a stern glare and he quickly puts both hands up in a defensive gesture.

Wait now, I didn't mean I was telling you to do or not do something, all I meant was that it worries me. I really care about you Grace. I'd like to see us have a future but especially I can't even think of you being in trouble.

With that I soften my look at him and sit on the edge of the bed. Look Eddie, I really appreciate that, and I care about you too. I care about you all, you a little differently obviously I say with a small wink, and he smiles.

I don't want to see anyone in trouble, that's why I offered to help. I don't trust Les or his brother one bit. I wouldn't put it past them to leave you guys hanging out to dry if it came down to them or you.

I can't say that I'm not worried about that also, but it doesn't change that I'm also worried about you.

That's so sweet Eddie and it makes me feel so good to know you care. I care also and I promise we are all going to be ok, we have to be. I have to make sure of it and I will.

He squeezes my hand tightly and it makes me a little emotional.

I look at him sweetly and stand up. Meet me downstairs when you're ready hun. I walk to the door, closing it behind me.

Downstairs I find the guys at the table still.

Hi guys, is everybody all done with lunch? Can I get anyone something else while I'm up?

No darling we're fine Preacher says.

Ok, well Eddie is feeling better, and he's going to eat and shower then come down and join us. I turn for the kitchen to clean up the trash from lunch.

I feel a hand on my shoulder, I don't even have to turn to know it's Jon. I would know the feel and presence of him blindfolded our connection is that strong.

You alright Gracie? You have a look in your eyes, kinda sad or distant maybe.

I turn and smile, of course I'm fine.

Grace. What is it?

It' nothing really, just...well, actually it's Eddie. I mean not Eddie but something he said. He's worried about the plan. Is he the only one or are you all worried?

I don't think it's so much about the plan as it's about you Grace. He really likes you. I think he's worried he'll lose you.

He said something kinda like that too. Maybe that worries me a little also.

What do you mean? Are you worried you'll lose him too? Because your plan seems pretty solid, even Preacher thinks so and it takes a lot to convince him of anything.

Well, that does make me feel better but that wasn't exactly what I meant.

Well, what do you mean?

It's just...I pause to collect a thought. Just that he seemed so, oh I don't know so serious when we talked a few minutes ago. Like he's jumping ahead 10 steps and I'm leaving for a year, and I definitely don't want to hurt him. I really like him Jon and he's great but I'm not in a rush and it kind of feels like maybe he is.

Oh wow.

Yup! Oh, wow indeed I say and hang my head a little.

So, you like him he asks? I shake my head in the affirmative.

And you don't want to end things with him he asks? I shake my head in the negative.

Ok so it seems to me that you just need to talk to him about slowing down a bit. Tell him it's moving too fast but that you want to continue on at a slower pace.

Jon, I know that. What I don't know is how. I usually turn tail and run when things get hard. I can't do that here. I really like him, and I love you. I love you all really and I don't want to lose any of you.

Awe darlin, you couldn't lose us if you tried. I promise, you're stuck with us forever.

This makes me smile, I hug him and look up into his eyes. Thank you, Jon, I'm so happy you said that. I'll find a way to tell him later and hopefully he'll understand.

I'm sure he will, if I had to choose between slowing down or losing a woman like you. I'd slow down. Trust me.

Thanks. Let's go sit with the guys while we wait for Eddie. There's a lot left to discuss and plans to complete. We only have a couple of weeks to be ready.

Eddie comes down and we all sit around the table quietly. Ok so I guess I'll start.

I go back over the plan starting with how we already started the process for the volunteer trip with shots.

I also signed you all up with the info you sent, and your names are in the travel manifests for the flights. We will be taking three flights actually and that's only after we get to Las Vegas by car.

So, what do we need to do Grace, Rob asks looking somewhat eager.

Well, I've booked all the flights and routed out the drive to Las Vegas. We got the shots and they're expecting us all in Ecuador on the 20th. Your job is on the 18th so that works out nicely.

You paid for our flights? Why would you do that, Jon asks, and I see the question in all the eyes looking at me.

I look back at them all and for a moment I feel nervous, like I've done something wrong.

I'm sorry, I didn't mean anything by it, you can pay me back if you want. I just had to book together to make sure we all got seats on the same flights. Please don't be upset, I didn't mean any offense. Looking around I wait for someone to say something.

Grace, Rob says then pauses with his hands on the table.

You didn't have to do that, any of this really. Another pause and I begin to dread what he is about to say. Everyone seems to be looking at him expectantly, like they can't believe he's saying anything let alone this.

What I mean to say is, thank you Grace. You are truly an amazing friend to us all, I don't know where you came from, but I think the Gods must have sent you to us.

I stare at him in stunned silence. Everyone does. It's seems like minutes tick by and then I jump up and race around the table throwing my arms around him. I have tears running down my face and he stands pulling me into a huge embrace.

I hear the guys clapping and whistling behind me and it melts my heart. The doorbell rings and it brings us all back down to earth so to speak.

I wonder who that could be? Maybe it's Lisa, Will says with a cheesy grin.

Oh, I don't think so honey, she comes in the back door, and she's never rang my bell.

What in the world? Lindsey, what are you doing here?

I hope I'm not intruding but Jon said everyone was coming out here for the weekend and I thought it sounded like fun. Is that ok Grace?

I can see so much hope in her eyes that I cave and say, of course it is. The more the merrier come in and join us.

Jon swaggers over, looking a little confused and maybe a little tiffed as well.

Lindsey, why are you here? How did you even know where Grace lives?

That's not very nice Jon, she says as she drapes herself all over him and kisses his cheek. I wanted to surprise you, so I looked her up online. Apparently, our Grace is quite well known.

My address is online? That doesn't seem very safe I say while shaking my head and closing the front door.

So, what was everyone doing before I got here?

We had lunch a bit ago, I'm sorry you missed it, but I could rustle you up a snack if you'd like.

Oh no, I'm fine. I ate earlier. So, what are the plans? Big night out maybe?

No Lindsey, we were discussing some future plans, this really wasn't the best time. You should have called first. I could have saved you the trip.

Jon! What's the matter?

Lindsey, you just showed up uninvited at Grace's house after driving hours to get here. Don't you think that's a little pushy?

Lindsey looks hurt by his words. She's looking at him but not really saying anything. We're all just standing around feeling uncomfortable at this point. I notice the guys all head into the kitchen except for Jon of course.

Why don't we all go sit down, Jon can I speak with you a moment? Lindsey, go have a seat in the living room and we'll be right in.

As soon as she's out of earshot I grab Jon's arm and pull him into the dining room. Jon, you are being very rude.

Me? Grace, she just showed up out of nowhere, uninvited. And she stalked you online to get your address. Don't you think that's a little bit rude?

Well yes, I suppose but she's here now so what are we gonna do, throw her out? She's young and probably insecure. Anyway, we should tell her about the plan, well just the volunteer part.

Are you crazy? Why would we do that?

Well, think about it Jon. You've sort of been seeing her for a couple of weeks, so if. You were truly planning this trip wouldn't you at least mention it to a girl you're "seeing" I say with the dreaded air quotes. Just think, it's someone who could corroborate the plan if asked.

I can see the wheels turning in his head as he weighs the merit of my words.

Ok, well that does make sense, I suppose we should all be telling family or whomever we have about it, so it seems more planned out and not like a cover.

Exactly I say, so let's go and smooth things over with our little pushy stalker and make her feel a little more welcome.

Ok, let's do that. Oh, and I guess I will switch rooms with Eddie, and she can bunk with me.

I roll my eyes and smirk at him, great plan.

After what can only be described as an awkward evening of dinner and card games, we all decide we should turn in. Everyone is leaving tomorrow.

Come on Lindsey, I'll show you to my room you'll be sharing with Jon. I take her hand and lead her up the stairs.

It's right in here, I'll just grab some PJ's for myself since I'll be in the room down the hall with Eddie.

Grace?

Yes Lindsey

Well... why is Jon in your room? I mean why didn't you have Eddie in here with you?

I look at her for a moment and see that she is worried about Jon and I.

Oh hun, it's not what you're thinking. I gave him my room because he gave me his when I stayed with him. We aren't romantic at all. Jon is like the best friend I've ever had. You don't need to worry about me, I promise.

I can see the doubt in her eyes for a moment before she smiles and hugs me.

Oh well, aren't you sweet I say.

I'm just so happy, I really like Jon! I wish I was going on this trip with you all, I don't want to be away from him for a whole year. I don't think I can stand it.

Oh Lindsey, I'm sure you'll be ok. There's email, phone calls and you can even video chat. You'll be fine.

But what if he forgets all about me, what if he finds someone else down there.

I seriously doubt that, besides the language barrier, we are going to work and help not find romance.

She looks so pitiful; I can't help but give her a hug.

You're right Grace, I'm probably just being foolish. I just hope he feels the same way I do, it's so hard to tell.

Just then, Jon walks in. What's going on in here, he asks looking at the hug skeptically.

Oh nothing, just a little girl talk I say. I take my jammies and head for the door.

I'll be right down the hall if anyone needs anything.

Lindsey, I'm still not sure why you are here. Jon, I thought we settles this earlier. I just wanted to come and surprise you. We haven't had much time together and I thought it would be nice. I like you a lot.

I like you too, but you can see how odd this is can't you?

Oh, I guess so, but your friends are so nice, and Grace is fine with it. I think she likes me.

Grace is nice, they all are, and they do like you. I like you too but I'm not trying to get serious, I hope you understand that.

I understand, but I do hope you change your mind in the future.

Ahh Lindsey, I can't promise that. You know I'm leaving and we're so different, I just don't want to hurt you. You're so young and I know it seems like I'm the perfect guy, but I can promise you I'm not. I hope you can understand that. I do like you, you're a sweet girl and lots of fun but I'm not in a serious place right now.

She hangs her head just a little, but says I was, well I am just hoping you'll change your mind about me. I think we could be happy together. I know you're leaving but I'll be here when you get back and we can call or text all the time. I wish I was going with you all, it seems like a great adventure, and we could do it together.

Looking into her hopeful, expectant eyes I don't know what to say. Awe Linds, see this is what I mean. You think it's as easy as you just tagging along, but it's not. There are shots, forms, medical exams and plane tickets to consider. Not to mention what you would do there, they have to need what you can offer to be accepted. This is what I mean, I don't want to hurt you.

I'm sorry Jon, I was just being wishful, I guess. If you want, I can leave now. I'll just grab my bag and head out, I'm sorry for coming. I feel like I ruined your weekend and plans.

I grab her arm before she opens the door. Lindsey, you didn't ruin anything, and I didn't say you have to leave. Put your bag down and come sit over here.

I like you, but you have to understand that we're not in the same place in life right now. I can't proceed with you if you can't or won't accept that, ok?

I see the tears are starting to build, I hate it when girls cry. Oh, please don't look at me like that.

She drops her chin and whispers I'm sorry. I feel like a fool to think you could want the same things I want.

You're not a fool, you're just young and sweet. I should have been more clear from the beginning that we were only having some fun, I'm sorry about that. I should have been more careful with your feelings.

Chapter 19

I knock quietly on the door. I can hear talking so I think it's ok.

Yes, come in.

I'm so sorry you guys, I hate to interrupt. I just need to grab an extra pillow and blanket from the chest. I need to go sleep on the sofa.

Why? What happened? Jon says and jumps up like something is wrong.

Relax buddy, it's just that Eddie is feeling sick again and doesn't want me to see him puking. Can't say I mind. I mean I can try to be supportive but there are some things better left unseen in a new...new... well, I don't know what we are but it's still better left unseen.

Oh no, can I help with anything? No thank you Lindsey but very sweet of you to offer.

I can't let you sleep on the sofa in your own house Grace, Jon says and tries to take the pillow and blanket.

Why don't you stay up here with Lindsey, and I'll go down to the sofa?

No way! I will not have a guest on my sofa. You two stay here and that's final.

Jon crosses his arms and Lindsey looks between us.

What? You think crossing your arms will stop me from doing exactly what I want?

No, but do you think I'm letting you leave this room to sleep on a sofa? It's a huge bed, we can all just share for one night.

I look at him in surprise and notice Lindsey doing the same. Jon, I'm not so sure you're considering how this would make Lindsey feel.

Her head swings to Jon but she says, oh it's ok with me I don't mind, really.

See, she doesn't mind. It's no big deal, it's just one night and there's plenty of room. I can sleep in the middle if it's easier.

No, you don't have to do that. I'll sleep in the middle. I'm the smallest Lindsey chimes in. I look at her and know she just doesn't want me next to Jon.

Ok, I say. If you're sure, then Lindsey in the middle and my side is the left side.

Perfect, I'll go to the bathroom and get ready for bed then Lindsey can go.

When he closes the door, I look at Lindsey. Are you sure about this? I can run downstairs while he's in there and I'm sure you can distract him after that.

No, it's ok, really. We were just discussing how we aren't well suited for anything serious, so it doesn't really matter.

Oh honey, I'm sorry. I really am, are you ok?

I'll be fine, I should have known better anyway.

No Lindsey, I know he likes you. You gave it a try and there's no harm done in that.

Well, no harm except my feelings but, I guess I'll get over that. He still wants us to hang out and have some fun if I think I can handle that.

Oh, that's harsh. What did you say to that?

Nothing, you came in then. But I guess it's better than nothing.

Honey, you have to value your time or no one else will. If you're just looking for fun then fine but if you want more, you should find someone willing to give it to you. You're a sweet beautiful young lady. Don't settle for anything less than what you want.

You're right, I know you are. I just want Jon, but I can't have him long term so I'll take him for as long as I can have him.

Just then Jon opens the door to come out and Lindsey dashes into the bathroom and closes the door.

I hear the shower turn on, so I know I have a few minutes at least to talk to Jon.

So, what did she say?

I punch his arm and shake my head.

What was that for?

You know what you did, that sweet girl is heartbroken. Couldn't you wait until you got back home before dropping all that "let's only have fun" stuff. She thought you wanted "more".

Oh, that. I'm sorry I hurt her feelings, but I don't feel right lying to her and letting her believe this is going somewhere. That's not fair to either of us.

I know. And I'm sorry I punched you. Maybe it's best if I go downstairs so you can talk with her.

No way! Please don't leave us alone tonight, I'll probably just sleep with her and make it worse. And if she starts to cry, I won't know what to do.

That's pathetic Jon, it really is. Ugh...fine I'll stay.

Thank you, Grace, and I am sorry about all this.

It's fine, I guess I can't say it was a boring weekend. So, is everyone clear on the plans? Is everything in order?

Yes, we talked while you and Lisa were walking Lisa's little dog. Everyone is clear on the timeline and what each of us have to do. And we will all be paying you back for the flights. We decided it will look more legit that way, so we'll get cashier's checks from our banks so there's a record. We thought that was just one more piece of proof that we had this all planned out and were serious.

That does make sense, good thinking. Well then, I believe we are all set. Just make sure you guys are on time to meet me so we can prove the timeline.

We will, and Grace?

Yes?

Thank you again, I couldn't ask for a better friend.

I lay my head on his shoulder and we hear the shower turn off.

Ok, I'm getting into bed. Just be nice and let's get through the night.

Yes ma'am Ms. Melody.

Hi Lindsey, I say when she comes out is tiny pajamas. Ready for bed?

Yes, she says and climbs in the middle. Jon hits the light and I feel him climb in on the other side.

Here we go I think and try to go to sleep.

I wake to an odd sound, I guess I must have fallen asleep. It's still very dark, I glance at the clock and see it's 1:12am.

Then I realize what I am hearing and feeling happen in this bed. Oh no! They couldn't be doing that here, now. Oh my God no. I'm frozen. I don't know what to do, should I sneak out or let them know I'm awake. What do I do? Maybe I should pretend to be sleeping, that could be better, less embarrassing for sure, but I don't wanna hear this...ugh gross.

Mmmm, ohhhh, yesss Jon, Jon, Jon...

NO, NO, NO! I should not be hearing this. I try to block it out, but I can't. It's actually kinda turning me on, which is so wrong on so many levels. I realize I have room to slide closer to the edge. If I can do that quietly, they probably won't even notice me over here at least not with all that going on.

I slide just an inch away and stop. I listen, seems like they didn't notice. Ok then Grace, let's try to move a little more. I start to scoot and my foot slips, uh oh I freeze. Who did I just kick? Oh no they stopped. I'm still frozen and I hear Jon whisper my name.

Grace...

I answer before I can tell myself not to. Yes.

Oh my God, oh my God they know I'm awake.

They're frozen, I'm frozen...no one is moving which means he's still, they're still... I feel like I might die of embarrassment.

Jon whispers, I'm sorry Grace and slips to Lindsey's side. I hear a loud exhale and then another more slippery sound.

Jon's in the middle now, I can feel his side next to me. It feels strangely nice. Oh no, no no no no. Don't even think like that.

I'm sorry I hear just above a whisper from Lindsey.

Um it's ok, I didn't mean to wake up I say. Like that matters I think, I mean they were doing it in my bed next to me.

You could join us she says. I feel Jon stiffen next to me, but he doesn't say anything.

I stutter but can't form a coherent reply.

It's ok Grace she says, and I feel a hand on my thigh, and I know it's hers. She's running her fingers slowly up and down and I can't say I don't like it. But it's Jon and Lindsey. I'm not sure this is a good idea. OH! She's shifted and is leaning over Jon and touching more than my thigh, a lot more.

Do you like that she asks? Yes, I moan, I can't help myself it does feel good.

Involuntarily I shift to my back and part my legs for her. What am I doing? My brain is saying stop this now, but my body has a different opinion.

My body decides for my brain, and I feel myself beginning to get wet and I arch into her hand. As my eyes adjust a little to the dark, I can make out her naked silhouette and I can feel Jon next to me. He hasn't moved yet.

Jon, Lindsey is saying. Why don't you join us?

I feel his hesitation, then I sense him moving. She moans and I know he's touching her. I reach up and cup her breast, rubbing my thumb over her nipple. She moans, I think she likes that. I feel Jon's hand on my thigh, he's gently rubbing it but nothing else. I can handle that, it's not too weird.

I shift and come up on my knees, I reach out and touch Lindsey. Her face, down her throat to her chest. She throws her he'd back and moans as I trail my fingers down over her belly and head down slowly. I reach her center and run my fingers over the smooth mound then slide them between. She's wet, so wet. She cries out and I can tell Jon has slipped his hand up to her mouth to quiet her a little. Shhh sweetie he whispers.

I feel his hand reach for me, he's touching me, she's touching me and I'm touching her.

I reach back for him. I graze his abs and I feel him flinch a little at my soft touch. I pull back but he grabs my hand and puts it back.

Ok I guess he likes that, so I continue to touch them both while they touch me.

Lindsey slowly pushes me into a lying position and comes over me, trailing her tongue over my neck and chest. I feel Jon come up behind her, I have my hands on her butt and hips. Our fingers touch, it's so erotic. Just his touch is electrifying, I feel an orgasm start to build and I moan softly.

I hear him slide into Lindsey and she exhales, I grab her breasts and twist her nipples firmly between my thumb and forefingers. I pull her closer to me so that our centers are pushed together, and I wrap my legs around them both. I hear Jon groan when I do that. It feels so good, I'm building with every thrust. He's not even inside me but I can feel every single movement and vibration. It's magical, like waves of sensation.

I can tell Lindsey is about to climax, she's gripping me firmly. I begin to push up against her as he pushes down and that sends her over the edge. I cover her mouth as she cries out and leans down against me.

Jon slows and starts to turn her around. She slides to my side of the bed.

She's panting heavily, I sense Jon right above me. My legs go up around him, he's paused at my entrance. I'm trembling, I feel him slide in and it's heavenly.

He leans down and kisses my throat and nibbles on my jaw line. I hear and feel him whisper my name in my ear so quietly. It's like a breath more than a whisper...Grace.

It makes me clench around him, and my climax starts, it's so intense. I tighten my legs around his back and grip my fingers into his shoulders. I slide my hand up to his face and touch his cheek, there's an electric shock an actual real shock. It makes me crazy. I pull him hard into me with my legs and pull his face down to mine and kiss him hard. It's different, his kiss never felt like this before... I'm shuddering all over, I've got him locked tightly to me with my legs, he's grinding against my center. It's forceful, I can't stop pulling him into me. I'm so hot, it's like a frenzy. I'm meeting him with every thrust, it's like an explosion of sensation when I climax. I have him caught in a tight grip as I clench him in waves. I feel him shudder and grunt as he releases. I grab him and wrap him up, arms and legs I can't let go. We both shake a little as we crash back down to reality.

What have I done? I don't know what to do or think, I have to get up, get out. I need to go away from this.

I slip out from under Jon and out of the bed. I go into the bathroom.

Staring at myself in the mirror I contemplate, what have I done? I cannot grasp what has just happened.

Who am I? What does this mean? I have no answer, so I turn on the shower, climb in and let the water run over me. I feel something very odd. It's not shame or embarrassment I know that for sure. But what is it then? I can't put a name to it, but it doesn't feel wrong or quite right either. Just wash I tell myself, that's what I should do now. Everything else can wait for 10 more minutes at least.

Lindsey sits up and reaches for Jon, how was that?

Stumbling to find words he finally manages to say, good.

Good? I would think it was better than good, is something wrong?

No, no, there's nothing wrong hun. I guess I'm just surprised at what just happened, I was not expecting anything like that. And anyway, Grace is sort of with Eddie and he's my friend.

Is that all? What about me? Don't you care how I am? You don't do you? It's her, that's who you're worried about. I knew there was something more than friendship between you two.

Jon takes a deep breath and reaches for Lindsey's hand, hun I never lied to you. Grace and I are just friends, what just happened is a shock to me and probably to her. Please don't cry. You already knew we weren't an exclusive item or even an item at all. I told you I didn't want anything serious, and you said you understood that.

Jon, I know what I said but I had hoped that you would eventually come around. I thought if you got to know me more you might want something more...something longer, more like forever with me. That was just stupid, I guess. I knew it was her you wanted, but you kept saying she was just your friend. You lied to me Jon, she lied to me too Lindsey declares sobbing.

Lindsey, you need to stop this. I didn't lie to you and neither did Grace. Not to mention this whole night is your fault, you initiated this, this...whatever this was.

Slap! Her slap rings out along with her tears as I open the bathroom door to face the music.

Lindsey, stop this instant. You will not hit anyone in my home. Now listen to me and stop that crying.

What happened tonight was a mistake, we all got carried away and this should not have happened. I am sorry if your feelings are hurt or you feel betrayed, but I did not lie to you. Jon and I are only friends and if he does not want to be in a relationship with you it has nothing to do with me. Now I hope you can calm down and accept that.

Lindsey rushes past me and into the bathroom shutting the door. I let out a long sigh and hang my head just a little. Jon comes over to me and places his hand gently on my shoulder, his head hangs a little too. We say nothing for long moments.

Jon moves his hand up to my chin and gently lifts it, so I have to look at him. I'm sorry Gracie, this is all my fault.

Listen, it's not your fault or mine or Lindsey's for that matter. It just happened.

Quiet moments stretch out. What do we do now? I can't lose you Grace.

Listen to me, you will never lose me. I love you with all my heart, I am so happy we found each other, and you are my best friend. I don't ever want that to change, I wouldn't know who I am or how to be without you. You've changed me Jon, for the better.

Oh Grace, he says as he pulls me into an embrace. I'll always be your best friend darlin. Life without you wouldn't be bearable. The day you came into my life was the most incredible day ever. I never want to live a day without knowing I have you as part of my life. You're the best part of my life.

Just then the bathroom door opens, and Lindsey is standing there openmouthed gaping at us as we embrace and confess undying friendship and how much we need each other.

I knew it! You love her and don't try to tell me you don't. And you, Miss we're only friends, you're a liar too! She's screaming at this point, every dirty word and rotten thing she can think to call us.

I step closer to her in hopes of settling her down, Lindsey, listen to me. It is not what you think it is, we were saying sorry to each other and promising to stay friends.

Yeah right! I don't believe you, whack!

Out of nowhere she's hit me, right in the face. I'm stunned, I don't think anyone has ever hit me in my entire life. I look up and see Preacher and Eddie standing there in the doorway looking at the scene in stunned silence.

Whack! Crash!

All of a sudden, I'm hit again and rolling on the ground with her trying to pull my hair out and punch me more. I take a hold of her arms at the shoulders and wrap my leg behind hers and flip her over pinning her down with my weight to subdue her.

Stop it right now Lindsey I scream at her. Jon is trying to pull me back, but I know if I let go, she'll scramble up and hit me again.

Preacher jumps in and is kneeling on the ground to hold her down, Jon does the same, so I let go. Eddie is right next to me with his arm around my shoulder pulling me away.

Grace, what in the hell is going on here. We could hear her yelling down the hall, and she's hit you. What happened?

They're in love, or didn't you know Lindsey is yelling as Jon and Preacher hold her back against her struggles to get free and attack again.

You are delusional I say to her, I told you over and over that's not true. Jon told you too, you're just angry that he doesn't want a serious relationship.

Oh, I am angry, angry that you both lied to me then jumped into bed with me having me believe it was all just some fun.

All eyes swing to me. What? Eddie says and turns to face me with searching eyes I can't quite meet.

It's not what you think. Well then what is it? I look at him and take a deep breath, it started out as nothing. See you were sick, so I came in here to get an extra blanket and pillow to sleep on the sofa. When I did, Jon said he would sleep on the sofa, and I said no.

After all he's the guest, but they both said I should just stay. So, I did, and I dozed off just fine.

I look around before continuing, I can see the look in Eddie's eyes, and it hurts me to know the next part will hurt him.

Then I woke up to...well they were um er... you see they thought I was asleep and were...well they were umm...

We were having sex, just spit it out already you lying bitch! Lindsey yells.

That's about enough from you Eddie says to her. Grace, please go on.

Well yes, they were having sex and it woke me up. I tried to just pretend I as sleeping and scoot to the very edge without them noticing...but they did notice.

And?

And then she tried to convince me to join.

And did you join? Eddie asks quietly, already knowing the answer.

Yes, I did. I say and hang my head in shame. I know I shouldn't have, I let myself get swept up in the moment and it was wrong. I'm so sorry I say quietly.

I feel his arm release me and he steps back. All of a sudden, he's yelling at Jon, how could you do this? You're supposed to be my friend. How long has this been going on? Having you been fucking her this whole time?

No way! You know I wouldn't do that to you brother. This whole night was just a mistake that got carried away.

Carried away? You had sex with my girlfriend, that's not what a brother does he says as he walks out and slams the door.

I stand there in so much shame I can't move. What have I done?

Lindsey starts laughing, well I guess he doesn't want you anymore. My, my, Grace, looks like you're just ruining everybody's night.

Shut up! You're like a petulant child lashing out at everyone around you. Get out of my house before I have you charged with assault for hitting me. Go home and grow up!

I notice Jon pickup up her bag and take it over to her as Preacher helps her to leave.

As soon as they are gone from the room, I sag down to the floor and begin to cry. I cannot even believe all that has happened tonight. I can hear voices coming from downstairs, but I don't care, I just lay down right where I am and close my eyes hoping it will all just go away.

Chapter 20

I must have dozed off because when I wake up the room is quiet, and the pre-dawn light is starting to peep through the windows. I shake myself awake and get to my feet. I head to the bathroom and then dress quickly, nothing fancy just some yoga pants and an old t-shirt. I head out the door, looking down the hall before quietly going downstairs. I need some coffee so I head for the kitchen, everything is quiet and dark, no lights are on.

In the kitchen I flip on the light and start the coffee. I hear my name, almost a whisper...Grace. I turn around and there's Eddie, so much hurt written on his face it makes my shoulder sag to see and my stomach flops.

Eddie, I say quietly, you're up...it's so early I thought everyone was still asleep.

I never went back to sleep. I've been sitting for hours trying to figure all this out. I just can't figure out why you would do that.

Oh Eddie, I'm so sorry. This is all such a mess, it never should have happened. I don't know how it happened. I mean I do but I just can't believe it happened myself. I wish it hadn't happened. I swear I never meant to hurt you. I am so sorry, I feel terrible.

I feel terrible Grace, I thought we had something you and I but obviously I was mistaken.

No, you weren't wrong, we do have something between us. I just made a huge mistake. I would never want to hurt you. I hope you believe that.

Grace, I...I don't know what I believe. It's hard to look at you right now. I think I should go home.

Oh Eddie, I reach for him, but he doesn't move. Not to step away or closer, so I stop and drop my hands. Ok then, maybe you should go but before you do I want you to know that I do care about you, and I hope that this mess hasn't ruined everything for us.

I don't know Grace. I just need to think. Alone.

Ok, but will you let me know when you get home safely?

I will Grace.

Thanks, I say as he turns to walk away, I see him head upstairs I assume to gather his things.

Grace, thank you for having us this weekend Will says with an oddly sheepish expression on his face.

No problem, Will and I'm sorry it got a little stressful today.

Don't worry about that Grace. I'm sure Eddie will come around, he says while looking down. We'll see you soon anyway, right??

Of course you will I say and give him a small hug.

Don't worry about anything Grace, everything will settle back down in a few days. We all do things we wish hadn't, we're human.

Thank you, Preacher, take care of him for me.

Oh, he'll be ok. You weren't married or engaged, it's all still new for you guys. He'll get over it in a day or two. It's not like it's a serious thing with you and Jon, right?

No, it's not. We're friends, best friends really. It's hard to explain what we are, I just know I can't ever lose him. And I don't want to come between two friends. I stop myself before I start to cry. Look up and breathe deep I tell myself.

Grace, it's ok I promise. Take care sweetheart, we'll see you in a couple of weeks.

Bye Preacher

Grace, I hear my name and tun back to see Jon.

I'm unable to speak and I just gaze at him as he gazes back at me.

Oh sweetheart, I'm so sorry. I feel terrible about all this. I don't know what to say, just please tell me I haven't lost you.

Jon... I feel so bad, this is all so much to process. I can't even believe this happened. You will never lose me, but I can't come between you and Eddie.

Awe Grace, you're not coming between us. Lindsey did that, on purpose, I think. I told her I didn't want a relationship and that I only ever wanted to have some fun. I said if she wanted more that I couldn't hang out with her any longer. I think that probably made her snap like she did.

Ok I say, you should go I don't want to hold you up or have Eddie out there worrying about anything else.

Ok sweetheart, I will call you later. I want to talk through this mess with you.

Ok, please drive safely I say and wave him goodbye as I close the door and sag with emotions I can't even name.

Hours later I wake up from a much-needed nap to find Lisa standing in my bedroom.

Here you are sleepy head, late night or should I even ask she says with a chuckle.

I sit up and look at her, with misty eyes I say you don't wanna know. It was horrible. I don't even know how or what exactly happened myself. It hurts my head to even think about it, I was hoping to just wake up and realize it never happened.

Oh honey, what in the world went on here last night? I'm sure it's not as bad as it seems.

It's worse than anything you can imagine I assure you, I messed up so bad. I'm not sure I can fix it and I'm so afraid I'm going to lose Jon and Eddie.

She sits on my bed and takes my hand in hers. Oh Grace, whatever it is it can be fixed, there's no way you could do anything to anyone that couldn't be forgiven.

Well... I'm not so sure about that this time. I slept with Jon, and Lindsey.

You did what! She yells in shock. How in the world did that happen?

Oh, Lisa it's such a long story that ends with me having a three way and everybody finding out. I drop my head and sag in pure shame. I feel so bad, this isn't like me. I think I hurt Eddie so bad and what about Jon. I've made such a mess of everything.

Whew! I guess you are in a pickle hun, maybe you just need to apologize and give them both a little time to get over it. But honey there were three people there so Jon can't be to upset. I thought there was nothing between you two anyway?

She's looking at me so kindly, puzzled but kindly. That's just the thing, there isn't anything between us or at least there wasn't. I mean it happened in the heat of the moment and it was...well it was actually incredible but that's what is also so confusing. I never felt romantic feelings for Jon, I even kissed him to make sure remember I told you that. Then last night it was just so weird, she was touching me and I was touching her then they started....and...then well he and I and it was just...incredible and confusing. Incredibly confusing. I'm not sure my head can handle all this. It's exhausting.

Wow, that's all I can say. But honey, I promise it will all be ok, and I'm hear if you wanna talk about it or drink it away or whatever you need. Anything you need I'm here for you.

Thank you, you're a great friend. I love you Lisa but right now I think I just need to go back to sleep. I'm so tired physically and emotionally I can't even process all this for now. Sleep, I just want to sleep.

Ok hun, I'll take my leave. But I'm right next door if you need me. Get some rest it will all be a little clearer after you're rested and refreshed.

Thanks, I sure hope so I say before rolling back over and dozing off again.

Next time I wake up I look at my phone and find a text from Jon.

Jon: Hey

Me: Hey, glad you made it home safely

Jon: how are you doing?

Me: I've had better days, how are you?

Jon: I'm so sorry Gracie, please don't hate me

Me: Oh Jon, I could never hate you. I love you, you're my person

Jon: I love you too, I just don't want what happened to ruin our friendship

Me: Nothing will ever ruin our friendship, I promise

Jon: Oh Gracie, I'm so glad you said that. I have been so worried all day. I feel like I ruined everything

Me: You could never ruin anything. This whole thing is just such a big mess. We made a mistake, but that doesn't mean we can't get past it...I hope??

Jon: Sweetheart, of course we can. And I know Eddie will come around too

Me: Do you really think so? He was so mad. I mean I don't blame him, but he wouldn't even look at me

Jon: He cares about you, and I know him, that doesn't come easily for him, but I believe he will forgive us. But honey I'm not so sure he'll continue a relationship with you. He was burned so badly before, I just couldn't say what will happen there.

Me: I can't say I would be surprised if he didn't want to see me anymore. I hope he and I can at least be friends someday. I don't want to lose you all as friends, you've become like family to me. You all know me and accept me like no one ever has.

Jon: We love you Gracie, we all do. People do bad things but that doesn't make them bad people. You are not a bad person, you re the kindest most generous person I have ever known, and I love you dearly. You are my family, our family and that won't change.

Me: Thank you for saying that; it helps. I just need to sort through all these feelings and emotions, it's been an exhausting day for sure. I think I'm going to have some supper and go to bed early.

Jon: That's a good idea, you need to take care of yourself. If you need to talk, I'm here, anytime. Otherwise, I will call you tomorrow darlin.

Me: thank you Jon, you should get some rest too. I'm here if you need me, anytime day or night and I love you

Jon: I love you too my wildfire

While I am texting Jon, I notice a text from Eddie has come in.

Eddie: made it home safely

Me: I'm glad, thank you for letting me know. Are you ok?

Eddie: No, I'm not ok. None of this is ok.

Me: I'm so sorry, all I can do is apologize. Please know I never meant to hurt you.

Eddie: I believe you Grace, I don't think you meant to hurt me, but you did. I really thought we could be together, but I just don't think that's going to happen now.

Me: Oh Eddie, I hate that my actions hurt you. I feel like I hurt everyone and I'm losing this amazing new family I found. It's so painful and I am so ashamed of myself. I'm not this person, I don't even recognize myself.

Eddie: Grace, you haven't lot us. I just know that I can't be with you the same way. You didn't do this alone. The blame is not all on you.

Me: The blame is on me. I know better or I thought I did. I always had a level head. And that Lindsey, I hope I never see her again. I still cannot believe she hit me, twice at that. But I do hope you're right about not losing you all, I care so much for you all. And I was serious about us Eddie, I never lied to you about that.

Eddie: I never lied to you either, I care very deeply for you, but this is just a lot to process. I think we could be friends in the future, we weren't committed yet. I thought it was going in that direction and I believe you did too. What bothers me most is that it was Jon.

Me: I know, and I never planned for anything to happen with him. That's not the kind of friends he and I are. Please don't let me come between the two of you, I will disappear before I let that happen. Jon was duped by Lindsey and got swept up in her jealousy and plotting.

Eddie: I already forgave Jon, he explained what happened to me on the way home. He and I will get past this, he's my brother. So, you don't need to disappear, we all want you in our lives. We're all going to Ecuador soon remember... but I'm not sure I want to see you before then. I think I just need some time to get it all worked out.

Me: Do you mean it? You're all still coming? And I'm so glad you and Jon are ok.

Eddie: Yes, we are all still going. Look I'm gonna go to bed early, so I'm gonna say goodbye. Try to get some rest, everything will be ok.

Me: You are such a good person, thank you Eddie and good night.

I flop back on the bed and let out a deep breath. Whew! I am so relieved. I can't believe he forgave Jon and could maybe forgive me and be friends again. My stomach growls and I realize I need food. I pick up my phone and order Chinese. It says 25 minutes which is perfect. I run to the bathroom to grab a quick shower.

When the doorbell rings, I take my food and head back upstairs and devour the food. Knowing they all don't hate me has lifted a weight off my shoulder and given me back my appetite. It's only a week until we leave, I need to finish getting ready and setup everything for while I'm gone. I mean a year is a long time really.

I grab the notebook from my nightstand and begin a new list, because let's face it I'm definitely a list kinda girl.

First, clothes. I need appropriate "jungle" clothing. It will not be too hot and there will be bugs...ugh that part will suck. I need lots of bug repellent and a net for the bed. Then I need to focus on the house, Lisa has a key so that's good. I'll leave the power on and shut everything else off until I get back. The payments are automatic through the bank, so the mortgage and utilities are covered. I'll throw out what little food I have or donate the non-perishables and make sure to do all my laundry.

I put down my notebook and grab my laptop, I need to shop. I order 6 net bedcovers and two cases of insect repellent for two-day delivery. Now I must look for where to find clothes. I see there's an outdoor warehouse store not far from me and decide to go there tomorrow and get everything I need. Ok, all that done I decide to go back to sleep. I turn the TV on for some background noise and curl up in bed and pass out.

Chapter 21

I wake up and it's already daylight, I look at my phone and see it's almost 8am. I feel better having eaten and slept the whole night. I see a text from Jon.

Jon: Good morning, I hope today is better

Me: Good morning, just woke up and so far, it's much better. How are you?

Jon: Good, at work. Eddie seems a little better too.

Me: I'm glad. I'm gonna head out and buy some "jungle" friendly clothing today so I can get packed and ready. It'll be good to focus on prepping for the trip.

Jon: Enjoy that sweetheart, I'm gonna head back to work. I'll talk to you later.

Alright, coffee sounds good, but I think I'll just grab some while I'm out and about. I hit the bathroom quickly and then get dressed. Grabbing my bag and keys I head out the door. I spot Lisa headed for her car also, so I wave and walk the 15 feet over to her.

How ya doing this morning she asks? Better for sure, I talked to Jon and Eddie, and I think everything will be ok, at least eventually it will. That's so good hun, I knew you all would work it out. You can't lose those friends. I mean I will need to see that Will again she says with a wicked grin and an exaggerated wink that makes me laugh. Ahh Lisa, you always manage to make me laugh and I love ya for it. Hun, there just isn't enough time in life to be upset. You just gotta find your joy and hold onto it with both hands. Grace you've always been so... well such a....uhh... well a like a wildfire. I look at her sort of stunned as she proceeds to tell me why. You know, You're just so full of life and ideals. You jump on things you care about, you grab opportunities and run with them. You're not afraid to grab onto what you want. And honey, you care about so much and so many people. My wonderful friend, and you are wonderful.

Oh Lisa, I throw my arms around her neck and hug her. I'm gonna miss you this next year, but I will email you all the time and call whenever I can. You are such a good friend to me, and I love you so much. She pulls me away and holding my arms says that she loves me too. Now hun you're wrinkling me, and I have a very important client to meet this morning and I'd really like to get a fat commission. I'm gonna go now but let's have dinner or drinks later and chat, you can show me all your new "jungle clothes" she says using the dreaded air quotes and it makes me laugh. Deal, now go and get that big payday.

I drive to the coffee shop and order a large latte and a scone to eat on the way to the outdoor warehouse. Walking in I see so much stuff, holy cow I think wow they have everything you could ever possibly need to survive the apocalypse much less a year in the wilds of Ecuador.

I'm so lost so I find a sales associate. Excuse me ma'am can you show me where I can find clothing appropriate for a trip to Ecuador? More specifically a remote area, more like a jungle where I'll be working for the next year. Oh my, well, yes I can. How exciting for you, what were you thinking you'll need?

Everything I suppose. Pants, shirts, shoes just everything, essentially an entire wardrobe minus underwear I say and chuckle. Well alright then she says and leads me over to a section of women's outdoor wear. It'll be hot there, right? So, you'll need lightweight clothes that dry quickly. Yes and no, it won't be too hot in the mountains maybe sometimes. So, I will need clothes for hot and cold. I read that it will rain some too so quick drying will be perfect. I also think I want pants and shorts just so I'm covered. Well then you may want these weather-proof lightweight utility hiking pants, they are long pants with zippered legs that break away into shorts. Oh wow! That is perfect, let me try on a size 6. I head into the dressing room and quickly try them on then check them out in the mirror. Hmmm... these ok pretty good and they length is good too. I quickly take them off and switch back to my shorts.

Ok, I look at her name tag and say Jan. These are perfect, I'll take 10 pairs. Well yes ma'am, all the same color or do you want to see what we have. Let me see what you have. She shows me the two shades of tan and a khaki green. I'll take three each of the tan and 4 of the khaki green. Now show me shirts and sports bras. She shows me the same type of shirts with zippered sleeves, and they are perfect. These come in a variety of colors including all the basics, so I grab a variety of ten as well. Then she shows me some moisture wicking tank tops and sports bras that will be perfect, good layers are best. I choose 10 sports bras and 15 tank tops along with five pairs of lightweight running shorts for sleeping in. I'll add 3 pairs of long johns just to be safe I tell her, and we choose them all in grey for ease.

Is that everything you'll need ma'am? Well Jan, I think I'll need some shoes. Utility ones that will hold up and be comfortable too, oh and socks do you have any that stay dry? Absolutely, follow me ma'am. Its Grace, please call me Grace. Alright, Grace, let's get you some shoes. We look at many pairs and I try on about twenty different ones before settling for a low cut pair of waterproof hiking shoes with steel toes and a pair of heavy-duty sneaker style water shoes. I add on thirty pairs of water-resistant socks as well, half ankle length and the other half crew cut.

I think this is perfect Jan, I am so glad you helped me, or I would have been here all day I say and chuckle. She helps me to the checkout, and I notice these really cool hats, sort of like a fishing hat but with a floppy sort of brim for the sun so I grab one and throw it on the pile. Nearly fifteen hundred dollars later I head out with many bags ready for an adventure. I stop by my favorite local cafe for a sandwich before heading home to start packing.

At home I drag everything in and start removing tags and washing everything. That started I head upstairs and root through my closet for my old ruck sack. I find it and grab my hiking backpack as well so I can pack up when the laundry is done. I grab 30 pairs of my plainest underwear and a pair of flip flops for wearing in the showers if necessary. I grab some bandanas and a whole pack of hair ties. Oh crap, I realize I will need a years' worth of deodorant and tampons, shampoo, soap, toothpaste etc. I jot down a list and dash out to run up to Target for all I need.

Back at home I throw the laundry in the dryer and start the second load.

I head back upstairs to lay out all my purchases and proceed to make a check list, so I don't forget anything. I sincerely doubt I can get what I need there at least not easily for sure with how remote we will be.

Before I know it, it's after five and Lisa is popping in my room holding a basket full of laundry. Wow, you had a busy day I see. Oh. And I swapped your laundry on my way up. Oh, thank you so much! Yes, I have been busy I say and take the basket to start folding my clothes.

Well, what did you get? Let's order a pie and you can show me these "jungle clothes" she says again showing a funny face and using the air quotes. Haha, I say, yes let me order a pie, I grab my phone and ask if she wants out usual. Of course, I do and some garlic bread too. Will do, placing the order quickly, I turn back to her and say twenty minutes. Now let's look at my loot.

While eating the pizza Lisa looks over my list. You sure bought a lot of clothes; don't they have a laundry facility there? Well yes, they have an electric washing machine, but we have to hang the clothes to dry. It's gets rainy so I figured I had better be prepared. Ok well that makes sense but why haven't you bought any laundry detergent? Looks like the only thing you're missing from what I can see. Oh no, you're right I never even thought of that. But my bags are gonna be so heavy as it is, and we're only allowed to bring two. Two bags she exclaims, how in the world will you get all this there?

Oh Lisa, I don't know. Hey, I know what to do she says, why don't you just take one of what you need right away and mail the rest to yourself there before you leave. You are a genius Lisa, that's perfect. I'll do that tomorrow. So, tell me, did you snag the big commission? You know I did she says with a huge smile on her face, I could take the rest of the year off with this commission. I could but I won't of course. I laugh and say, never of course and congratulations.

What about you honey, will you be ok not working for a whole year? Oh yeah, I say, between my saving and investments I could manage a few years easily. Plus, I will manage my investments from there, I will have internet and my accountant will handle the rest. Well good then I don't have to worry about you losing this place and moving far away. Nope, not a chance, you're stuck with me. Good she says.

She helps me neatly roll all my new clothes and we put them into plastic sealed bags before putting them into my ruck sack. A trick I learned from camping as a kid. I sort out enough necessities for about a month and pack those as well. That done, I set all the rest to the side so I can pack it up tomorrow and ship it. It's getting late sweetie, I'm gonna head home and get ready for tomorrow then bed. I'll see you before you leave, right? Absolutely, I don't leave until Friday so I will see you all week. Perfect, good night I'll let myself out and lock up. I hug her goodbye then grab a shower and get ready for bed myself.

I check my phone when I get out of the shower and see I missed a call from Jon, so I sit down and call him back.

Hey you he says, hey I say. Sorry I missed your call. I was grabbing a shower. It's been a busy day. Oh yeah? Did you buy up all the clothes? You joke but I might have, I dropped about fifteen hundred dollars on the clothes alone before I even started thinking about all the toiletries for a whole year.

Wow Grace, sounds like you're prepared at least so that's good. Yes, it is, I have to ship most of it to myself tomorrow. We can only bring two bags each so don't forget pack carefully and only what you absolutely need. I will and I'll make sure the guys do the same. Maybe I'll ship a few boxes of necessary items for us guys as well. That'll be good I say.

It's quiet for a minute before I hear Jon say, Grace? Yes Jon? I'm so sorry, I should have sent Lindsey home after dinner or when she showed up uninvited. If I'm being honest, I never should have been with her in the first place. She is too young and immature. I knew it was never going to go anywhere, I told her that and she said she could handle it but obviously not.

Oh Jon, it's not your fault at all. I am just as much to blame, and Lindsey is twice as much to blame as us put together.

You're right of course you are. You're my amazing Grace, he says with a chuckle.

What? I say.

Oh nothing, I just said amazing Grace. A song name and you're my Miss Melody. Just made me chuckle. But you are an amazing person Grace, truly.

Thank you, I appreciate that. I don't feel it much right now but thanks for saying it. Makes me feel better.

Well good, I'm glad. I only want to see you happy.

I know you do, and I feel the same about you.

Thanks, it means a lot Grace. Listen, I gotta get back to work but we'll talk later, and I'll see you soon. We all will for our big trip.

Of course. Take care Jon, goodbye

Bye sweetie

Chapter 22

I open my eyes and realize it's today. I lay there unmoving for a few minutes, mentally preparing myself for this new phase in my life. I'm ready, at least I think I am. If one can actually be ready for such a big change. I know I'm prepared. I'm always prepared. I've shipped my supplies, packed and re packed, checked every item off the list and gone over the plan in explicit detail with Jon at least fifty times. I know we are all as ready as we'll ever be, but I still have this feeling of... what?? It's not quite dread but it's definitely unease. It's probably just nerves and the anticipation of seeing Jon and Eddie again after the "big incident".

Ok Grace, get up and get moving I tell myself. Shower, get dressed and then eat. I begin my day like I'm ticking items off of a check list.

After breakfast Lisa comes in with two glasses that I can only assume contain mimosas. What's all this I ask?

Well, when your best friend is leaving on an adventure for a year, you have to toast the occasion and since it's morning I thought, why not toast with mimosas?

Why not indeed, I say and take my glass. To best friends and adventures, clink.

Cheers love, will miss you so much, but I am so excited for you and I can't wait to hear all about it when we talk or message. Well, whatever works out in this jungle anyway.

Oh Lisa, I love you. At this point we're both crying and hugging. And it's not really a jungle, at least not like you see in the movies. It's just very remote, I think anyway. I guess I'll find out soon.

Well, you had better take good care of yourself and you tell those men that I said they had better keep you safe and bring you back in one piece. I mean really Grace. I don't know how you managed to get five men to spend a year with you in a jungle wilderness for free at that. It's like sorcery, my witchy friend. You are so amazing; you just astonish me.

Are you ready? Yeah buddy, you? Ready as I'll ever be, Preach. Where are Will, Eddie and Rob? They are by the tree line over there, waiting for the signal.

Alright, what about Les? This shit is supposed to go down in the next few minutes. No idea brother, he said he'd be here. Well, he better be, because if he doesn't show, the deal is off. I never wanted to do this shit in the first place, and I'd be glad to walk away.

I hear ya Jon, but we gotta wait long enough to be sure he doesn't show. I know we do, let's take a quick look around and see if everything is like Les said it would be. Good idea brother.

Twenty-five minutes later we spot Les coming from around the back side of the house.

What the hell man, we've been here waiting for over an hour. That's pretty fucked up to leave us hanging out to dry like this.

It's not like that Jon, he says. Well, what is it like then?

Look man, I had to meet up with our employers and they called it off. Said they were going another way and that was it. I came as soon as I could to tell you all to take off out of here.

What the hell man? This doesn't make sense. First, we can't say no, then it's just off...just like that?

Look Preacher, it ain't my call. I'm just the messenger. I'm getting the hell out of here and I suggest ya'll do the same.

Yeah alright, Jon says. Let's go get the boys Preach. We need to be somewhere remember. Right, let's go then. I give Les one last long look and think something just isn't right.

At the tree line we give the signal and Will, Rob, and Eddie step out. Is it go time Will asks? No man, it's off and we need to get out of here. Grace is waiting for us I say and see a look in Eddie's eyes. That look, seems a little angry and a lot sad. But we have to go, we can't leave her waiting and we really should stick to the plan I suppose.

In the truck, I give everyone the run down while Rob drives us to the meeting point with Grace. When I'm done, I ask, so what does everyone think, should we go on to Ecuador with Grace?

I don't know man, Will says. Why should we if we haven't done anything? Plus, we didn't even get paid so shouldn't we go back to work?

Hey, Rob says. Listen up. They all fall quiet and listen, Rob doesn't usually talk a lot so when he does it's probably important.

It seems to me, that there is more to this story that Les has said. Without knowing what that is, I think it makes sense to continue on as planned. All of us. It would look suspicious if we did not.

It's quiet for a minute after that. First to speak is Preacher. He's right, I say we follow along as planned and just wait to see what if anything happens. It's a couple of weeks, and it'll be good for us all.

I agree, Eddie and Jon say at the same time, Eddie cracks a smile for the first time in a while and everyone takes that as a good sign.

Alright Will says and with that the journey begins.

They make is to the airport in Las Vegas and head to long term parking.

Let me text Grace and see where she's at, Jon says.

Jon- hey, where are you? We just got here.

Grace- I'm near the ticket gate, ready to check my bags.

Jon- ok, perfect. Wait there for us, we'll be there in a few.

Grace- sounds good.

At the ticket gate they spot Grace and walk over.

Hi guys, long time no see. Hope everything is good since I last saw you, I say while looking from one to the next. I don't see anything wrong on their faces, but something is definitely up. So... who needs to check a bag?

I think we're all good Eddie says, we packed our sacks to be carried on, to make things easier.

I look at him and smile, that's good. I had a bit more to bring so I checked two bags and shipped a few boxes ahead of time. I also packed my backpack and brought some snacks too for the flights. It's a long trip. We'll leave here in a couple hours and our first stop is Phoenix, then we head to Mexico City where we have to go through customs before our final flight to the capital city of Quito Ecuador. Whew! That's a lot, I know. And unfortunately, after we get there and clear customs again, we have to take a bus for several hours to get to the camp site. It's a couple days of travel, so why don't we get through security and grab a good hearty meal. Who knows what we'll get to eat along the journey, sound good?

Definitely, Will says. I'm starved and we definitely have some news to tell you.

Oh my gosh! Are you serious? They just cancelled the whole thing with no explanation.

That's what Les said, but we really don't know more than that. Preach is right, he didn't give us much to go on. But we talked about it in the truck, and all agreed we should continue on as planned. Rob made us see that not to do so would look suspicious even if we didn't do anything, Jon says.

Jeez! Well, I think Rob's right, and I definitely think the whole thing is fishy. But...I can't say I'm not glad you got out of it. I mean the money would have been nice, but the risk just wasn't worth it. You can always make money if you're legit, but if you're in jail or on the run it could get really difficult. And hey, now we'll all go on an adventure, and we don't have to worry about anything or be looking over our shoulders.

For that I am thankful too, cheers to Grace and to Ecuador. May the adventure be safe and enlightening.

Here, here, chimes in Will and everyone raises their glasses. Thank you, Jon, that was very nice, and I appreciate it. Honestly, I am not sure what we will find when we get there. I know that I will be testing soil and water sources, they said that you will be helping with wells, building, and other things that utilize your building skills and strengths. I also know it will be spartan living conditions, but they do have clean water and tents with beds for us. I tried to think of anything we could possibly need and shipped it ahead of time in hopes that it will be there when we get there.

Awe darling, we'll be fine Preacher chimes in. We've all either been in the military or been camping and hunting for years. We'll be alright, don't worry about us.

And something tells me you're a tough cookie too, so I'm not too worried about you either.

Well, thank you Preacher. I'll be fine, I grew up in Florida where almost everything in nature can hurt or kill you. It's hot and humid most of the year so the weather shouldn't bother me too much in the summer. I am told it gets pretty cold during summer in the mountains there. The seasons are reversed there, summer is cold and dry while winter is hot and wet. But I think we will all be just fine. And we'll have each other at least for a couple weeks until y'all head back, and by then I should be all settled in.

An announcement comes on to announce our flight and Will says, listen to that, sounds like we're about to start boarding. Let's get this fiesta under way. We all laugh and get ready to head for the gate.

Chapter 23

They arrive in Phoenix with only 40 minutes until their connecting flight to Mexico boards.

I'm headed to the restroom before we board, the next flight is much longer, and I hate airplane bathrooms with a passion.

Great idea Grace, I'll go too says Preacher. In fact, we all should.

At the gate, Jon leans over to Grace and asks, how ya doing sweetheart? Oh, I'm alright, I guess. A little nervous, maybe a bit anxious but nothing bad... why do you ask?

Grace, I was talking about how you are in regard to the whole Eddie situation. He can't keep his eyes off of you for more than 30 seconds and I know it was killing him not to be sitting beside you on the plane.

Oh, that. I don't know how I am about that. I know that Eddie is not happy, and he has not forgiven me and really why should he? I mean what I did was unforgiveable. I still cannot believe I did that to him; I hang my head in utter shame as I say this last part.

Grace, you did not do this to him alone. I was there to remember? I am just as much to blame for the hurt he feels, maybe more so. I mean I know better, there is such a thing as bro code.

I whip my head up at that and look at him in a bit of shock, did you really just throw "bro code" out there like it's worse than what I did? I mean yes, he is like a brother to you and that could be deemed worse, but I was in a relationship with him, well, sort of and it wasn't just physical. We had spoken about, about...possibilities, future type possibilities. I betrayed him in a way that if I was the guy and he was the woman, no one would expect him to ever forgive me. In my mind, what I did was worse. As a woman I know what it would feel like to be on the other end, and with a friend makes it so much worse.

He sat for long minutes really taking in my words, I could tell he was letting what I said wash over him.

He looked at me level in the eyes, I can't be sure, but they even seemed a little misty and said, Grace, oh Gracie... have I ruined everything? How could I let this happen? I am so very sorry, sweetheart. Can you ever forgive me?

I look at him astonished, forgive you Jon? For what, taking what I offered like a sex crazed wanton? You didn't do this to me, I did it to myself. I knew what I was doing in that moment, at least for that moment I did. I wanted...needed... I don't say anything else; I just look into his eyes, and I think he knows what I am trying to say. I'm not even sure I really know, but I definitely feel it.

He gently touches my hand for a brief moment, then pulls his hand away before saying Eddie and then glancing in that direction. As he does, I look that way too and notice that he is looking at us. I lock eyes with him and try to convey how truly sorry I am, a single tear falls, and he looks away. I stand and pace away a few steps then make a pretense of stretching and smoothing my clothes. Aw Grace, what are you doing, I think for not the first time recently? Luckily, they call for boarding to begin, I grab my carry on and go to line up.

Maybe I will sleep on the flight so I can stop thinking about the mess I've made of everything.

I sit down in my window seat, take out the book I brought and push my bag under the seat in front of me. Book in my lap, I lean my head back and clothes my eyes.

Good book? Preacher's voice snaps me back to reality.

What? He's pointing to the book, and I comprehend the question. Oh, yes, it is very good. An old friend really, I've read it many times, but it never gets old.

I have a few of those he says and holds up a copy of The Old Man and the Sea.

Hemingway? Really, I say. I never would have pegged you for the classics, but I suppose you should never judge a book by its cover.

I hold up my book so he can see the title. Hmmm? He says, I wouldn't have pegged you for the wishy-washy romantic type.

OH! I say and smack him in mock indignation. I'll have you know this too is a classic. What would you know about it?

Plenty, I read it, read a lot of things over there in the desert. I found Tess to be quite a mess. A child really, always making the childish decisions. Yes, she had it difficult, but I think she caused most of her own pain with her choices. Just my take, he says putting his hands up in surrender.

I think about that a moment and realize he isn't wrong. Well, I do see your point. I see it more like she was idealistic, living not quite in reality. To me she is childlike in her dreams. I like that in a way.

I can see that, Grace. You know, you also have some idealistic ideas. Don't get me wrong, yours are very noble.

Well, thank you Preach. I always worry about making the right decisions, for the longest time I didn't make any out of fear I would make the wrong ones. But now, after meeting you all, I don't think I could ever be that way again.

Aw shucks, well I sure am glad but Grace, most of that is Jon. If you think about it, I think he's the reason. I can't begin to understand this weird, odd, kind of amazing connection the two of you have but it's real. Anyone can see it.

I know, I think it's wonderful, but I don't understand it myself. Everything is just such a mess right now and I don't know how to fix it. I don't want to ruin everything.

Hey now, first of all, you could never ruin our friendship. And second of all, I think Jon would walk thru fire for you so I wouldn't worry about him. Ah hell, don't worry at all. If I know Eddie, he'll get over this in time. Maybe he won't want to have a romantic relationship with you, but I just bet you'll still be friends. And if not, then it's his loss and he couldn't ever keep the rest of us from caring about you.

I lean my head on his shoulder and begin to softly cry. Thank you, Collin. He wraps his arm around me and it's so comforting that I fall asleep, just like that.

I wake up as we are landing, the plane's brakes screeching and we're bouncing on the runway. I sit up straight in my seat and look at Preacher. Wow, did I sleep the whole flight?

Yes, ma'am you did. No worries, I slept a little too. It was nice really.

Stretching as much as I can, I thank him. I really appreciate you letting me sleep, I think it really helped.

Good, because if I know anything about traveling, I think we have an odd journey from here out.

I think you might be right. From here we have quite a layover before we connect to Quito. A prop plane too, so I hope no one gets airsick.

No worries from me, I've been on worse, I'm sure.

Well alright, let's get off this plane and see what Mexican customs is like. How's your Spanish?

Muy Bueno y que tal el tuyo? Well now, mine is very good also I say laughing as we deboard.

In line for customs, we are all together again. I inch closer to Eddie and ask how he is doing?

I'm ok, and you? He asks. I'm ok, I slept most of the flight to be honest. He looks at me a moment then says deadpan, I know. The whole plane heard you snoring.

My eyes shoot up, wide as saucers and he cracks a slight grin before laughing out loud. I do not snore I say all the while laughing so hard, I'm doubling over.

Oh yes you do, Will chimes in. Ain't that right Preacher? She was right next to you, poor bastard, you had a front row seat for the whole flight.

I swing my gaze over to Preacher who looks somewhat amused but isn't laughing.

He just shakes his head as if to say no way.

Well…I say?

Nope is all he says, shaking his head, and at that we all start laughing harder.

I'm wiping tears from my eyes as I reach the guard at the counter and offer him my passport.

He's looking at us like we are all crazy, so in my best Spanish I tell him that we are all laughing at the little one for being a baby and sucking his thumb while he slept on the plane.

The guard looks at Will who looks back and nods as if he has any idea what I just said. At that, the guard also busts out laughing and proceeds to point at Will and tell the other guards the joke and make the thumb sucking gesture. They all have a good laugh at that as we all proceed thru customs.

Grace, hey Grace what did you say to them? I look around and not knowing who all speaks Spanish I say, just that you were sucking your thumb while you slept on the plane and that was why we were all laughing so hard.

At that, his face turns 20 different shades of red and he looks like he might explode, so Preacher claps him on the shoulder and says fair is fair man. I mean you did call her out for snoring on the plane.

Yeah, but I didn't tell the entire Mexican government.

Awe Will… I'm sorry if I hurt your wittle baby feewlings, I say in baby talk and everyone erupts into laughter again. But I do go over and put an arm around his waist and say truce?

Alright, truce he says and gives me a little squeeze.

Chapter 24

We land in Quito and I'm exhausted, it feels like we've been traveling for weeks not 2 days. But I know we have quite a way left to go.

At baggage claim we all gather together to wait for our bags. I can see everyone looks as tired as I do, and no one is talking.

Jeez, I say. What a bunch of tired grumps you lot are. You'd think I'd dragged you all the way around the world and not just part of the way.

They look at me a little stunned and I crack a big grin to let them know I'm only joking. I get little grins all around and Will states matter of fact, I'm starving, and I hope I don't get the shits the whole time we're here.

To that there will be no controlling the raucous laughter from us all as we make our way yet again to customs. Although at least this time we get thru easily, seems they knew we were coming and were very welcoming.

We have a small wait for our transport out to the camp so I suggest we all use the "modern" facilities while we can and grab snacks in case my care packages haven't yet arrived.

I head straight for the restroom and then over to the store to grab some things. I remember that I do not have anything but American currency and hope they take that or plastic. I ask the cashier and get the answer I'm looking for, whew.

Browsing the little store grabbing things that look good or I think someone may want my arms quickly begin to fill up. I notice Eddie noticing me but try not to look like I'm in need of help, which of course I am. He strolls over to me and begins to take items from my arms.

Let me help with that Grace, no sense in you making a mess with all this stuff. Also, why are you buying all this? There's no way you can eat all this, he says, and I see a glimmer of the old him, I think. Or hope anyway.

Well, I thought maybe someone would want it. I don't know if my care packages have been delivered yet or if you all will like the food, they provide for us. So, I just thought why not, I'm sure someone will want it or maybe someone at camp will. Hey, can't hurt right?

I suppose not he says while holding the majority of my loot while I continue to browse. So, Eddie how did you travel? Everything ok? I know it was a lot of flying.

I'm fine, I slept a little and walking around is helping me get stretched out. How are you doing?

I turn and look at him, I see a searching in his eyes but don't exactly know what to make of it. So, I take a small breath and say, I'm fine too. Like you a little stiff and I could for sure use a shower and a bed. Uh oh I think and freeze. Oh, why did I have to say bed? I take a breath and chance a peek at him. He's looking at me, but he doesn't seem angry, it's something else. Hurt maybe.

I'm sorry I say at once and try to look as sincere as I feel.

After a pause he says, what for? Heck, I'm tired too, so why don't we pay for all this and see about where our transport is?

I smile a small smile at that. Absolutely, I think I have enough for a month anyway.

Outside a bus is waiting for us, it looks about as old as I am if not older but solid enough, so we all load the bags and pile in.

On the bus to meet us is Mark Simpson, the camps director and driving is Emanuel a camp worker.

It's so good to meet you all Mark says, shaking hands all around.

Thank you I say, glad to be here. About how far do we have to go to get to camp.

Well, ma'am it takes about 3-4 hours because the roads are not so good once we leave the towns behind us says Emanuel.

I thank him and then look at Mark and say, this old bus gonna make it?

Hell yeah! He says and smacks a seat. This is Juanita and she's as trusty and faithful as they come. She'll get us there safe, no problem. If we are all ready to go we should get started so we can make it before dark. I'd like to show you at least the living quarters and such so you can find your way around tonight.

At that we all chime in ready or not let's go.

We get to camp with at least an hour before dark, it's very nicely setup and the scenery on the way up was breathtaking for sure.

All right campers, we're here Mark announces as we pull into an area designated for the bus to park. Welcome to Loja, this is camp Endor as we like to call it. Grab your bags and I'll show you to the sleeping tents.

We do as he says and follow him. I say hello to everyone as I pass them here and there.

We arrive at the first tent and Mark announces here's the first stop. Half of you will stay here in this tent, he pulls these curtain dividers to show how they can have privacy. Each section has a twin bed and side table with two drawers.

I don't care where I sleep as long as I get to do it soon, Will says, drops his bags and flops down on the first bed he comes to. Dibs I guess he says.

Well, that's one down I suppose, who's else would like to be in this tent?

I don't mind if I do Mark, Rob pipes up and takes the next bed.

Alright, that just leaves one he says and looks at the four of us.

I look at Jon and Eddie and then at Preacher, I know what I have to do. I'll take it, I say and drop my bags next to the third bed. I do not look back at them because I don't really want to see the look in their eyes. I know Eddie will be disappointed, but how could I possible have shared a tent with Eddie and Jon? No way that's how.

Perfect Mark says and then turns to Jon, Eddie and Preacher and says follow me gentlemen, your home away from home is just next door.

They follow him out of the tent, and I let go a sigh of relief. I suppose I made that a little too loud as I look up and both Rob and Will are looking at me with knowing grins.

Dodged that bullet didn't ya, Rob says. Yeah, for now she has, but I'm going to enjoy seeing how this all goes down.

I throw my pillow at Will and say, grow up. Nothing is going to "go down" I say using the silly air quotes when I do so.

We'll see he says, and Rob gives me a small shrug but turns back to his bed. I flop back down and to think about just that. And I have no idea just what I am going to do or what will happen next.

We hear a bell of some sort to call us out for dinner, I sit up and let out a huge sigh and grunt.

Well, that was real lady like Will says, I can't see him, but I still roll my eyes and say shut up. A little grumpy, are we? Rob asks with a raised eyebrow.

I sigh again, maybe a little. I'm sorry, I think I'm just tired and a little stressed. Why don't we go see what's for dinner, that should make us all feel better? I take Rob by the arm, and we head out of the tent. As soon as we exit, there they are… Jon and Eddie. They look like little puppies waiting for a treat. I squeeze Robs arm a little and I think he knows why as he gives me a little squeeze back as if to say, "you got this", and with that, I say; dinner anyone?

I remember where the dining tent is from the initial tour, so I take the lead and assume everyone is following because there is no way I am turning around.

Dinner is pretty good, although I can barely eat. We are sitting mixed in with all the camp staff and it's it a good thing. Not just because I have no idea what to say to Jon or Eddie but because I need to get to know the people, I will be spending the next year of my life with. I make a little chit chat but find I just don't have much to say tonight.

After dinner everyone migrates here and there, there is a fire pit area with log benches around and I decide a few minutes by the fire might be nice. I sit and sort of loose myself looking into the flames. I am not sure of how long I have been sitting there lost in thought, well, maybe not thought exactly. It is more like blissful nothing, no thoughts swirling in my head, just quiet for once and it is very nice.

Hey.

I look up and I see Eddie standing there, but no words come out. I'm just looking or staring to be honest, but no words come out.

Grace?

Nothing, I still can't find a word to speak, and I feel so drained. Like if I tried to stand life would cease to exist for me. I continue to look at Eddie, I'm almost looking thru him at this point. I feel tired, no exhausted is a better description of how I feel. I let my head dip just a little, it was getting so heavy to hold it up.

Gracie, are you ok? I hear the words just before I feel the darkness taking over, and then nothing.

Help, someone find the doctor I think Grace is sick or something. I've got you Grace, Eddie croons. What's the matter honey? Can you hear me? Can you wake up for me Gracie?

Jon, Will, Rob and Preacher run over to where Eddie is cradling Grace on the ground. What's happened? Jon asks. I have no idea man, I came over to talk to her, but she never said a word, she was just staring kinda funny like and then she just passed out or fainted or something.

The doctor rushes over, what happened here? No idea, she was just staring kinda funny and not saying anything. Then just passed out.

What's wrong with her doc? Will asks.

Well, I don't know. I've only just gotten here. Has she been sick lately or exhibited any odd symptoms or behaviors?

They all look at each other and shake their heads or say no. But Rob says, before dinner she was a little grumpy. I mean nothing bad, she just snapped at a joke Will made but that's pretty normal for most of us.

She has been under some stress, Jon adds. What kind of stress? The doctor asks. Jon looks at Eddie then at everyone else. Umm, just normal stress, I guess.

It's me, Eddie says. I caused her stress; I didn't forgive her when I should have. Preacher puts a hand on Eddie's shoulder, nah man you had a right to your feelings. It was a bad situation that's all.

Ok, the doctor says. Well, it seems to me she is slightly feverish, or it could be from sitting by the fire for so long. Let's get her to the med tent and I will give her some fluids and see if she actually has a temperature. Yes, that's where we will start. Are any of the rest of you feeling ill?

To that question there are five resounding nos. Ok then, let's pick her up and take her now.

I got her Preacher says as he sees Jon looking at Eddie as if they don't know who should offer to carry her. He picks her up and follows the doctor. The other four follow in a line behind them.

Standing in a circle close to her but out of the doctor's way, the five best friends look as worried as they ever have been. She seemed ok on the flights, Preacher says. I mean a little tired, but I assumed it was jet lag. Do you think I missed some signal that something was wrong?

No way, Will says. She seemed fine all day, same old Grace cutting jokes and everything. Well, something is wrong, Jon says. I know Grace and she doesn't just faint or pass out. You all know she isn't some weak woman.

That's true Rob says, she is one of the strongest I've ever known. Maybe it is just jet lag and stress over the um, situation.

Situation? Eddie says. You mean me, that I caused this? No man, I do not mean that. But you all have to be honest with yourselves, the whole thing was stressful on all of us in a way. I mean we are a family, aren't we? And we invited Grace into this family. So, if any one of us failed to protect her, that's on all of us.

But no, Eddie, I do not blame you or Jon or any of us. She was fine until she wasn't, she seemed to be doing well until right before dinner. She was still fine then but she did seem grumpy.

Hell, who doesn't get grumpy sometimes? Will asks. That's no big thing, right? He asks looking to the older men for reassurance.

Jon puts an arm around his shoulder and gives it a squeeze. That's right buddy, we do all get grumpy. Maybe she is just tired and stressed from all the travel and it was a long trip.

The doctor clears his throat to get their attention. They turn and look at him expectantly.

Well, she does have a very small fever but that could be anything. I have her on fluids to make sure she is well hydrated. Nothing else seems to be wrong, when she wakes up, I will need to ask her a few questions and then I can go from there.

What kind of questions? Eddie asks. Anything we can help you with? I mean we do know her well.

Not sure, he says. Would you know about her medical history or female um her menstruation?

Oh! No, no not that. I do know she had her tonsils out and her appendix but I'm sure you've already figured that out by examining her, Eddie states.

Yes, I do see that. Well, gentlemen I think you should head to bed. I will keep Grace here tonight and make sure that she is ok.

I will stay with her Eddie and Jon say at the same time and the doctor looks between them, well I suppose one could stay but you all really should rest. I will come get you if anything changes.

No. This time it's Will. She can't be alone in a foreign country. What if she wakes up scared or confused? No, she needs one of us with her all night to be sure she is ok.

Ok, the doctor says, but only one at a time. Maybe you can take turns so that you can all get some rest.

Fine, Eddie says. I will go first Will says, I can't stand to see he tension between you and Jon to see who goes first. Not tonight, our Grace needs us.

Well said, Preacher chimes in. Will can start, then in a couple hours he can grab me and after me I will grab? He asks looking between Jon and Eddie.

Him Jon says, pointing to Eddie. Preacher shakes his head to agree and then says, and he will wake you to relieve him Jon. And Jon you will wake Rob, and hopefully by then she will be awake, and we might know more. But doc is right, we all need sleep. We won't be any help to Grace if we can't stay awake, so let's go to bed.

See you in a couple hours he says to Will, who shakes his head in the affirmative and goes to sit in the chair the doctor has placed next to Grace's bed.

Will wakes Preacher, letting him know there's no change. Preacher takes his turn and still there's no change. Eddie is next, he sits with her holding her hand and desperately willing her to be ok.

Jon walks up and taps him on the shoulder.

She'll be ok man. How do you know? I've been sitting here quietly apologizing and begging her to wake up, but she just sleeps.

I don't know how I know; I just do. We have this connection Grace and me. It's like nothing I have ever know or experienced before. From the first moment we met it was there. It's like a pull to her and an understanding of her, her spirit or soul or something. Like I said, I can't explain it, I just feel it. If she wasn't going to be ok, I would know.

That's all fine for you to feel it, but I am so worried. She hasn't moved a muscle all night, she just lays there so still and quiet. Is this my fault? Maybe I was too hard on her. But, Jon you have to know what happened was such a blow. I thought she and I could really work, you know?

I do man, I thought that too. I am so sorry, it's all my fault. It just happened; it wasn't planned. Somehow, I think Lindsey pushed us as some type of revenge for my unwillingness to commit to her. But that's a copout, I am an adult and should have known better. I am sorry, you're my brother and I love you man. I would never hurt you on purpose.

He sighs heavily, then turns to face Jon. I know that in my head, but my heart still hurts. I think maybe I was wrong all along. She was never going to be mine. I know you both said over and over you were just friends and that there was no connection romantically, but I think you were just fooling yourselves. The way you explain your connection is the same way she did. I always had a doubt in the back of my mind, I just told myself what I wanted to hear. I wanted Grace; I mean who wouldn't but still. I messed up man.

Oh man, no you didn't. You wanted something real and meaningful, no one could ever blame you for that. And you're right, Grace is worth it. But I tell you truly, I never thought of her romantically until that night. We even kissed to see if there was something there, and we told you all that we had done that. But there wasn't anything, nothing at all. She just felt like a best friend, like the closest kind. I am so ashamed of what I did. I let you both down.

No, you didn't, I did. They both swing their heads to Grace to see her eyes open and looking at them.

It was me. I shouldn't have ever come between two best friends. I'm so sorry to you both.

Oh Gracie, no, no, no, sweetheart. You did nothing wrong Eddie says as he's still holding her hand. Jon steps up closer and puts a hand on her as well. He's right you know.

I look at them both for a moment and realize just how lucky I am. I want you both to know how sorry and ashamed I am.

Grace, you don't…

Wait, let me finish. I want to be done with this and hopefully put it behind us. They both nod and wait for her to speak.

Jon and I have this connection, I couldn't explain it if I tried. And Eddie, you are so wonderful, I never lied to you. I truly did see a possible future. It was still very early on, but we did have a connection, you weren't wrong about that. It was very real. I have no excuse for what happened that night. I have thought a lot about it, and I still have no idea why I did what I did.

What we did, Jon says. Yes, what we did, but I have to hold myself accountable. It's who I am, I don't blame others for my actions. I'm an adult and could have stopped everything, I should have used better judgement and not been there in the first place. And that is on me. I want you both to remain best friends, brothers. Please don't let me come between you, it would kill me if it did.

Awe, Gracie. You didn't come between us, Eddie says and looks to Jon. Nothing could ever do that; we might get mad or argue but we'll always be brothers. I know I was hard on you both, my feelings were hurt, are hurt, and I took it out on you two. For that, I am very sorry, and I hope you will forgive me.

Nothing to forgive brother. I think we all need to put this behind us, so we can move forward together.

I agree, let's all be friends. Jon and Eddie look at me and both shake their heads in agreement.

Uhhhmm, can I interrupt?

Doc, yes of course. Grace is awake Jon says. I gather that, let me just take a look at the patient. How are you feeling Grace?

Ok, I guess. Pretty tired but that seems to be it. Can you tell me what happened?

I only remember sitting by the fire then waking up here.

It seems you fainted, and your friends and I brought you here to the medical tent. You were running a small fever, nothing too serious. Were you feeling ill before or on your trip?

No, not at all. I was a little tired, but I assumed it was just jet lag.

Do you take any medications?

No, just multi vitamins.

What about birth control? When was your last menstrual cycle?

My eyes get big at those questions and the doctor notices the guys standing and watching.

Yes, right. Gentlemen, why don't you go tell your friends the good news and give us a bit to go thru these more personal questions. It's nearly time for breakfast so why don't you all come back after that?

Of course, yes. Come on Eddie, let's go. I watch them leave before turning back to the doctor.

No, I do not take birth control pills and my last menstrual cycle was…let me think. Surely, I can remember. Um, ok it was about 4 weeks ago. Yes, I'm due to start any day this week. Maybe that's it? Do you think my period is coming and with all the stress and traveling it was just too much?

It could be Grace. Why don't we have you rest here a bit longer just to make sure you are ok?

I do feel a lot better, but a little more sleep wouldn't hurt, and I definitely wouldn't say no to some food.

Food huh? An appetite is always good, I will get you something to eat and drink. Lots of fluids. Working here you will learn that staying hydrated is very important.

Thank you, doctor.

You're welcome, Grace, and may I just say that you have some very good friends. They took turns staying with you all night and I thought the young one was going to cry he was so worried.

Will, really? Poor thing, I must have scared everyone. I swear I am not a fainter; I don't think I have ever fainted in my life. I'm usually so healthy, barely ever a cold or even a headache.

Well, good then, you should be an easy patient. Now let me see to that food.

Chapter 25

Grace?

I wake up to the doctor standing there with a tray of food calling my name.

Oh, I fell asleep. Food. Oh, thank you so much, I'm starving. Smells good. He hands me a big bowl of oatmeal and a banana.

I want you to eat all of it if you can and drink this bottle of water.

No coffee? I ask. No, maybe later or tomorrow, it can dehydrate you and I don't want you fainting on us again.

Ok then, water it is. So, doc you think I can get out of here after breakfast? I am here to work and that's what I want to do. Really, I feel fine now. I'm sure it was just the travelling and probably a little stress.

Well, I am inclined to agree as your vitals are all good and you've had fluids and rest. But I want you to take it easy, nothing too strenuous today just to be safe.

Agreed. Mmmm this is either really good or I'm just that hungry because I can't stop stuffing my face I say with a small laugh. Truly, I want to thank you for helping me and I promise not to be such a burden in the future.

No problem at all Grace, it's why I'm here. In a camp like this you have to have a doctor. We're so far from anything and I see a lot of sprains and exhaustion. Oh, and plenty of insect bites and sun burns.

Hopefully, not from me doc. I jump down and shake his hand, thanking him again and head over to the dining tent to find my friends.

I spot them at a table together and walk right over and sit down. Hi guys, how's it going this morning? Five sets of eyes turn on me with what seems to be a mixture of relief and question all at once.

Will jumps to his feet and nearly hauls me up into a bear hug.

Grace, oh Grace! Boy, am I glad to see you are ok? Put me down Will, I'm ok I promise.

He sets me down but keeps a hold on me looking into my eyes and says, don't do that to me again. I was so worried about you.

I put my arms around him and hug him close. I'm sorry Will, I promise I won't do it again. What did the doctor say? Are you really, ok?

Yes, I say stepping back and looking from one to the other of them. He thinks it was stress and the long travel day, it all probably just overloaded me. He gave me fluids and rest and I feel much better. I am ready to tackle this day. How about the rest of you?

All at once they stand and encircle me. Oh! Before I know it, I'm in the center of a group hug. Ok guys, take it easy. It's not like I was going to die or something, I say laughing. But

I'm very glad to know that you were all so worried about me, makes me feel good. And I'm very sorry that I made you worry, I promise I'll try not to do that in the future.

Why don't we go see what our assignments are for today and try to put this all behind us? Sounds like a good plan to me, preacher says. Everyone agrees and we had off to find Mark.

It's midday and I am buys testing water samples when Mark comes in to see how I am doing.

Grace, how are you doing? I heard you had rough evening. Yes, it was rough but I'm good. I honestly just think it was stress and all the traveling. I'm fine now, but I appreciate you asking and to be honest, I am a little embarrassed. No need to be embarrassed, it's a long trip and a big adjustment. We're just all glad you're here, we've really needed someone here to do this so we can begin to make further progress. Our last engineer left us nearly 4 months ago. We had just about done all we could until you contacted us. So, believe me, when I say how glad we are. To have you here. And your friends. They are proving quite handy. Seems like they know their way around tools and construction. Lydia, our resident architect said they are a godsend.

I am so glad to be here, I have wanted to do something like this for a long time. As for my friends, they are pretty great. I'm glad they agreed to come, and I knew they would be very helpful.

Don't overdo it though, I know it can be easy to get excited and try to do too much all at once. Just remember it's a marathon and not a race, he says. We need you well and hopefully within your year here, we can accomplish a lot.

Thank you, Mark. I promise I'll try not to work too hard.

That's good, Grace. And if you feel ill at any time, go straight to see doc. OK?

Absolutely, I say. Mark, can I ask you a question? Sure, you can. How long have you been here? Just wondering, I say so he doesn't think I'm being too nosy.

Nearly four years, though I go back to the states for 2 weeks every six months. Wow, that's a long time, I say. Yes, it is, I guess, but I love this place. I mean I suppose I could find another project somewhere or go back to the states, but I really just want to see this thing through. Eventually, we'll be done with what we came here for and then I'll have to figure out what's next.

You are very dedicated, but I know what you mean. I try never to start something I don't intend to finish.

Grace, why are you here? He asks, looking at me pointedly. Well now, I say, that's a long story. The short of it is this, I have always wanted to help or make a difference where I can. I became an environmental engineer with that in mind. Ever since I was little, I have always wanted to save the planet, I laugh at that. I know, very cliché. But in all seriousness, I just want to do what I can to help. Even if it's just in a small way.

That's a very good reason Grace. I'm glad you're here. We definitely need the help you can provide.

Thank you, Mark. I appreciate that. It feels good to know that.

Alright, well, I will let you get back to it then. If you need anything at all, just let me know.

Will do, I say and turn back to my samples.

Sitting on the end of my bed, I am changing into my sneakers. Whew, I need to break in these boots. Or maybe order some different ones, my feet hurt. But I think, it's a good hurt. I've had a productive day.

Just then, Will and Rob walk in. How was your day, dears? I ask and grin at them both. Don't grin at me Will says. Tell us how you are. Are you feeling ok, Grace? Jeez, I am fine. Will, it was just an episode and it's over I promise. I feel fine, other than my new boots hurting my feet.

Wear two pairs of socks tomorrow he says. Really? But they're tight and my feet are a little swollen.

He's right, Rob chimes in. Your feet shouldn't be swollen in the morning and wearing two pairs of socks will stretch out the shoes a little bit so they will fit better.

Thanks guys, I will definitely do that. But was your day good? Mark said that he heard you guys were a godsend and being so helpful.

It was good, Will says. And that architect, whew what a hottie she is. Grow up, Rob says. Her name is Lydia and she's a smart woman, not just some hottie for you to drool over. I look at Rob intently. Hmmm, I think. That's not like Rob at all.

Will must have thought the same thing because he immediately pounces. Why Rob, you wouldn't happen to have a crush on the hottie architect would you? Sounds to me like you just might have taken a liking to her.

Shut up Will, he says but winks at me in a secret conspiratorial sort of way. I flush a bit but say nothing.

Will just keeps chirping on about it, so I say, man am I hungry. Why don't we head over to the dining tent and wait for dinner?

Rob nods so I turn to Will and say, you just about done so we can all go eat. He has the decency to flush, so I take him by the arm, and we start for the dining tent.

We see Jon, Preacher and Eddie standing outside the dinning tent, so we head over to them. Hey guys, how was your day? Preacher speaks up first. Pretty good Grace, how was your day? You feeling ok today? I'm good, I say. Much better and it was a great day. I was testing water samples from all the different wells and some new locations we're scouting. That's good sweetheart, I just want to be sure we don't have a repeat of last night. I see them all looking at me expectantly when he says this last part. Guys, I promise

I am fine. I feel great. I am starving though, so why do we see if the food is ready. Deal! Will says and heads in first.

At the table plates full of food, we start to eat. So, nobody answered my question. How was your day? I heard from Eddie, Will, and Rob but what about the rest of you? It was good, Jon says between bites. Hard work but nothing we can't handle. I can see why they agreed to take us. The architect hasn't had a lot of skilled help, she seems to mostly have had laborers only for a while. Will, chimes in at this. And I know Rob is happy to serve her, in any way she wants. Will! Shut up, are you twelve or what I say. Rob looks at me with appreciation written all over his face and I give the slightest nod in return. Jeez, can't anybody take a joke. We all look at him and say no, in unison and start to chuckle at that. Well, I had a good day Eddie says. I got to build some shelves for a storage unit that will house more building materials. These are some good people. That's great I say, and I am so happy you are all here to share this with me for a while. It has made coming so much easier, I can't thank you enough. You don't need to thank us Grace, this plan of yours is good for us too, plus I think we are all seeing a different side of things being here, Jon says. I mean I surely never would have thought something like this even exists much less come half-way around the world to be here helping. It feels good to do this, and for me I appreciate that. Not a lot has felt good lately, it's a nice change. At this, I put my arm around his shoulder and lay my head on his shoulder. Awe, I hear Preacher say. That's so sweet Jon. I joke, but he's right. Grace, we've done plenty wrong. I wouldn't say we're bad people, we've just done some bad things and this, what we're doing here, maybe it will help to wipe a little of that clean. And that darling, is a blessing to me.

I stand up and walk around to Preacher, he stands to meet me, and I fall into his arms for a huge hug. Tears in my eyes, I say; Preacher you are a good man. You all are, I say looking around at them each. We have all done things we aren't proud of or wish we could undo. Sometimes we even hurt people, but that doesn't make us bad it just means we're human. And I believe that good actions make us better, help to ease some of the hurt we feel. At least I hope so, I say.

You're the best person I know Grace, Eddie says, and I look at him in surprise. You help everyone, without question. You see the best in people. And you're so generous. I for one am glad Jon brought you home, I don't even want to imagine life without you now. Oh my gosh you guys, I love you all so much. But I think we had better all sit down and quit all this blubbering before everyone else starts to think we're crazy. They're starting to look at us funny. We all sit back down quickly, and I wipe my tears and clear my throat. We finish eating quietly and head out to sit around the fire pit.

I stretch my feet out closer to the fire. It's a little chilly after dark, this fire is nice. My feet are so sore, I think I'm going to grab a shower and go to bead early tonight. I'm excited for tomorrow, lots more samples to collect and test. I stand and stretch, goodnight my friends. Goodnight, Grace, I hear Jon say and the others echo, and Will stands up too. I think I'll do the same, he says and holds out his arm to me. Shall we? I take his arm and we head off towards our tent.

After I finish my shower, I head back to the tent to get some rest. I walk in and Jon is there waiting for me. Hey, you. Long time no see. Grace, I know you're tired and I won't stay long. I just wanted to check on you one last time. I won't be able to sleep unless I know for sure you are ok. Last night scared me, made me realize just how incredibly important you are to me, hell, to all of us. I put my arms around his waist and hold him tight. Jon, I promise you, I am fine. Last night scared me too, well actually this morning when I woke up and realized what had happened. I realized thru all of this just how much we all mean to each other. But you, especially you Jon. I know we've talked about it, this connection between us and I still don't know what it is, but I know it's real and that I need you. You are a part of me. I love you. I love you too Grace. I'll let you get some sleep, but soon I want to be with you alone, I feel like we need to talk. Just me and you. I look up at him and say, are you breaking up with me Mr. Observation?

He's taken aback a bit, what? No. Why would you say that? I giggle, and he sees it was a joke. I'm teasing you, of course we can find time to talk. Why Miss Melody, teasing isn't very nice. Whoever said I was nice; I quip with a little sass. Oh, you're nice and you know it, he says with a chuckle. Ah well, keep that between us would ya? I'd hate for everyone to find out, I say with a laugh. Sorry, cats already out of the bag on that one. You're nice and you can't hide it. It's just who you are. Well then, I suppose there no sense in trying I say and flop down on my bed. I'll be testing samples most of the day tomorrow. So far, I'm usually all alone in the lab. If you get time, why don't you come by, and we can talk. Otherwise, we can go for a walk after we're done working. That'll work for me, let's plan on a walk after work. Now to bed with you, you need your rest and I need a shower. Yes, sir I say with a salute laughing. Good night, Mr. Observation. Good night, Miss Melody, sweet dreams.

Chapter 26

Hey, you, I say seeing Jon coming up to outside my tent. Hey yourself, he says. Wanna go for that walk now or later after showers and dinner? We can go now, I'm anxious to hear what you want to talk about. Ok then, let's walk over to that wooded area at the edge of camp, seems peaceful there. Sounds like a plan to me, I say and take his arm as we stroll that way.

So, tell me Jon what's on your mind? Well, you know all that has happened between us since we met. Including that incident with Lindsey. I lower my head, yes of course I remember, how could I ever forget. I'm sorry Grace, he says lifting my chin. That's not exactly what I wanted to talk about. I only brought it up to say that I well, I wanted to ask if you are really, ok? I mean, I want to be sure that we are ok. I have had this feeling ever since it happened that something is changed between us. It feels like there is a shift, I have new feelings and I don't know what it all means. Oh Jon, I am so sorry for all that happened. I don't want to lose you. Are you saying you don't feel the same way about me anymore?

Grace, no, I don't mean that he says taking me by the arms and pulling me close. I could never feel like that. I feel more, if that's possible. This thing that's always been there between us, it's more if that's possible. I don't know how else to say it, Grace. I am so conflicted. Conflicted how? I ask. Well, I'll try to explain it. I don't fully understand it myself. As you know, we met and there was an instant connection. Yes, I say. Well, we both knew it was something special. I knew for sure anyway. I did as well I say, taking his hand and leading him over to a log so we can sit. Sit here and try to explain what you mean; I say and give his hand a comforting squeeze.

Ok, here goes. I have these new feelings for you Grace. They're confusing and new to me. I feel this overwhelming draw to you, almost like a pull to be close to you. I have this urge to know you more and this need to be with you. Like, be with you in a romantic way. And I know you don't feel the same, you have always made that clear and Grace, I swear I felt the same way. I promise I never lied to you. But now… everything is so different.

He looks at me now, eye to eye. Have I just ruined everything? I see the hopefulness and maybe fear in his eyes. Jon, you haven't ruined anything. I'm a little shocked by your words. I never thought you could feel that way for me. That night, when we were together it was… I trail off and look away. Grace, what is it? You know you can say anything to me.

I know I can, but this is hard and I'm not sure how to say it. Just say it, blurt it out and then we'll just deal with all that we've said. You'll never lose me; I hope you know that. Oh, I do, I know it with all my heart. Good, he says and gives my hand a squeeze in reassurance.

Oh Jon, that night was like magic. In those moments we were together, it was like no one else in the world existed. It felt like my soul woke up, like it had been asleep up until that very moment. I have never felt a connection like that before. You are part of me, a part I didn't realize was missing until that very moment. Jon, I know I don't make any sense. What we did was wrong, and we hurt people. But I can't regret being with you, I just can't. I begin to cry and drop my chin. I look up and see he is just looking at me, a look in his eyes that I don't understand.

Please say something. Jon, you have to tell me you forgive me. I'm crying harder now; I feel like my world could be ending. Does he hate me, have I ruined everything? I don't know what to think. I can't breathe, I feel like I am suffocating. I struggle to breathe; I think I'm hyperventilating.

Grace! He's got me by the shoulders now. Grace, take a deep breath and try to relax. I try and double over in an effort to gain control of my breathing. It takes long moments like this. Jon is saying soothing words and rubbing my back. By the time I sit back up, my breathing is better but still a little ragged. I look at Jon and he's looking at me, almost in shock. Did. I. ra ra ruin everything? I finally manage to say. Oh God no Grace, he says and pulls me into a hug. Oh, honey no, you didn't ruin anything. You're amazing. Do you know that, Grace? Amazing Grace, that's funny but it's true. We stay there in an embrace for a long time, just holding on to each other. Holding on for dear life it feels like.

I have no idea how long we've been like this, but it seems like forever. I pull back and look at him, he looks back into my eyes. Do you love me? I ask.

Yes sweetheart, I love you. More than the love of a friend, I am in love with you Grace.

You're in love with me? You love me? Yes, I do he says. How does that make you feel?

I don't know what to say. Oh, he says with a crestfallen look. Oh Jon, no, no, no, please don't misunderstand me. I put my hands on either side of his face and look into his eyes. Jon, I am in love with you too. I love you with every bit of my heart and soul. You do? He asks. Yes, I truly do. I can't believe it. How could you love me? I'm nobody, just some guy and you're... Grace you are amazing. There's no way a woman like you should ever be in love with someone like me. I'm nothing, no one. It doesn't make sense. Jon! How dare you say that. You are a wonderful man. How about you let me decide who is worthy of my love, I say with a little grin. Next thing I know I'm being swung around and kissed. I surrender myself to the moment. His arms, his lips, the smell of him, it's all so intoxicating. By the time he puts me back on my feet, I'm smiling from ear to ear and laughing with pure delight. A little breathless, I place my hands on his arms and look up into his beautiful blue grey eyes. They're like these endless pools of liquid steel. I am in awe of this man.

Oh Jon, I say. I feel so happy in this moment. What are we going to do? I don't know he replies honestly. We're here in this faraway place with all of our friends, and with everything that has happened and so many feelings to consider. I just don't know.

I'm not sure we should say anything about this, whatever this is to anyone just yet. Don't get me wrong, I am happy for all we have said to each other, and I don't regret it at all. I love you so much, you incredibly wonderful man. I'm just worried about hurting Eddie with everything still so raw. I truly did care for him, I didn't love him, but he is special to me. But you Jon, you are everything to me. I still can't believe this. How did I get so lucky to find you and for us to be here in this special place together and realize how we feel? I'm the lucky one he says. You have no idea how happy I am and how happy you've made me today. But I agree with you, it's not the right time to reveal any of this to the others. First, I think we need to figure out what it all means and what we will do. It may take Eddie some time to come to terms with it, but Grace if you'll have me, I'm yours, forever. Forever, I say in return and just wrap my arms around him.

I think we should go back now, he says. It's nearly dinner time and the guys will be wondering where we are. You're right of course, and I don't want to worry them.

OMG! This dinner is so good, Ms. Norma is a marvel. Woo, yes ma'am she is Preacher adds. I don't think I have ever had rice and beans this good in my whole life, and this chicken, it's awesome. Looking around I see everyone is so engrossed in dinner that they don't see the looks Jon and I are exchanging across the table. I need to stop this before someone does notice, I think. So, did you all have a good day? I ask between bites.

I did Rob says and we all swing to look at him. What? He says looking up from his plate. I did. You are weird here bro, Will states matter of factly. I think it's Lydia, that's got you so happy. All eyes swing back to Rob, waiting for him to either confirm or deny the accusation. He slowly puts his fork down and looks around the table before speaking. So, what if it is? Am I not entitled to like someone? For a moment no one says anything, maybe we're all stunned a little bit. Jon speaks first, brother you are more than entitled. I'm happy for you. Eddie goes next, does she like you? Well, I see him talking to her a lot while we're working, Will adds. I think she does, we have talked to each other quite a bit. I've never met anyone quite like her and I'm going to get to know her better. Good for you man, Preacher says. Who'd have thought, you come all the way down here for an alibi and you find a special lady. Good for you, man. I notice he's smiling, and I smile back at him. I'm so glad, Rob. Now I want to meet her, I mean if she's turned your head, she must be special. Plus, I'll be here for a year so I should meet more of the people here. A year I say aloud, not meaning too. I am just realizing; I'll be here a year and they're all leaving in like 10 days. What's wrong Grace? Preacher asks, noticing the odd look on my face. Oh, I say. It's nothing. Are you sure? You said, a year then just looked all funny, Will observed. I'm good, it just hit me. I'll be here a year and you're all leaving in less than two weeks. I look around the table at these men, my friends, my family, and my love, Jon.

Jon, I think. He loves me, I love him, how will ever go a year without seeing his face. I'm sorry, will you excuse me. I say and stand. I turn and walk away without saying another word.

Uh oh, Preacher says. Guys, I think something is bothering Grace. Like she just realized she would be here alone. She knew all along, it was her plan Will says. Yes, that's true Eddie says, but something is different. You took a walk with her earlier Jon, Rob says, did she say anything to you? Uh oh Jon thinks, what do I say. Well, we did have a long conversation. What about? Will asks. All eyes on Jon now. We talked about a lot of things. Nothing to make her upset. Then why is she upset? I don't know Will. At least I'm not sure, I think but don't say aloud. Well, something's up, Eddie says. Maybe she's just afraid to stay on her own, Will says. I don't think so, Eddie says. Grace isn't the type to be afraid, it's something else and I think it has to do with whatever happened between you and her today, he says looking directly at Jon from across the table with eyes that seem to be accusing. Again, all eyes swing to Jon. Look, I promise I didn't do anything to upset, I never would. But I do think she's upset that we're all leaving. You know that we are all close. I hope they believe me; I am not ready to reveal the real reasons she is upset.

Well, Rob says. To be honest with you all, I may not be leaving. What? Will says a little too loudly. Keep it down little buddy, he scolds. I mean what I said, I may choose to stay a little longer. Depends. Depends on what? Will, you cannot be that dumb, Eddie adds. He's thinking of staying for Lydia. Ohhh... But you barely know her, why would you stay here, for her? Preacher is just shaking his head. Somebody else take this one, Eddie says. Little buddy, Preacher starts, if he doesn't stay, how will he get to know her better? I don't know, Will replies. But here? I mean it's okay for a couple weeks and it's kinda cool doing this all together, but staying here... You're crazy man. No, he's not, Jon says. I'm actually thinking of staying too. Now they're all looking at Jon. Look guys, I like this work and I'm just not sure about leaving Grace here alone. I know she's capable of taking care of herself, she's an incredibly smart and capable woman, but I can't explain it. I just feel responsible for her. Preachers' eyes seem to comprehend everything, but he just says, that's good brother. I think we will all feel better knowing she has you here to look out for her. I look at him gratefully and notice Eddie has a far off look on his face. Well, that's true Will says. I was worried about leaving her here alone, but man how can you stay? What about work and us? Awe, I say, you'll be fine with these guys for a year. It's not like I'm staying forever. Look buddy, we're brothers and nothing will change that. I know he says, but it feels like all of a sudden everything is different.

Back in my tent now, I grab my shower caddy and some clothes and head off to the shower tent. I just need to think. I don't know why I reacted like that, what's the matter with me? I love these guys; I knew they were leaving. It was always the plan, but now... It's all different. Jon loves me. That changes everything.

After my shower I'm back in my tent and Rob is sitting on the end of his bed. He looks up as I come in. Hey Rob, didn't feel like hanging out after dinner? Nah, he says. I wanted to come talk to you Grace. Talk to me? Of course, I say sitting down beside him after dropping off my shower caddy in my little cubby. What's up? Grace, are you sure you're, okay? Yes, I'm fine. I'm a little sad about you all leaving but, I always knew it was the plan. But, even still, it's tough. You're all so important to me. Well... I may not be leaving. That's one reason I wanted to talk to you. What? I say and grab his hand. You want to stay? Why? Is it Lydia? Are you are? Whoa Grace, one question at a time please he says with a chuckle. Okay, sorry you're right. It's like this, I do like Lydia. A lot. I may want to stay longer to see how things go between us. She's different Grace, I have never felt this way about anyone before and I feel like I should at least give it a chance. Know what I mean? Oh Rob, yes! I absolutely know what you mean. Can I tell you something, but if I do you should know it's just between you and me for now? Of course, you can Grace. No one can keep a secret like me. I believe that about you Rob, I say with a grin.

So?? What is it he asks? I begin to tell what happened today between Jon and me on our walk earlier today. We realized we're in love and we want to be together. But neither one of us wants to hurt Eddie and Rob, I swear this is not at all what I expected to happen. I never had these feeling for Jon before that...that night, I say and drop my head. I believe you Grace, he says. I can't say I'm surprised though. Why would you say that? I ask.

Grace, seriously? You cannot be that obtuse. I mean all of a sudden you two find each other and you have this "magic" connection? He says using the obnoxious air quotes with his hands. You two have been almost inseparable since then. It was like you both were going out of your way to prove you didn't have those feelings or maybe you were just fooling yourselves, I don't know but it was obvious to anyone around you.

I'm stunned silent, I sit there looking at him like I cannot fathom the words he's just said. Grace? I'm sorry if what I said upsets you. No. I manage to say. I'm ok, I just had no idea that is what you thought. Did anyone else think this also? He pauses for a moment, then answers. We all did, well except you and Jon. I think even Eddie knew it deep down, though maybe he just didn't want to believe it.

Grace, something like that doesn't happen often. This thing between you two is plain for anyone with eyes to see. It's special, I mean I wish I had what you have.

Oh, Rob I say. Maybe you do, with Lydia. Who knows, right? Maybe, he says. It's the closest thing I've ever come to it for sure. That's why I feel I should stay. Would it be a problem? I mean they still think we're staying, don't they? Yes, they do I say. It's no problem at all. I'm so happy for you Rob. And me too a little, I say. I mean, it will be nice to have a friend here. Don't get me wrong, everyone is so nice, and I am already getting to know a few of them but they're not family like you all are.

Well, he says that's very true. We are family, and we always will be. No matter where we are. But Grace, after you left dinner, Jon said he might be staying too. What?! I say, very surprised. You didn't know? No, I say. I had no idea; he didn't say anything to me. Wow, I think.

Well, maybe he just realized it himself when I said I was thinking of staying. But that's good, isn't it? Oh, it is. It's wonderful actually. It would make me so happy, I say. Happy? He says, you don't sound happy about it, he says. My head swings up quickly and I look into his eyes. I promise you it makes me very happy. It's just that, well, Rob I am so confused about everything. I mean, not about loving Jon. That I am one hundred billion percent sure about, I say and smile brightly. Then what is it that's got you confused Grace?

Everything else, I say in a matter-of-fact way. What about Eddie? I never meant to hurt him; I swear. And the rest of you, what does this do to all of us. I don't want to be that woman who comes between a group of friends. I would rather have you all as friends than lose anyone of you for anything. Being here, for a year now that I know I love him is going to be hard. I can handle it, but can he? And what happens next? I mean, I feel like I was always destined to go places and help people. I'm just getting to a place in life where I can make those dreams come true and I'm not sure I want to give up on my dreams.

He takes my hand and squeezes it before speaking. Grace, why can't you have everything? Do you think Jon would cut and run because you are chasing your dreams? That's not who he is. I think we both know that. Why can't you both plot your course together? As for Eddie, he'll be ok. I promise you that. I know him, and I know deep down he knew what the two of you had could never have worked. He's strong. You'll never lose any of us, no matter what happens. Life is a wild ride. It's like wildfire, it goes in whatever direction the wind takes it. I think we're like that too. We go wherever life takes us, we're just here for the ride. And if you can do good along the way Grace, that's a good thing. Jon loves you; he'll support what you want and need from life. As for the rest of us, we have lives to live too. But we'll all still be a family, no matter where life takes us.

I know you're right and thank you for saying it. This has helped me so much, thank you for talking with me. Maybe I should go see the guys, I'm sure I worried them. I didn't mean to, I just needed to think.

Good idea, he says. I think they're all by the fire. Let's go let them know you're fine. Turns out Will worries like an old momma hen, he says laughing. I know, I say. He's very sweet.

We walk up to the campfire and sit down with everyone else. Hi guys, I say. Sorry I left dinner so abruptly, but everything is okay now. I had a shower and did some thinking. Also, had a long chat with Rob and I feel much better. Will looks at us shaking his head. I said it before and I'll say it again, Rob is weird here. We all laugh at that. The evening goes very nicely after that, we sit chatting about this and that. Just enjoying each other's company. I look around and I feel so lucky.

Chapter 27

The next couple of days fly by, I am so busy with samples and testing. The guys seem to be busy also with this building project and plans for more. I've fallen into a nice routine, and I've had a lot of time to think about everything with Jon, but also about what I want. It's been four days since our discussion in the woods. Four days of knowing I'm in love with him, well at least four days of coming to terms with it. Maybe I always knew, like Rob said but I just don't know. Today, I want to talk to him again. I'm ready, I know he's been so patient, giving me time and space. I decide that when I'm done working today, I am going to find him and see if he wants to go for another walk and talk some more.

Just as I'm packing everything away for the evening, Jon walks into the lab tent. Hey you, I say. Hi, he says. Wanna go for a walk, we both say at the same time and laugh. Jinx! I say and we laugh some more. Yes, I say. I was actually about to come find you. Good timing then, he says. I'm here. You ready to go now? Yes, I just wrapped everything up.

We head out walking in the same direction we went a few days ago. I figured we'd just follow the same path as before, he says. Good idea. We walk along a few minutes quietly. Suddenly I stop and then he does too. Grace? I love you, Jon. I blurt it out more like a question than a statement. What I mean is, I am in love with you. I have thought a lot about it, I've basically thought of nothing else since our last walk. I am in love with you to Grace. Wait, I say. I need to say a few things, before this goes any further. If that's ok. Of course, Grace, what is it?

I love you Jon, and I want to be with you. I mean together, with you. But first, I want to tell you what else I want. I mean for myself, so you can be sure you know what you're getting into if you want to be with me too. Ok, he says. Then just tell me. Grace, nothing you say will change my mind.

I believe that Jon, but I want you to know everything before we take this any further. I love what I do and being here has already started to show me that I help people and make a difference. It's only been a week. In a year I don't know how I will feel or where life will take me. I can't see myself wanting to give up on my dreams and just go back to Fresno or Reno and settle down. I think you know that's not who I am. I do know that I have no expectations of that happening.

Ok, good I say. I mean, I don't think I will necessarily want to travel nonstop, and I will have to make money at times. I mean, I have enough for several years and if I sold my town house, I would have a lot more but, I am only 35 and I can't afford to retire and do volunteer work forever. Jon, I have to go and do more, see more, at least for a while. Does that make sense? I feel like my life is just beginning and I can't give it up.

Honey, where is this coming from? I have never asked you to give up anything, and I never would. I love you Grace, I am in love with you. I want to be with you, go where you go and do what I can to help you make these dreams come true. I don't care where that takes us, if we're together it doesn't matter. And if you have to go alone, then I'll miss you like crazy, but I won't stop loving you. I'd wait forever for you Grace.

I throw my arms around him. Jon, thank you. That means so much for you to say that. Are you sure? What about you? How can following me around the world make you happy?

What about your life back home? Grace, without you what point is there? You came into my life and changed everything, and it's so much better. Before you I was just wandering around without focus or purpose.

My life is with you now. Where you go, I go. As long as you want me there, consider it done. I feel like I've finally found what I've always been searching for. You are amazing, you always think of others first and you want to help everyone. I love that about you, I want to be more like that myself. I'm not worthy of you Grace, but if you'll have me, I'll be yours forever.

Tears in my eyes, I grab his face and pull his lips down to mine. Between kisses, I say; I want you Jon. Forever, wherever I go I want you with me. His arms tighten around me, and I put mine around his neck enjoying the pleasure of kissing him.

I pull back for a moment and look into his eyes, passion is burning there. I feel a strong longing. I need you, I say. Here, he asks. Yes, now, it has to be now. He groans and grabs me pulling me hard against him kissing me again this time with heat and passion. The urgent need is overtaking us both.

I step back and pull off my shirt then grab the buttons on his jeans. He pulls his shirt off also and I notice not for the first time how incredibly sexy he is. Oh my God, I say with so much need and longing. I kick off my shoes as quickly as I can, I don't even care that we're in the woods. I want him now, hard and here. This cannot wait. Both of us undressed now, he picks me up and I wrap my legs around his waist as he lowers me down onto him. Oh, Jon I groan, wrapping my arms around his neck. Our mouths crash together in searing kisses. He's deep inside me and the feeling is incredible. I grip his shoulders and back, the pleasure is immense and I'm building to climax. I grip his shoulders tightly and throw my head back, crying out in ecstasy as I explode all around him. I drop my head to his should, I feel his hands grip me tighter as he picks up the pace of his thrusts. One last thrust and I hear the low growl in his throat as he lets go. His arms grip me tighter, his lips on my neck. He lifts me to my feet, but I hang on to him knowing I'm not ready to stand on my own yet. Breathing deeply, we hold onto each other. You... are... everything, he says. I love you, Grace. I love you, Jon. That was amazing. He steps over and grabs our shirts and spreads them out, sit he says. Gladly, I say still breathing heavily. He sits next to me and takes me into his arms. Rubbing my arms and back as I lay my head against his shoulder, I feel perfect. Absolutely perfect.

I lean my head up to look at him and I meet his steel blue eyes. There's so much depth in his eyes, like he can see into my soul. I love you, I say. He answers me with a kiss. Sweet and tender at first. It feels like he's putting all the love he can into this kiss. He's showing me without words, how he feels. I place my hand over his heart and kiss him back with all the love I have. I move to sit on him, not done with loving him yet. This time it's slower, we take our time having slaked our urgent lust already. This time it's deeper, more connected, we pour everything we have into each other. It's all passion and love. We express everything to each other. It's pure magic.

We stay there holding each other, naked, no barriers and no words. We don't need them; we just know everything in this moment.

Having no idea how long we've been gone, I notice the dark shadows starting to come thru the trees. I could stay here forever with you, but maybe we should head back soon. I'd hate them to come looking for us and find us like this, I say grinning at him.

I am so happy Grace, he says. I want to stay like this forever too, but you're right. We have to go back. We stand and try to shake the dirt and leaves out of our clothes. I need a shower I say, and food. Definitely food. Me too, he says kissing me softly. How about dinner, then a shower? Works for me I say, lazily.

I look at him, he looks at me and we both laugh. We look like sex; we both say at the same time. Jinx, I say, and we laugh again. Nothing to do about now, he says. Maybe they won't notice, I say. Yeah right, he says. They'll know the minute they see us. Would you rather go to the showers first he asks? Do you still want to keep us a secret, Grace? No, I say. Rob already knows and I guarantee Preacher does too. He knows everything, I say with a chuckle. Will won't mind and Eddie, well, Eddie will just have to come to terms with it. Rob said he thinks it will all be ok. Are you ok with telling them?

I am. And I'm staying here with you Grace. I love you, and I don't care who knows it. I love you too Jon. Well, I'm hungry so let's get this over with.

We meet up with everyone in line for dinner. They're looking at us, but no one says anything. We sit next to each other at the table, I take his hand under the table, and he gives mine a squeeze. Grace and I are together he says, absolutely deadpan. I look around to try and gauge their reactions. Rob is the first to speak, congratulations he says. It's about damn time. I let a breath out that I wasn't even aware I was holding. Exactly, Will says too. Preacher smiles warmly, I am so happy for you both. I know you'll be very happy. Thank you, I say. I look over to Eddie, there's something in his eyes I can't read, but he smiles slightly and says, I'm happy for you both. I look into his eyes, trying to convey my gratitude and how sorry I am if he's hurt. He gives me a slight nod and with that I know we will be ok. I'm so hungry I exclaim, this food smells great. I bet you're hungry, Will smirks and Rob gives his arm a playful punch. We all chuckle and dig into dinner.

After dinner, we all head to the showers. Me to the ladies' side and them all to the men's side. Afterward back in the tent, I'm sitting on my bed with my tablet writing a few emails to check in with Lisa and my family back home. I quickly reply to a couple of emails from work and one from my mom. Next, I begin writing to Lisa, I need to tell her all about what's happened here so far.

Dear Lisa,

I've been here a week already and so much has happened; I don't know where to begin. It was a long trip getting here. Three flights and hours on a bus. I think all the traveling and recent stress affected me poorly, I fainted. Me, fainted…crazy I know. I'm fine now. The work here is good. I am really making a difference. But the biggest news has to do with Jon. I can't really explain how it happened, but we're in love. Like in love, love. We want to be together. He said where I go, he will go. This is it. I feel it in my bones, he is the one. I can hardly believe it, I never thought about us like this. After that terrible night, something changed in us. I can't really explain it. It's like coming together that way, flipped a switch or something. Then here, when I fainted, it scared these guys so bad. Poor Will was in tears and sat by my bed for hours refusing to leave me unless one of the others stayed with me. Lisa, they took turns sitting by my bed all night long. I was amazed. I'm so happy I found this whole new family. Enough about me, how are you? I miss you like crazy. You would hate it here by the way. Sleeping in tents, we have beds but still. It's dirty and hard work, but I love it already.

Write me back when you have time and stay out of trouble if you can.

Love you bunches, Grace

I shut off my tablet and stretch out on the bed. Will and Rob come in, clean from their showers. Hi Grace, Will says. You going to bed already? Kinda early, isn't it? Nah, I'm just stretched out, I had a few emails to answer and send. I'll probably just read a while. I have a bunch of movies I downloaded if you're interested, he says. That sounds nice, I say. What do you have?

Deciding on a Clint Eastwood movie he sets his laptop on the little table, and we all sit around and watch. Jon comes in and sits beside me. I love this movie he says. The shut up and watch Will says. Grumpy much? I remark, but we all shut up and watch.

When the movie is over, I ask Jon where are Preacher and Eddie? I feel bad, we didn't ask them to watch with us. Preacher was reading a book and Eddie was on his computer when I left. They're ok. That's good. How are you, I ask? Good, great actually he says with a wide sext grin. Me too, I say blushing a little. We're speaking just above a whisper, so the others don't overhear us. You tired; he asks? Yes, I say. What about you? So tired, he replies. But I don't want to leave you. I know how you feel, but we need to sleep. Why don't I just stay here with you? Jon, I cannot have more sex today. If you stay, we must sleep. Agreed, he says. I just want to be here with you. Me too, I say. We climb into bed and lay there holding each other. Goodnight, Miss Melody he whispers. Goodnight, Mr. Observation I reply. He kissed my head and I close my eyes.

Next thing I know, I a waking up to Jon's gentle shake. Sunlight coming in the tent. Good morning sleepy head, he says. I stretch out and say good morning yourself. What time is it, I ask? Around seven, I think. You getting hungry? We could go over to the dinning tent and grab breakfast. The guys already went. We're alone I ask. Yes, he says with smirk like he knows why I ask. I wriggle closer to him. How long do you think we have? They just left, so at least half an hour, he says. Perfect, I say and begin to slip off my pajamas.

A little later we make our way to the dinning tent. I'm ravenous, I whisper to him and wink. Have a care woman, he teases. Let's eat first, then we can decide what to do with the day. Oh yeah, I say. I totally forgot it's Sunday, there's no work to do.

We grab food and sit down to eat eggs, sausage and flat bread. I think Mark said Emmanuel is taking the bus to town for supplies. He said anytime they go we can go with them. Some of the others go to but things or have a mean in the town. Some just go for the ride. If that's what you want to do Grace, it's okay with me. Hmm? I think aloud, what I'd really love to do is spend the whole day alone with you. Now, that sounds amazing but how are we going to be alone all day, here, with all these people? Good question, I say as I continue to eat my breakfast.

I got I, I say. Why don't we pack a picnic lunch and go for a hike, just me and you? I heard from a few people here that there are some nice places to see if you can hike a little way. I'm game he says. If it gets me alone with you for the day, we can hike to Timbuktu, he says. I laugh at that. I don't think we need to go that far, it's only a couple miles. We'll take lunch and just see what we see. Deal, he says.

After breakfast we head over to the bath tent to get cleaned up and ready for the day. Back in my tent, I grab my backpack and add four bottles of water and two rolled blankets for us to sit on. I notice my tablet and quickly check my email. I scan the one from my sister quickly and decide to reply later. I see a reply from Lisa and open it to read it.

WHAT!!! Grace, you're in LOVE??? I am so excited for you honey. I always knew you two were meant for each other and what a hunk…whew girl, you have good taste. I'm good, just selling houses and taking names. I'm glad you're okay, I have never known you faint. How scary. I want to hear more about everything in your next email. I need details, all the details. Take care of yourself. Talk soon, love you sweetie.

XOXO- Lisa

I put my tablet back down and grin. Lisa… gotta love her, I think.

I walk over to the dinning tent to see about a couple of sandwiches or something and see that Jon is already there loading his backpack with zipper bags of food. He looks up and says, Mrs. Norma said to keep the food in these bags so wildlife can't smell it. That makes sense to me, I say. We have sandwiches, apples and protein bars he says. Will that be enough, he asks? I think so, I say. I put four bottles of water in my pack and blankets to sit on. Awesome he says, I have a blanket too and some water as well as a bag of wasabi almonds. Yum! Sounds like we're good to go.

We hike for a while through the trees, up and up before we come to a meadow by a creek. Wow, I say. This place is beautiful. There are flowers all over and the grass is so green and tall. The breeze feels so good, it's a cool day but it's not cold. Will this do I say to Jon. Absolutely he says, coming back to reality. Where'd you go, I ask? I was just looking around, he says. This place is special, I can feel it. I agree.

Why don't we look around for a bit, then we can spread out our blankets here for lunch? Sounds like a good plan. Let's go over and check out that creek, he says. I bet there are fish in there. We walk over, it's not really deep but you can see fish and rocks. Kneeling down, Jon reaches in and feels the water. Feels nice, a little cold but really nice. I follow suit and reach in as well. That is very cold, I say. But it's so clear, I can see the bottom and look at all those fish. This place is perfect, I say feeling it deep in my soul. We stroll around hand in hand looking at everything around the meadow. I pick a few flowers and bring them up to my nose to smell them. Mmmm... I feel so happy in this moment, I think. You getting hungry he asks? I look at him and smile, very I say with a wink. We lay out two of the blanked and leave the other rolled up to lay back against. I sit and lay back, looking up at the bluest sky. Just a few puffy fat white clouds float by. Jon lays down next to me and takes my hand to his lips and kisses my palm sweetly. I sigh, utterly contented. I begin to hum a little tune. Penny for your thoughts, he says. Oh, I was just thinking how happy I am and how perfect this place is. It's just incredible that we get to be here in this beautiful please, together in this moment. Just us, no one else in the world. I'm so happy, I love you Jon. I love you right back Miss Melody.

We make love right there, enjoying our time together and each other fully. This moment is all that matters and whatever comes next, I know that we will face it together.

Epilogue

The guys stay two more weeks before packing up and heading back to reality. Jon and Rob have decided to stay, and I couldn't be happier. These weeks here, doing this work and being with Jon and my wonderful friends has been everything to me. Jon and I are now sharing my tent with Rob having moved to the last bunk, he's barely there anyway as he's been spending most of his time with Lydia. Will has moved into Jon's old bunk, and we've settled into an easy routine together.

I'm crying as I hug Preacher, Will and Eddie outside by the bus. I will miss you all so much. We will miss you too, Will says. But it's time to get back to the real world, it's been an adventure for sure. Thank you for bringing us here he says. Awe, Will. You're so welcome I say and kiss his cheek. Preacher says to Jon and Rob, take care of our girl. We will they say and to me he says, I know you'll be fine Grace. I have never met a woman like you before, you're so strong and I just bet you're going to kick this world's ass. Take care of them for me. I will I say and hug him again. Thank you, Colin, look out for Will and Eddie for me. You know it, he says. And no more tears, we'll write and see you at the end of the year. Remember you promised to come home for a good long visit before the next adventure. I know, and I promise to spend at least a month with you all before even thinking about what's next.

I walk over to Eddie and take his hand. I'll miss you I say. You too, he says. I'm truly happy for you and Jon. I see how happy you are together and that makes me happy Grace. I want only the best for you both. I hug him tightly for a moment, then pull back and say, thank you. I love you.

I walk back over to Jon and Rob; Lydia is standing next to Rob holding his hand. They have gotten so close over the last few weeks. Travel safe and let us know when you get back home, Rob says. I'll miss you brothers.

As they all get on the bus. Rob and Lydia wave goodbye then turn to walk back to camp. Jon and I stand there and watch the bus pull away. When the bus is no longer in view, we look at each other and say, what now, at exactly the same time. Jinx, I say, and we laugh. I don't know, I say. But whatever it is, let's just face it together. Deal, he says, and we turn to walk back to camp together, hand in hand. Confident that no matter what, we are better together.

The End